D0201404

Love Finds You™

on *Christmas*
Morning

Love Finds You™

on Christmas Morning

BY DEBBY MAYNE
AND TRISH PERRY

summerside
PRESS™

Summerside Press, Inc.
Minneapolis 55438
www.summersidepress.com

Love Finds You on Christmas Morning: Deck the Halls
© 2011 by Debby Mayne

Love Finds You on Christmas Morning: 'Tis the Season
© 2011 by Trish Perry

ISBN 97-8-160936-193-8

Scripture references are from the following sources: The Holy Bible, King
James Version (KJV). Scriptures marked NIV taken from the Holy Bible,
New International Version®, NIV ®. Copyright © 1973, 1978, 1984, 2011
by Biblica, Inc.™ Used by permission of Zondervan. All rights reserved
worldwide. www.zondervan.com.

The town depicted in this book is a real place, but all characters are
fictional. Any resemblances to actual people or events are purely
coincidental.

Cover Design by Koechel Peterson & Associates | www.kpadesign.com

Interior design by Müllerhaus Publishing Group | www.mullerhaus.net

*Summerside Press™ is an inspirational publisher offering fresh,
irresistible books to uplift the heart and engage the mind.*

Printed in USA.

Acknowledgments

....

We would like to thank Tom Byrd, author of *Around and About Cary*, for providing historical information about the charming town of Cary, North Carolina.

Thanks also to Howard Johnson, president of the Cary Chamber of Commerce, and Paul Ashworth, proprietor of Ashworth Drugs.

—Debby Mayne and Trish Perry

Deck the Halls

BY DEBBY MAYNE

Lord, thou hast been our dwelling place in all generations.
PSALM 90:1 KJV

Chapter One

....

Early autumn 1926

Lillian Pickard shifted her weight to take some of the load off her aching feet. There always seemed to be one customer who lingered at the end of the long day, keeping Lillian from locking up Joachim's Five and Dime and going home. She took a couple of deep breaths and tried to remain pleasant as Mrs. Gooch carried her handheld basket of odds and ends to the counter.

Lillian rang up the woman's selections and bagged all the items then handed them to her. "Have a nice evening, Mrs. Gooch. See you again soon."

"You are a mighty sweet girl," Mrs. Gooch said as she took her bag. "It's a shame you have to work such long hours. Give my regards to your mama."

"I will."

As soon as Mrs. Gooch made her exit, Lillian scurried to the door and locked it, just in case anyone had the notion to walk in. She counted the money in the cash drawer, tucked it inside the deposit envelope, and slid the envelope into the slot on the side of the safe.

Finally she was ready to leave for home. The tiny house she shared with her parents was less than a half mile away, but on evenings like this, it might as well have been ten miles. Her feet throbbed and her mind raced over all the things she still needed to do when she got home.

Her daddy's factory injury five years ago had rendered him incapable of working most of the jobs he was qualified for. He'd needed Lillian's mama nearby to take care of him in the earlier days, so it had been up to Lillian to support the family. She didn't mind at first, but as time went on, it became painfully obvious that her lot in life wasn't what she'd always wanted.

The first raindrop plopped smack-dab in the middle of her head as she crossed the road. Lillian groaned. As if her situation weren't already bad enough...

She heard the rumble of an automobile coming toward her, so she jumped back, closer to the building. She turned to see which of the rich people were out riding around. There weren't many automobiles in Cary, North Carolina, and it was after business hours, so Lillian assumed it was someone showing off.

The automobile pulled to a stop, and the man driving it leaned over and cranked down the window. "Hey, gorgeous! Need a ride?"

Thank the Lord the sun wasn't shining or William Tronnier would see the redness of her flaming cheeks. "Mr. Tronnier!" But before she had a chance to say anything else, the occasional raindrop progressed to a steady downpour. "I always walk home from work, but thank you for the offer."

He laughed. "You shouldn't have to walk in the rain when I have this perfectly fine automobile. Get in before you drown."

She only hesitated for a few seconds before deciding that taking him up on his offer was much better than getting drenched. As she stepped up into the automobile, her ankle wobbled.

"Whoa there, Miss Pickard." He leaned across the seat, opened the car door from the inside, and reached for her hand, which she gave without a second's hesitation. He pulled her up to the seat and quickly let go.

* * * * *

There was no way William would let this opportunity slide by. He'd all but given up on breaking through Lillian's shell when he spotted her walking home. Ever since meeting Lillian Pickard last Christmas season, he'd tried to come up with a way to get to know her better. His first idea of shopping at the store where she worked had backfired. He'd spent the better part of an hour gathering some items to purchase. But while she rang him up, he saw the glazed look in her eyes that he'd come to recognize as the barrier between the classes. And it broke his heart.

"Turn right at the next road," Lillian instructed, snapping him from his thoughts.

"Yes, I know where you live."

She turned and gave him a questioning glance. Her long, dark eyelashes framed what he remembered as being light blue-gray eyes that twinkled when she talked.

"I took Merv for a spin when my family first got this automobile, and we happened to drive by your house," he explained.

"Oh." Lillian fidgeted with the purse in her lap.

"We went all over the place," William continued, hoping to ease some of the discomfort he'd caused. He nervously rambled on about where he and Merv had gone that day. By the time he realized he'd monopolized the conversation, they'd reached the cottage where Lillian lived with her parents.

As they pulled to a stop, Lillian reached for the door handle. "Thank you for the ride, Mr. Tronnier."

"Wait." William cleared his throat. Lillian let go of the door handle and turned to face him. "I wondered... Well, I thought maybe..."

Lillian's forehead crinkled. "Did you need something?" She tilted her head and pursed her lips.

"Would you like to do something with me sometime?"

"Like what?"

William shrugged. "I don't know. Perhaps I can take you for a ride in my automobile."

The corners of her lips twitched, as though she might be repressing a smile. "You already have, Mr. Tronnier, and I thank you for it. Between the rain and my aching feet, I have to admit, I dreaded the walk home." She got out and leaned over to look him in the eyes. "Thank you again for your generosity."

He exhaled slowly and nodded. "You're quite welcome, Miss Pickard. Have a nice evening."

As William drove away, he wanted to kick himself. One thing he'd been known for, besides being the son of a wealthy farmer, was his way with words—and now those words had escaped him.

* * * * *

"Lillian, did I just see you getting out of an automobile?" her mama asked. Before giving Lillian a chance to answer, she shook her head and clucked her tongue. "It's not a good idea to take rides from people you don't know."

"I know him."

Mama lifted her eyebrows. "You know someone with an automobile? Or do you just know *of* him?"

"That was William Tronnier." Lillian paused when her mother pulled back in surprise. "I met him at the Jordans' Christmas party last year."

"Honey, I know who the Tronniers are, and they're out of our league. I hope you don't—"

Lillian lifted a hand to stop Mama from continuing. "It was just a ride, Mama. It was raining, and my feet were killing me. Mr. Tronnier took pity on me and offered me a ride."

Myriad emotions slid across her mama's face—first a tad of

disappointment that transformed to acceptance and finally satisfaction. "As long as you don't forget who you are and where you stand in society, you'll be fine."

"Yes, I know, Mama." She headed toward her bedroom. "I'll help set the table after I put my things away."

Lillian stood in front of the scratched mirror that rested atop her equally distressed dresser. Rain and unruly hair were a bad mix. Frizzy ringlets drooped over her shoulders, and her feeble attempt at dressing stylishly clung to her in unkempt folds. Knowing who she was and where she stood in society wasn't difficult, considering what a mess she was. Mr. Tronnier was definitely a nice man, but the tiny tingle of attraction she'd felt when he helped her into his automobile needed to be tempered with reality.

She changed into some dry clothes and flat shoes before joining her parents in the small dining nook between the kitchen and living room. Mama had put food on the plates rather than in serving bowls because the small table was already overcrowded. As soon as she was seated, Daddy took her hand to say the blessing.

"Lord, thank You for the meal my wife has prepared, as humble as it may be."

As soon as Daddy finished praying, Lillian started eating. They'd run out of the meat she'd purchased with her last earnings, so their plates were filled with potatoes, onions, fried okra, and a slab of corn bread—the standard meal on the Pickard table at the end of a pay period.

"So tell me about that Tronnier boy." Her daddy set down his fork.

Lillian shrugged. "There's not much to tell. He drove me straight home."

"You must have talked about something. Did he ask you about your work?"

"No." Lillian didn't mention the fact that William had stopped by the Five and Dime periodically since she'd met him, loading up on silly, nonessential things she never would have wasted her money on. But then, she didn't have spare money; he obviously did.

"You had to talk about something. I can't imagine a young man being completely silent with a pretty girl sitting right there beside him."

Mama cast a glance in his direction. "I don't think it's appropriate for someone in Mr. Tronnier's position to consider someone like our Lillian, even if she is the prettiest girl in town."

Lillian held up both hands. "Please, let's stop talking about this. Mr. Tronnier saw me walking in the rain, so he was kind enough to offer me a ride home. Nothing else."

"I agree. That was a very kind gesture, and we shouldn't read more into it than what it is." Mama sighed and forced a smile as she directed her attention to another topic. "How was work today?"

As much as Lillian didn't feel like discussing work, she was happy for a different subject. She dug deep and came up with a few anecdotal stories to share with her parents.

"Joachim needs to hire someone else," Daddy said. "You shouldn't have to run that place all by yourself."

"He was there most of the day," Lillian said in her boss's defense, even though she wholeheartedly agreed.

Daddy pushed away from the table. "I sure hope he finds someone to work through the holidays. The way people spend money these days, you'll be swamped. You might want to ask for a raise."

"I plan to," she replied.

"Good. After you get more money, all that work won't seem so bad."

Lillian disagreed. She didn't particularly enjoy her job, and she suspected that Mr. Joachim wouldn't have hired her if he'd had more qualified candidates. But everyone in town who wanted to work had a job, and she'd arrived at the Five and Dime when he was desperate for help.

Over time, she'd learned that when people walked into the store, they generally knew what they wanted. And if she spotted an opportunity to sell them something else based on what they plopped onto the counter, all she had to do was mention it. Occasionally they even took her suggestion. As for the numbers…well, she still had trouble counting money. Mama said she got that from her. She wished she had a fraction of her father's math skills.

"Got any dessert?" Daddy asked.

"Just some shortbread I made from the recipe your mother gave me." Mama smiled. "Maybe we can budget for some store-bought cookies after Lillian gets her raise."

"There's no guarantee Mr. Joachim will give me a raise. I just said I planned to ask for one."

"The way he's raising prices in that store, surely he'll see that you can't afford to keep working there on the salary he pays you."

Lillian couldn't afford *not* to keep working there, but she kept her comments to herself. Mama didn't understand business, and Daddy had lost touch with reality after not working for so long.

She sat and listened to her parents go on and on about the state of the economy—about how people were foolish and spending every dime they had as though it would never run out. Lillian suspected it wouldn't run out for many of them since they had decent jobs that paid well.

"You look like you could use a little more rest tonight, Lil. Why don't you go to bed early?" Mama said. "I'll take care of the dishes."

Lillian wasn't about to argue. Her feet throbbed from trying to wear the high heels one of the women from church had given her. She didn't care how in-style they were. Tomorrow she was wearing flats, even if they were dowdy. What did she care? It wasn't as though she could fool anyone into thinking she was a fashion expert.

She went back to her bedroom, closed the door behind her, turned around, and studied her reflection in the mirror again. Her long, curly hair was terribly out-of-date. She lifted the ends and tucked them beneath her collar, trying to imagine herself with one of the shorter bobs so many of the girls in town were sporting. *Maybe one of these days...* She tilted her head and studied her look some more. Mama and Daddy would have a fit, but a cute bob might be just what she needed.

* * * * *

"We expected you home an hour ago," William's mother said. "What kept you so long?"

William grinned as his face grew hot. "I had a little fun showing off the automobile."

"I bet it was a girl," his brother Mason retorted. "That's the only thing that'll set a man's face on fire."

Their mom turned to him with a grin. "Did you meet up with a girl, William?"

"Well...not exactly." He shot his brother a pretend fierce glare.

Mason folded his arms and leaned against the doorframe. "Wanna tell us her name?"

"You don't know her," William said.

"Try me." Mason tilted his head, lifted an eyebrow, and grinned.

"Lillian Pickard."

"Oh, I know who she is," Mother said. "Isn't she the girl who works at Joachim's?"

"Yes, she's the one."

"Pretty girl," Mason said. "Maybe a little old-fashioned for you, though, Will."

"What's wrong with old-fashioned?"

Mason shrugged. "Nothing's wrong with it. I just thought you could do better. You're the looker in the family."

"Mason!" Their mother frowned at the older of the two sons. "If Will likes a girl who is old-fashioned, what business is it of yours? And it would certainly do you some good to stop chasing after all the silly, prissy young women you seem to fancy."

William shot his brother an I-could-have-told-you-so look. "It doesn't matter. She's not interested in me. I took advantage of the rain and offered her a ride home."

"How do you know this girl?" Mother asked.

"She was at Ina and Merv Jordan's Christmas party last year."

"Yes, I remember." Mason narrowed his eyes. "In fact, you had her cornered for almost an hour. Even if she'd wanted to meet other people, she wouldn't have been able to."

"I didn't have her cornered. We enjoyed chatting."

"That's not how I remem—"

Their mother cleared her throat. "Boys! That's enough. So when do you plan to see Miss Pickard again?"

"I don't know if I'll ever see her again."

"That doesn't sound like the brother I know."

"Oh, I'm sure you'll see her again, William," their mother said. "Cary isn't that big of a town."

William smiled and gave her a hug. "I'm sure I'll see her, but that might be as far as it goes. She doesn't seem interested in me as a suitor, and I'm not about to push myself on her."

He started for the stairs but was stopped by the sound of his brother coming from behind. William glanced over his shoulder and saw that the two of them were alone in the foyer. "So what have you been doing all day?"

"Amos wanted to get out of the office, so I helped Pop with the books. His accountant told him he needed to hire someone, but he doesn't know anyone who needs a job."

William chuckled. "I'm surprised he was able to get you to sit still long enough to work on the books."

"Trust me, it wasn't easy." Mason ran his fingers through his freshly cut hair. "So tell me more about Lillian Pickard. Sorry about some of my comments earlier. I was just joking. She would be very pretty if she'd update her hairstyle and wear better clothes."

"I've never cared about that. In fact, I like how she wears her hair. She's different."

"Yes, you can say that again. She is definitely different. I didn't want to say this in front of Mom, but one day I stopped in to pick up a few things at Joachim's and I caught her eating a pickle sandwich. She quickly stuck it beneath the counter, but she had a big mouthful to swallow before she could offer to help me. I thought, 'How odd. What kind of girl would eat a pickle sandwich?' "

"Why do you care what kind of sandwich she eats? Not everyone likes a side of beef for lunch every day." William gave his brother a once-over glance. "You might do yourself a favor by eating a pickle sandwich every now and then."

"Touché, brother." Mason patted his belly. "Some of the girls like me this way. There's a whole lot more to love."

"Good point," William said, grinning.

"You could use a little more meat on those long, lanky bones of yours."

"I'll keep that in mind." William took a step toward the stairs then stopped. "By the way, no offense intended."

"None taken."

William loved his brothers, even when they got on his nerves. Mason was the oldest of five children, three of them boys. William was the middle child, and Amos was the youngest. Their two sisters, the second oldest, Loretta, and the second from the youngest, Virginia, had both married young, and they already had five children between them. William loved his nieces and nephews and hoped he'd be blessed with children of his own someday.

* * * * *

Lillian arrived at the Five and Dime five minutes before the store opened the next morning. Mr. Joachim pounced on her the second she walked in. "You're late."

She glanced at the wall clock. "I still have five minutes."

"You know I need you here early to get the place ready."

With a sweeping gesture, she shook her head. "I swept and dusted yesterday before I left, so there shouldn't be anything left to do."

"I don't want you cleaning while we have customers in the store."

Lillian opened her mouth to argue and say that she cleaned between customers, but she knew it would be a losing battle. Besides, Mr. Joachim already seemed to be in a bad mood, and there was no point in infuriating him further. "Have you looked at the receipts?" she asked. "We had a good day yesterday."

"That's nice. Now get back behind the counter. I'll open up."

Within an hour, the store was packed with customers—mostly women picking up personal items and things for their homes. During the lunch hour, working girls came in looking for accessories and hair products. None of them wanted to be bothered taking advice from a girl who obviously didn't use what she was selling. Following a brief afternoon lull, a more eclectic crowd arrived—women pushing strollers, children who'd gotten out of school, and a few regular customers.

Mr. Joachim remained at the store until closing. Afterward, he stood at the end of the main aisle as she walked up and down the rows with the feather duster. When she finished the last of the rows, he held out the broom and dustpan. Good thing she'd worn her flats, or she'd be limping. As it was, she had a blister on her foot from the day before. It hurt, but it wasn't unbearable.

After she finished cleaning, he handed her an envelope. "Get your things and get outta here. See you Monday morning."

She gladly did as she was told, and she clenched her jaw to keep from saying anything. Mr. Joachim wasn't as bad as he came across, but as tired as she was, her thoughts weren't exactly pleasant. She stuffed the envelope filled with her weekly pay into her purse and walked out the door.

The first thing she spotted when she rounded the corner toward home was William Tronnier standing on the side of the road, leaning against his automobile. When he noticed her, he lifted a hand and motioned for her to get in.

"Thank you," she said, "but I can walk."

"Why would you want to, with me right here?"

Good point, but she couldn't get in without an argument. "I like walking?"

"Maybe so, but you've been on your feet all day. I'm giving you a chance to ride home in style." A playful smile teased his lips.

She paused then got into his automobile and waited for him to run around to his side. "What are you doing here again today?" she asked when he joined her inside the car.

"Waiting for you."

"Tell me the truth."

He lifted one hand as he shrugged and gave her a quick glance before turning his attention back to driving. "That is the truth. I just happened to be in town, so I hung around to take you home."

The sliver of hope dashed, and she sighed. She should have known better than to think he'd drive all the way into town just for her.

"So how was your day? Better than yesterday, I hope."

"It was good." She smoothed her hands over her dress. "Busy."

"I like hearing that. Business seems good for everyone. These are some very good times all around."

Maybe for some people, but Lillian wasn't exactly feeling the effects of such great times. "I suppose."

* * * * *

Lillian wasn't very talkative today, and William felt awkward. He racked his brain to think of something interesting to say.

Finally he forced a laugh. "My brother Mason told me he caught you eating a pickle sandwich."

"He caught me?" Confusion replaced her look of exhaustion. "Is there anything wrong with eating a pickle sandwich?"

"No, not at all." William hated that he'd made her defensive.

She folded her arms and slumped in the seat. "I eat pickle sandwiches when I don't have anything else to bring for lunch."

Of course. It had never dawned on him that she ate something odd simply because that was all she could afford.

"I am so sorry, Lillian. I had no idea."

"I bet there are a lot of things you have no idea about." She pulled herself straighter as they stopped in front of her house. "Like what it means to have to work for someone at a job you don't love and go home too tired to do anything—and then have to repeat it all the next day."

"Hold on there, Lillian. I never meant to insult you."

"But you did."

"I'm sorry, okay?"

She cleared her throat and nodded but wouldn't look him in the eye. His mouth went dry as he tried to figure out what to say or do.

He reached out and gently touched her cheek. She slowly turned to face him. "Please don't feel sorry for me, William."

"I don't." More than anything, he was embarrassed by what he'd said. "My apology wasn't about feeling sorry for you, but more about asking forgiveness for sticking my ugly foot in my mouth."

Her lips curled into a grin as she glanced down at his feet. "I bet those boots taste terrible."

"Oh, trust me, they do." His hand lingered on her cheek for a few seconds before he finally pulled away. "I'll see you again soon, Lillian."

She started to say something, but she closed her mouth, nodded, and got out of his automobile instead. "Thank you again for the ride, William. I hope you don't feel obligated to make this a regular thing."

He didn't feel obligated, but he fully intended to make this a regular thing. Waiting for Lillian was torture, but seeing her had become the highlight of his day. He waited until the front door closed behind her before pulling away—but not before the front window curtain fluttered back into place. Someone had been watching them.

Chapter Two

....

Lillian walked into the house in time to see her parents pretending they weren't spying from the front window. "Before you say a word, yes, I did get a ride home in William Tronnier's automobile."

"Be careful, Lil," her daddy warned. "I'm sure he's a very nice man, but people like him…well, they have different expectations."

"I don't want you to get hurt," Mama added. "I have no idea why he's giving you all this attention, but it can't be good."

Her mama had stepped over the line with her last comment. Lillian spun around to face her. "Why do you say it can't be good? You don't think he's merely a nice man who wants to do a girl a favor?"

Mama and Daddy exchanged a knowing glance before Mama took her by the arm and led her to the sofa. Daddy disappeared to another part of the tiny house. "There are some things that you learn from experience. I was once courted by a young man of means. I thought he liked me for who I was, but he just saw me as a temporary diversion between more suitable young women."

"That was a long time ago, Mama. Besides, a couple of rides home in an automobile don't constitute courting."

Her mama lifted a finger in the way that annoyed Lillian. "Mark my words. Either he feels sorry for you or he wants something a girl from his social class won't give him."

"Mama!"

"I know it sounds harsh, but it's better to learn this now than to find out later the hard way."

Daddy reappeared at the doorway. "When's supper going to be ready? I'm starving."

Mama hopped off the sofa and scurried toward the kitchen, her voice trailing her as she went. "It'll be ready in two shakes of a bunny's tail."

Lillian rose and started to follow, but Daddy stopped her. "Your mama is just trying to protect you. She knows what it's like to be a young girl with a broken heart."

"You didn't break her heart," Lillian reminded him.

"No, but I was right there after it happened." He offered a self-satisfied grin. "In fact, when I saw her in distress, I swooped down and claimed her for me. I was glad to do it, too. I couldn't have found a better woman, even if I'd gone looking in the upper class."

"Daddy, that's all good, but this has nothing to do with looking for someone." Why couldn't her parents get it through their heads that she and William Tronnier were not seeing each other?

"Speaking of looking for someone, what's wrong with Walter Adams? He's a hardworking man, and he would be better suited for you." Daddy rubbed his chin as he pondered his suggestion. "In fact, I think he'd be very understanding about you working."

Walter Adams didn't have a gentlemanly bone in his body. "I'm not interested in Walter."

"He might not be as handsome as Mr. Tronnier, but you should look past all that. If you'd like, we can invite him over one evening so you can get to know him better."

"No, Daddy, I've known Walter long enough to know that he's not a good match for me. Besides, I can't see myself ever wanting to be with Walter."

"Don't say no so fast, Lillian. Age tends to advance quickly, and as the years go by, you may not have the luxury of being so picky."

* * * * *

The next morning, Mama entered Lillian's bedroom and swished open the curtain. "Time to get up and ready for church. I'm ringing bells, so I have to be there early for our final rehearsal."

Lillian slowly sat up in bed. She felt as if she'd been hit by a steam locomotive. "Where's Daddy? Is he ready yet?"

Mama laughed. "He's still sawing some Z's. Give him another five minutes before you try to get him up. Ever since it's cooled off at night, he's been more difficult to wake up. Maybe if I yank the blanket off the bed and hide it, he'll be more agreeable to join the land of the living."

Lillian watched Mama leave for church before she stood and pulled on her own robe. At least Mama had made the coffee. She poured herself a cup and sat down at the table to enjoy a couple of sips before making an attempt to wake Daddy.

She was about to go get him up when she heard the sound of movement in the hallway. When she glanced up, she saw him trudging toward her. "Where's your mama? Has she already gone off to church?"

Lillian nodded. "Want some coffee?"

"Sure." He limped toward the table.

"Are you hurting?" she asked as she poured the coffee and added cream and sugar.

"A little." He rubbed his leg. "Sometimes I can almost kid myself into thinking I might be able to go back to work someday, but then on days like this, I wake up feeling like it happened yesterday."

Lillian knew there was no point in getting her hopes up about Daddy going back to work. The doctor had said he'd never be able to hold a job that required any standing or walking for long periods of time, and that was the only type of work Daddy knew how to do.

"I'd get a job at the bank if they'd hire me, but you know how it is. All those jobs are held by relatives and friends of the old bankers."

She offered him a look of sympathy as she set the coffee cup in front of him. "Eggs?" There were two eggs in a small bowl in the icebox.

He nodded. "Scrambled, if you don't mind. And some toast. When are you getting paid again?"

"I got paid yesterday," she replied.

"Good. You can give your mama some money to get some decent food. I'm getting sick of potatoes and onions."

Lillian was sick of a lot of things, but she didn't mention it. Instead, she prepared the eggs and toast for her daddy and then served him.

"Aren't you going to eat?" He shoveled a forkful of eggs into his mouth and watched her as he chewed and swallowed.

"I might fix myself a piece of toast after I get ready for church. Do you feel like going?"

"No, but I'll go to make your mama happy. She hates when I miss church—especially when she's ringing bells."

An hour later, Lillian and her daddy were on their way. Fortunately, their church was only a couple of blocks from their house. A group of people hovered near the door. When she got close enough to see their faces, she spotted someone she never expected to see.

* * * * *

William knew the instant Lillian saw him. Her face lit up with recognition before doubt and distrust covered her like a shield. Her father didn't seem to know what was happening. He hobbled up the three steps and edged past the few people who stood in his way, while Lillian hung back.

"What are you doing here?" she asked in a loud whisper.

"Same thing as you. Worshipping God."

"I've never seen you here before." She diverted her gaze. He glanced over his shoulder and saw her father chatting with Walter Adams.

"That's because I generally attend church with my family," William replied, pulling her attention back to him. "But I thought—"

"You thought you'd come to this side of the tracks where all the poor people worship God."

Instead of arguing with her, which he knew would be pointless, William countered her with what he knew was true. "We all worship the same God, so what does it matter?"

She opened her mouth, but nothing came out. Walter pulled away from Lillian's father and approached them.

"Hey there, Lillian," Walter said in a husky voice, "I've been thinking me and you might should get together sometime."

William pulled back in astonishment. That took some gall.

"It's very sweet of you to think about me, Walter, but I don't think our getting together is a good idea."

Walter now seemed stunned. "But I thought...your daddy...well—"

"Now run along and find a seat near the back, Walter. Those pews are always the first to fill up."

William had to hand it to Lillian. She sure didn't pull any punches if she wasn't interested. Then it dawned on him—she'd never spoken to him like that.

"Would you mind if I sit with you and your father?" he asked.

"Suit yourself." Lillian barely glanced at him before setting out for the front of the church toward her father.

As they sat down, her father extended his hand. "I would stand, but I have a gimp leg. I'm Frank Pickard."

"William Tronnier. Pleased to meet you," William said as he shook Mr. Pickard's hand. "I don't expect you to stand. I just thought it would be nice to visit Lillian's church this morning."

"It's a fine church," Mr. Pickard said as he nudged Lillian. "Isn't it, Lil?"

"Yes." Lillian fumbled with her Bible and squirmed in the seat between the men.

Occasionally, William spotted some of the other church members leaning forward and staring at him, until he turned around and met their gazes. All of them offered brief smiles and quickly looked away. Some of them probably knew who he was, but many didn't. Regardless, he was sure they wondered what he was doing there.

As the pastor preached his sermon, William thought about how similar the service was to his own. His mother was in the bell-ringer group at his own church, and when they started playing a familiar tune, he leaned over and whispered this to Lillian. She gestured for him to be quiet, so he did as he was told.

Finally, when the service was over, William stood and helped both Lillian and her father to their feet. "This was very nice—almost exactly like the service at my church."

"Only the people at your church dress much smarter, I'm sure," Lillian blurted.

The instant she said that, her father gave her a stern look. "Where are your manners, Lillian Pickard?"

"That's all right," William told Mr. Pickard. "I can't say I didn't expect something like that. It's really my fault, showing up uninvited."

"Well, the way I was brought up, you should never have to wait to be invited to any church," Mr. Pickard said. "The Lord's house is for His believers, no matter who you are."

"Thank you." William extended his elbow toward Lillian. "Would you like to go outside?"

"It's cold out, and I don't intend to leave this building until it's time to go home."

"Oh, that reminds me. I'd like to offer you and your parents a ride home."

Lillian shook her head. "That isn't necessary, Mr. Tronnier."

"William."

She rolled her eyes and sighed. "William. Like I said, that isn't necessary. We are perfectly capable of walking home. We do it every week."

"Your father's leg…well, I think he might enjoy a ride in this cold weather. And your mother too."

"That sounds like an excellent idea." The female voice behind William sparked his attention. It sounded similar to Lillian's voice, only slightly huskier. He turned around. "Mrs. Pickard?"

"Yes, you must be William Tronnier. I would love a ride home in your automobile. I've only ridden in one once, although my husband has been in several."

William noticed Lillian pulling away, but she didn't leave. "Then it will be my pleasure to take you all."

"You can stay for dinner afterward. We've been a little lean lately, but I put aside a chicken for Sunday's meal."

William was taken aback by her open admission of the family's lack of food. "I couldn't…I mean, I'm sorry, but I can't stay for dinner." He shuffled his feet. "My mother is expecting me home for our own family meal."

When he looked over at Lillian, he instantly knew she could see right through him.

"Well, if your mama wants you home for dinner, that's where you should be," Mrs. Pickard said. "As soon as my husband finishes chatting with his friends, I'm ready to go home."

William helped two of the Pickards into his automobile. Lillian resisted any assistance, so he left her to do what she wanted. But he was more determined than ever to get to know her better.

"Oh, this is fun," Mrs. Pickard said as he pulled away from the church. "Does this thing go very fast?"

"Faster than a horse," William said. "And I don't have to worry about it tiring out."

"One of these days perhaps Frank and I can purchase an automobile."

Silence fell among the Pickards. William suspected that Mrs.

Pickard had a tendency to dream of a future she wasn't likely to have, and her family appeased her by not arguing.

He pulled up to the front of their cottage, got out of the automobile, and helped the elder Pickards out. "Have a good day, folks. See y'all soon." He glanced at Lillian, who abruptly turned and stomped toward the front door.

"Lillian!" Her mother ran after her and grabbed her by the arm. "Where are your manners?"

"Oh, sorry." Lillian squared her shoulders, lifted her chin, and forced a smile. "Thank you for your generosity in giving us a ride home in your fine automobile, Mr. Tronnier."

He had to stifle a chuckle. Lillian's pride was hilarious and very attractive.

"I enjoyed driving you." He waited until the Pickard family was inside their house before taking off for home.

All the way back to the farm, he thought about how to appeal to Lillian. She was an enigma, caught between her pride and her manners.

His parents arrived home right behind him. Mom was the first to hop out of the buggy. "I thought you went into town to spend the day with the Pickards."

"I thought so too, but my timing might have been off."

"You did go to church, didn't you, son?" Pop asked.

"Yes, of course. It was a very nice sermon."

Pop grinned. "I find it interesting that you mention the sermon since we all know the reason you went to town had nothing to do with church."

William shared a look with Pop before turning his attention back to Mom. "Mrs. Pickard plays the bells in her church."

"I would love to talk to her. I suspect we have quite a bit in common."

"I'm sure you do."

* * * * *

As the Pickard family sat down to their chicken dinner, Mama didn't waste any time before jumping on the topic of William Tronnier. "What a sweet young man. He went to an awful lot of trouble to see you, Lillian. Perhaps I was mistaken about him."

"Don't assume that, Helen, just because the boy visited our church one time."

"At least he came," Mama argued. "Not everyone does. I think it says something about him and his upbringing."

"Anyone can go to church."

As her parents discussed William, Lillian considered bolting from the table and running to her room. Why did they feel it necessary to go on and on about something that didn't matter anyway? It wasn't like she'd ever allow her head to be turned and leave them to fend for themselves. And they certainly couldn't make it without her.

Their voices buzzed as she thought about how she'd never be able to realize her own dreams. But that's all they were...dreams. When she was younger, she'd imagined herself dressed in her mother's wedding gown and walking beside her daddy down the aisle of the church toward a dashing groom.

"Don't you think so, Lillian?" Mama's voice startled her from her thoughts.

"Don't I think what?" Lillian lifted her glass and sipped some tea.

"You weren't listening to a word we were saying, were you?"

"Sorry, Mama, but I have a lot on my mind. Mr. Joachim is already talking about the Christmas season."

"Oh my. Isn't it a bit early for that? It's barely October."

"Apparently he thinks he needs to get started on it or we might miss out on some business. Sears has already started promoting their Christmas mail order."

"This isn't Sears we're talking about," Daddy said. "Joachim doesn't have to compete with that giant."

"He seems to think that getting a head start on it will lock up some business. We'll be decorating, and he wants me to make a display with gift ideas."

"Who has room to store gifts now, even if they do buy them?" Daddy said. "That's ridiculous."

Mama shrugged. "If we had a bigger house, I might consider it."

Lillian shook her head. "Most people don't have a bigger house, so I think it's a waste of time to start this early, but he's the boss."

"Yes, he is the boss," Daddy agreed. "And you have to do what he says."

"Mama, I'll give you the household money from my pay envelope after we finish eating."

"Good. I was thinking I might pick up some ham hocks and greens for supper one night."

"Just don't spend too much on it," Daddy advised. "I don't want to run out of food and get stuck with potatoes and onions again." He made a face.

"Frank! You should be thankful you have any food at all. If it weren't for Lil—" Mama cut herself off and glanced down. "We are blessed to have food on our table, no matter what it is."

Daddy cleared his throat. "Yes, of course we are."

The tone at the table had changed from lively to somber at the mere hint of Lillian's having to support the family. She knew Daddy's pride had been wounded, and she would have done anything to make it better.

* * * * *

Lillian walked to work the next morning with dread. She suspected that Mr. Joachim would be waiting by the door, with boxes of store decorations beside him, ready to pounce on her before she took off her jacket.

To her surprise, she arrived before he did. She had to fish around in her purse for the key. Once inside, she prepared the store to open.

Mr. Joachim didn't show up before the first customer, either. As she rang up Mrs. Gooch's order, she found herself worrying about her boss. This wasn't like him at all—especially not right before the holidays—and it annoyed her, since he'd probably come in barking orders and asking why she wasn't doing whatever it was he wanted her to do.

It was practically noon before he finally walked through the door looking haggard. "My wife got sick after church, and we were up all night."

Lillian instantly felt remorse for her earlier thoughts. "Do you need to go back home and take care of her? I can manage without you for a few more hours."

"No." He rubbed the back of his neck. "Her sister came to help, so I can stick around here all day."

"If you need to leave, I understand."

He looked her in the eyes and started to smile, but he caught himself before it happened. "We have work to do. Christmas is coming whether we're ready or not, and I don't want to miss out on any business. This is the time when we can make enough to get us through the worst of times."

"Times have been very good lately," Lillian reminded him. "Everyone is talking about it."

"Yes, but mark my word, it's just a cycle. We have good times and then we have bad. Nothing will ever stay the same."

* * * * *

William loved nothing more than helping out on the farm. Pop tried to give his sons less strenuous tasks by hiring some laborers to do the hard work, but William wanted to be out in the fields with the rest of the men.

"So tell me what you see in this girl," his brother Amos said as they walked along the rows where they planned to plant soybeans in the spring. "Mom says you're completely smitten."

"She says that?" William walked in silence for a few seconds, until he finally stopped and turned to face his brother. "I s'pose she's right. In fact, I haven't been able to get Lillian out of my mind since I first talked to her at the Jordans' party last year."

"Do you think she feels the same way?"

"Hard to tell. She's very guarded."

"I wonder why."

"It's hard to say. I'm thinking there's some pride involved, but I don't know for sure."

"I would think any girl would be proud to be seen with you," Amos said as he started walking again.

"That might be the problem. She might be embarrassed about her own situation. Her dad had to quit work, so he depends on her to support the family. I'd suspect her income to be very meager."

"Pride gets people into all kinds of trouble."

"Or people use it to keep from getting their hearts into trouble."

Amos smiled and nodded. "You just have to show her that your heart is right with the Lord and let Him lead the relationship."

"That's the problem," William said. "There isn't a relationship. All I've done is taken her home from work a couple of times, and I took her family home from church once."

"Maybe you can visit her at home sometime. Get to know her parents and show them you're a decent guy."

William nodded. "That's probably a good idea. They seem nice enough, and they didn't mind getting a ride home from church. Her father's leg was injured at the factory, and from what I understand, he's not likely to go back."

"Seems he'd be able to do something else…like a job that allows him to sit. A desk job, maybe. Perhaps at a bank."

"You and I both know how tight the banking business is. He'd have to have some connections to get on with one of them."

"True," Amos agreed. "Maybe we can get Pop to pull some strings for him."

"I don't know if that's such a good idea right now, though. Mr. Pickard hasn't given me any indication he's interested, and I don't even know if banking is something he'd like to do."

"Banking is definitely something I wouldn't want to do."

"Same here," William said. "Well, looks like we're on the right track with next year's crop rotation. The soil looks good, so we should be able to get it fertilized and ready for planting as soon as spring comes."

* * * * *

Lillian worked on the display between customers. Her mind wandered as she worked, and before she realized where her thoughts had gone, she found herself thinking about William Tronnier. His surprise visits had quickened her pulse each time, which annoyed her. How dare he continue to pursue her when she'd made it clear she wasn't interested.

"Lillian!"

She nearly fell off the small stepladder at the sound of her name. Josephine Finley stood behind her, arms folded, a scowl on her face.

"Where did you move the cold cream?"

"It's in the same place it's always been, Mrs. Finley. On the second aisle from the left."

"When you say left, are you facing the back or the front of the store?"

Lillian felt her pulse in her head and had to take a deep breath. Some people tried her patience more than others, and Mrs. Finley had always been one of them. "Facing the back..." She pointed. "Over there."

"You should have said so to begin with."

Lillian climbed off the ladder and headed in the direction of the beauty aisle. "I'll get it for you." Lillian continued toward the beauty products and stopped. "It's right here."

Instead of getting a jar, Mrs. Finley planted a hand on her hip and stared at Lillian. "When did you start seeing one of the Tronnier boys?"

"I—I haven't been seeing any of the Tronnier boys."

"Well, then, who was that at church yesterday? He certainly looks like the middle Tronnier boy."

"He was. But I'm not seeing him." Lillian tucked her hair behind her ear and wished she'd stayed on the ladder.

"Then what was he doing at our church? He and his family attend somewhere else."

"I suppose he was worshipping God, just like we were."

"Young lady, I've known your mother since long before you were born, and I just happen to know she wouldn't appreciate your smart-aleck mouth."

Chapter Three

By the end of the day, Lillian had held her tongue so many times she was ready to let loose and scream. Mr. Joachim's demands hadn't stopped with the display, and customers from church had come in throughout the day. Most of them asked about William and wondered what he was doing there on Sunday—and everyone seemed to have an idea of what she should do.

Mr. Joachim left an hour before closing to see about his wife, even though there were at least a dozen customers in the store. That was fine with Lillian. It was easier to handle the busy store all by herself than to have to deal with constant criticism. As usual, one straggler remained in the store after-hours, and Lillian had to remind her of the closing time. The woman paid for her handful of items, but she didn't leave right away. Instead, she struck up a conversation about the changing weather. She wasn't someone Lillian recognized.

"Yes, it generally does start to get cold out at night this time of year," Lillian agreed. She glanced at her watch. "I don't want to be rude, but I was supposed to lock up the store ten minutes ago. Do you need anything else?"

The woman's grin widened to a full-blown smile. "I just want you to know that it's nice to see such a hardworking girl who cares so much about her family. Back when I was your age...or maybe a little bit younger, I did the same thing for my family. But then I met Claude, and he was able to support—" Something outside the store caught her attention, and she abruptly stopped talking. She grabbed her bag off the counter and scurried toward the door. "Thank you, Miss Pickard. You are a delightful young lady."

Curious, Lillian turned around and spotted William Tronnier outside the window, standing beside his automobile. He waved when their gazes met. She flipped her hair over her shoulder as she turned back around. What was he doing here?

The bell on the door jingled. "I thought I'd stop by to take you home. Anything I can help you with?"

"No, there is nothing you can help me with. And for your information, I don't need you to always be around to take me home. I'm perfectly capable of walking."

After he didn't respond for a few seconds, she turned to see if he'd heard. "Having a bad day?"

"You don't know the half of it."

"I'm a good listener." He took a tentative step closer.

"Well, that's all fine and dandy, but I'm not in the mood to talk about it."

"Must be very bad, if that's the case. You don't have to say a word until you're ready. Just know that when you want to talk, I'll be here."

"Mr. Tronnier, I don't know of a polite way to tell you this, so I might as well go ahead and let you know that I'm simply not interested in your charity."

"Charity?" He folded his arms and rocked back on his heels. "What kind of charity are we talking about?"

Lillian tried to look directly at him, but his gaze made her tummy flutter, so she pretended to look at something on the counter. "You know exactly what I'm talking about. All those rides in your automobile and…" She couldn't think of anything else.

"And?"

She fluttered her hand. "I don't know why you're doing this, Mr. Tronnier."

"Let me explain this to you in the simplest manner possible. I am a man. You are a woman. I find you immensely attractive and interesting. I would like to get to know you better."

She ventured a brief glance in his direction and caught him smiling. The walls seemed to close in a little around her, so she edged farther back behind the counter to put more distance between them.

"That's not all," he said. "After we talked last year, I asked around about you, but no one had much to say except that you took care of your family. I find that quite attractive as well."

She forced herself to laugh. "Oh, it's so attractive. I get up every morning, come here, work all day, and practically drag myself home every night. Can't get any more gorgeous than that."

"I would have to agree. You have purpose in life, and people with purpose in life have something special." When she looked him in the eyes again, he leaned toward her. "Want to know what I find the most attractive about you?"

"Sure, go ahead; you're on a roll."

"You love the Lord, and you don't let your circumstances get you down or keep you from worshipping Him."

"You haven't seen me on my good days."

"Is that a challenge?"

She twisted her mouth to one side, lifted one eyebrow, and slowly moved her head from side to side. "Maybe."

"Then I'll take it."

Lillian wasn't sure what to say next, so she didn't even attempt to respond. She went about her end-of-the-evening routine and started for the door.

"Would you mind if I stopped off at your house and visited with your parents?" he asked.

"Can I persuade you otherwise?"

"Not a chance," he replied.

"Then why bother asking?" She walked outside and didn't even put up a fuss about getting into his automobile.

When they arrived at her family's cottage, she turned to face him. "I have no idea what my parents might say or do since they're not expecting you."

"Lillian, you never have to make excuses for anyone, including your parents. Besides, they seem like nice people, so I'm sure they'll be polite even if they don't want to see me."

"You are one strange man," she said as she got out of the automobile.

He caught up with her before she reached the door of her home. "That's a compliment. I don't want to be like everyone else—especially with you."

"Oh, trust me, you're nothing like anyone else I've ever known."

"Lillian, is that you?" The sound of Mama's voice rang through the house.

"Yes, Mama, it's me, and I have company."

In less than a minute Mama showed herself in the living room, a confused expression on her face until she spotted William. "Hi, Mr. Tronnier. It's so nice to see you. I apologize for the mess."

Lillian glanced around and saw that everything was perfectly clean and in place. "Mama, the house looks nice. Mr. Tronnier just wanted to stop by and say hi to you and Daddy."

"Would you like to stay for supper?" Mama asked.

William didn't waste a moment before shaking his head. "No, I'm expected at my parents' home for supper. Besides, I wouldn't want to pop in unexpectedly and expect a meal. That would be rude."

"In that case, why don't you come by tomorrow night?"

Lillian spun around and glared at her mama. She started to make up a reason why he couldn't, but he was faster to respond. "I would love that. That is, if Lillian doesn't mind." He looked down at her.

What could she say? "Of course I don't mind."

"Then I'll be here. Would you like me to bring something?"

Mama wore a false smile as she lifted her chin. "Just yourself, and make sure you come hungry."

"Don't go to too much trouble," he argued without an ounce of conviction in his voice.

"It's no trouble at all. I haven't cooked for one of Lillian's friends in a long time, so it will be my treat."

Lillian wanted to cringe. Her mother didn't need to tell him everything.

* * * * *

William felt bad for Lillian. He could tell that her mother had embarrassed her, but she needn't have felt that way. He was used to his own mom talking too much. It came with the territory.

"I'd best be getting home." He glanced at Lillian. "Walk me to the door?"

"Sure. The house is small, so we don't have to walk far."

They stopped when they reached the door. Mrs. Pickard shot them a glance, smiled again, and disappeared, leaving him alone with Lillian. Lillian, however, wouldn't look at him, so he took a chance and tilted her chin up. He held his breath until he realized she wasn't going to resist.

"What are you thinking?"

She lifted one eyebrow. "Do you really want to know?"

William laughed. "You are one feisty woman, Lillian Pickard."

"And you are one presumptuous man, William Tronnier."

"Sounds like a very good match to me."

She stepped back, freeing herself from his touch. "All depends on the perspective."

"True." He hesitated before opening the door and taking a step.

"Since I've officially been invited over tomorrow evening, why don't I stop by the store and pick you up?"

"I'm surprised you bothered to ask," she replied. "You always do whatever you please."

Laughter bubbled from his throat, but he stifled more than a slight chuckle. "This is more fun than I've had in many years."

"So glad I'm able to amuse you."

"Until tomorrow." He didn't budge.

She stood at the door and narrowed her eyes. "Are you planning to leave or just stand there bantering with me?"

William sighed. "I guess that's a hint."

Now it was her turn to laugh. He heard her voice as she closed the door. "Good night, Mr. Tronnier."

All the way home, William rehashed his conversation with Lillian, and he couldn't stop laughing. Lillian definitely kept him on his toes. All the girls he'd seen in the past were too agreeable and bored him to tears. Lillian didn't have an agreeable bone in her body, yet she wasn't unpleasant. In fact, she was quite pleasant. The soft, husky tone to her voice, her fragrance as she breezed past him at the store, and the silky-smooth feel of her skin beneath his calloused fingers brought him an immense amount of pleasure.

She obviously wasn't a slave to style, yet she had more style than all the other women in town put together. Her long hair that had been coerced into waves defied the current trend of copycat short bobs on the working women he knew. She wore a very subtle shade of lipstick that enhanced her lips without drawing too much attention away from her sparkling eyes.

William pulled up in front of his house and tried to think about something besides Lillian. He didn't feel like fielding questions he didn't have answers to—at least not yet. And knowing his family, there would be plenty of questions as soon as he mentioned that he wouldn't be home for supper tomorrow night.

"What gives with the silly grin?" Mason said as soon as William walked in the door.

"I've been invited to dinner with the Pickards tomorrow night."

Mason whistled. "Can't stay away from her, can you?"

Amos came around the corner and joined them in the foyer. "Leave him alone, Mason. Can't you see the man's in love?"

"Stop it." William lifted his hands. "Or next time you even look at a woman, it'll be payback time."

"Trust me," Amos said through his laughter. "This is probably the last place I'll bring any woman I like—at least until I marry her."

"Who is bringing a woman home?" Mom said as she joined the brothers. She glanced around the room then settled her gaze on William. "Is someone hiding a woman in the house?"

"No, Mom," Amos said, "we're just harassing William because he can't stay away from Lillian Pickard."

"She must be quite a girl." Then Mom waved her hand the way she had since they were children. "Go get cleaned up. Supper is almost ready."

"Speaking of supper, guess who won't be home for dinner tomorrow night?"

William darted a warning glance in Mason's direction before speaking for himself. "I've been invited to join the Pickards for supper."

"Well, I hope you accepted," she said. "It's time you boys follow in your sisters' footsteps and start thinking about settling down."

"Why would we settle down when we have you?" Mason teased.

Mom groaned as she quickly turned toward the kitchen. "That's what I'm afraid of. Looks like I might have to resort to strong-arm tactics to get you all married off."

After William and his brothers washed up, they joined their

parents in the dining room. One of the household help kept glancing at William as she set the food on the table.

"What are you looking at, Nelda?" he asked.

She cut her gaze over to his mom, who nodded. "I hear you're sweet on some girl in town."

"Someone give me a break, please. Is that all anyone around here is talking about anymore?"

"It's all anyone in Cary is talking about," Amos said.

"Really?" William had started to pick up his fork, but instead he folded his hands and rested them on the table. "Are you serious?"

"No, of course I'm not serious." Amos nodded toward Mason. "It's your turn to say the blessing."

After they said "Amen," the conversation about William and Lillian resumed. Pop remained silent until Mason asked why Lillian had to work so hard.

"Why does it matter to you, son?"

Mason's face turned red, and he lifted his glass of tea.

"People work hard for a variety of reasons. Perhaps she likes having her own money. There's no better way to have money than to work for it."

William squirmed. "Let's change the subject, okay? This one is getting old."

Mason nodded his agreement and added, "We'll give you a break now, but don't think this will be the last of it."

"Oh, trust me, I realize that." William lifted his glass of tea. "Cheers."

* * * * *

Lillian fretted all day about how the evening would go. From the moment she awoke, she thought about what to wear, how to act unfazed, and where she should look when William gave her one of those long, appraising stares. It always unnerved her when he did that, but deep down, she sort of liked the flutters in her tummy.

Still, the question remained, what was going on with William Tronnier? Someone of his stature and position in the community could have his pick from any number of girls who were much better suited. What did he want with her?

She would have enjoyed being courted by William if her life had been different. But the fact remained that her parents depended on her to support them, which meant she'd most likely wind up as an old maid.

An image of Daddy's older sister popped into Lillian's head, and she had to stifle a giggle. The woman had a perpetually puckered mouth, looking like she'd sucked on a lemon for too long, and her hair had a gray stripe on either side. She pulled it up into a bun so tight, the skin on both sides of her eyes was stretched. No wonder she never smiled; her face must have hurt. Lillian and her brothers used to laugh at the woman they called Aunt Grim, although her name was really Grace. The one time Lillian's younger brother slipped up in front of Grace was the first time Lillian had ever seen Daddy so angry that his face turned bright red.

And now here Lillian was facing the same fate as Aunt Grace. Would her nieces and nephews call her "Aunt Grim" or perhaps something worse? She shuddered.

Before Daddy's accident, Lillian had never doubted she'd eventually find a suitable husband, live in a small but nice house in Cary, and have children. She wasn't in a hurry because there had been so many options back then. David Hampton was one possibility, but he had a nervous tick that could be rather off-putting. Then there was Mrs. Gooch's son Maverick, whose stare could make the most confident woman self-conscious. At the time, she thought she'd leave her options open to see if someone better would come along. But that didn't happen until it was too late.

Lillian closed her eyes as she remembered the night she met William Tronnier. She knew about his family, the successful soybean farmers who'd inherited thousands of acres of land. In spite of their assumed wealth, she'd learned that they were down-to-earth, God-fearing people who treated everyone as their equal.

Mama had been doing a little mending on the side to bring in extra money, and Ina Jordan, the wife of one of Daddy's former coworkers, had stopped by to pick up her dresses. She'd offhandedly invited the Pickard family to the party she and her husband Merv were throwing the next night. Mama said it was difficult for her and Daddy to get out after dark, but she asked Mrs. Jordan if Lillian could go. Without a blink, Mrs. Jordan said, "Yes, of course, we'd be delighted for Lillian to attend."

Fortunately, the party was the next night. If it had been further into the future, Lillian would have talked herself out of going. As it was, she barely had time to find a suitable dress and make arrangements to get to the house on the other side of town. Mama had another customer who was attending, and she agreed to stop off for Lillian on the way. Lillian knew the elderly couple had to go out of their way to pick her up, which was why Mama wouldn't take money for the mending she'd worked so hard on.

When Lillian arrived at the party, she instantly felt out of place and very dowdy. She was the only woman her age with hair past her shoulders. Most of the women wore stylish bobs, and those who'd kept their hair long had it professionally coiffed. As if that weren't enough to set her apart, her dress was ridiculously out-of-date.

Lillian would have turned around and run the several miles home, but before she had the chance to take a step back, William Tronnier had taken hold of her elbow and guided her across the room. The rest of the night was like a dream. Sometimes it still didn't seem real. William had turned his full attention on her and engaged her in the type of conversation she only imagined people having.

"Lillian! What's taking you so long? If you don't get a move on, you'll be late for work." Mama stood at her doorway shaking her head. "Are you not feeling well?"

"I'm feeling just fine." Lillian ran her fingers through her hair and fluffed the ends. "Just getting a late start."

"Don't lose track of time. Good thing I made biscuits and sausage for breakfast. You can eat that on the way to work."

"I'm not hungry, Mama, but thanks."

Mama's expression softened. "Are you nervous about tonight?"

Lillian started to pretend she'd forgotten about William coming over, but that would be pointless. Mama would know. "A little."

"Don't be. He seems like a nice man, and I feel obligated to pay him back for all those rides he's been giving you. Just don't let yourself fall in love, or you'll wind up getting hurt."

Lillian forced a laugh. "Fall in love? I don't even know him all that well, so that should be the least of your worries."

"Good girl. Now get moving so you can keep that job of yours. We can't afford for you to lose it."

The reminder wasn't necessary, but it did get Lillian's thoughts back on track. She didn't need to be daydreaming about having company for supper or reminiscing about the night she met William. Her job was to bring money home so her parents wouldn't wind up in the poorhouse.

Chapter Four

....

"The way you're primping, one would think you were getting ready for a royal ball."

William adjusted his tie, studied his reflection in the mirror, and then started over. "I can't get this thing right."

"Here, let me help you." Amos closed the distance and took both ends of the tie William had been fiddling with for the better part of ten minutes. He got it right the first time. "There ya go. This girl is pretty special, huh?"

"I would tell you to mind your own business, Amos, but that wouldn't be very nice, now would it?"

Amos propped his hand on the door frame and grinned at William. "You still didn't answer me."

"My answer?" William pulled out his comb and raked it through his hair a few times before turning to face Amos. "Yes, Lillian Pickard is very special."

"She's not exactly an easy one to read either, is she?"

"What are you getting at?"

"Just make sure you like the girl and not the fact that she's a challenge."

"That's ridiculous," William said with a huff.

"Maybe. Maybe not. I remember the chase with Annie Jergens. It was fun as long as the game was on, but once she let me catch her...well, I lost interest."

"This is different."

Amos pulled away from the door and lifted his hands. "If you say so." He took a few steps away and stopped. "At least have a good time while you're...involved."

Rather than keep up this line of conversation, William nodded. "I will. Now if you'll excuse me, I have a date to keep."

He'd made it to the door when he heard Mom holler, "Don't forget to bring something!"

"Like what?"

She appeared in the foyer carrying a platter. "You should never show up to dinner empty-handed. We didn't know what kind of cookies the Pickards like, so Nelda and I made peanut butter, chocolate, and gingerbread."

William laughed as he took the platter. "So that's why you were baking so many cookies. I'm sure they'll love all of them."

"I hope so." She stuck her hands in her apron pockets.

He'd planned to stop off for some flowers on the way, but perhaps that would be too much, now that he had the cookies. He didn't want to appear desperate or too charitable.

"Why don't you go by the florist and pick up some chrysanthemums?" Mom said.

"You don't think that's too much?"

"Of course not. The flowers are for Lillian. The cookies are for her family."

William couldn't help but think about how inept he felt. Seeing other girls from his social arena had been easy. No one ever doubted his motives when he arrived with arms filled with gifts. Now he had so many other considerations that could make or break his standing in Lillian's eyes. Not that he was courting Lillian, as she frequently reminded him, but he fully intended to if she'd accept.

He arrived an hour later at the Five and Dime to pick up Lillian. The store lights were on, but he couldn't see her through the cluttered window. He sat and waited a couple of minutes then decided to just go on in and see how much longer she'd be.

Mr. Joachim came from the back of the store the moment William walked inside. "Hello there, William Tronnier. How's the family?"

"Quite good." He glanced around. "Is Miss Pickard still around?"

"No, I sent her on home. She said she had company coming over. Based on the way she was acting, I suspect it might be a suitor, and I wouldn't want to stand in the way of my best employee finding love."

Obviously Lillian hadn't mentioned that he was her potential suitor. He tipped his hat and reached for the door. "It was good to see you, Mr. Joachim."

With a puzzled look, Mr. Joachim tilted his head. "Did you need something?"

"Um…as a matter of fact, I could use some…" William glanced around the store. "Candy."

"Candy?" Mr. Joachim echoed.

"Yes, I would like some candy. Chocolate, if you have it."

Five minutes later, William walked out the door with a sack of chocolate candy. He sure hoped Lillian had a sweet tooth.

The short drive to the Pickard house gave William some time to gather his thoughts. He'd hoped to arrive with Lillian. Now he'd have an armful of gifts instead.

* * * * *

Mama let the curtain slip from her fingertips. "He's here."

Lillian ran her hands down the front of her skirt as she strode toward the door. Her heart hammered and her lips were dry, so she took a deep breath, licked her lips, and lifted her chin.

"Don't forget who you are, Lillian." Her mother's voice gave her pause before she touched the doorknob.

"Trust me, Mama, I can never forget who I am." She refrained from reminding Mama who'd invited William for dinner.

As soon as Lillian opened the door, her gaze locked with William's. He shuffled and glanced down, directing her attention to the bundles nestled in the crook of one arm and a bouquet of flowers in the other hand. He thrust the flowers toward her. "Presents. For you."

"Presents?" Lillian started to smile as she took the flowers, but Mama's presence loomed behind her. "That's not necessary."

"I realize that, but Mom and Nelda baked some delicious cookies." He shifted the Five and Dime bag to his now-empty hand. "And candy."

"That's an awful lot of sweets."

"Come in, Mr. Tronnier, and let me take your coat," Mama said as she came around from behind Lillian and took him by the arm. "Where are your manners, girl?"

"That's quite all right," he said as he stepped inside. Mama took the cookies and candy, leaving him and Lillian to stand there staring at each other. "I didn't want to come empty-handed."

"But cookies, candy, and flowers? You didn't need to bring anything, but one of those would have been sufficient."

"Sufficient?" A grin tweaked the corners of his lips. "For what?"

She was aware that he watched her reactions, so she tried to keep a straight face and changed the subject. "Why don't you come on back to the kitchen and talk to my father? Mama made him stay there so he wouldn't pounce on you the instant you came in."

"Why would he pounce on me?"

Lillian shrugged. "He's suddenly developed an interest in farming, for some odd reason."

"Then lead me to him. I love a good farming conversation."

Lillian couldn't tell if he was serious or kidding, but regardless, she motioned for him to follow. Daddy stood up by the table when they entered the room.

"You don't have to get up, Mr. Pickard." William glanced down at Lillian and winked. "I'd love to sit down, if it's all right with you."

"By all means," her daddy said.

As the men chatted, Lillian helped her mother prepare dinner. The whole scene felt cozier than she was comfortable with.

Mama had a pot of turnip greens cooking beside a larger pot filled with chicken. She'd rolled out the dough for dumplings, and her favorite cast-iron skillet was well-seasoned and oiled, waiting for the corn bread batter. Lillian worked in silence as she wondered if this was a typical meal for the Tronniers. It used to be for the Pickards, until Daddy lost his job. Lillian's paycheck didn't stretch far enough to indulge in such a lavish meal very often.

Every once in a while, when the men's conversation stalled, William offered to help with something. "Mom sometimes gives me a task in the kitchen to keep me from raiding the cookie jar," he explained.

"Our cookie jar is in the cupboard, and there hasn't been anything in it since…" Mama's voice trailed off as Daddy glared at her. "You and Frank go on and finish chatting."

After another half hour of preparations, Lillian set the table. Daddy and William poured and placed the tea while the women put everything in serving bowls and set them on the counter. "I hope you don't mind buffet style. The table is so tiny—"

William held up his hands and smiled. "I enjoy buffet suppers. Mind if I say the blessing?"

Her daddy nodded. "Go right ahead. That would be very nice of you."

As William thanked the Lord for the food they were about to eat, Lillian had no doubt that his words were sincere. She was amazed at how humble he came across when he had every reason not to be.

"So tell me about the soybeans," Daddy asked between bites. "Why did your father decide not to grow tobacco?"

"That seems to be what everyone else is growing, so we thought soybeans filled a need."

Daddy squinted before slowly nodding. "Supply and demand. Good business move."

Lillian cringed at the very thought of Daddy coming across as though he knew anything about business. Even though William must have been a good fifteen years her father's junior, he probably knew more about the farming business than her daddy would ever know.

"Pop was talking about adding some crops for rotation. Any thoughts on that?"

Her daddy swallowed his food and rubbed his chin as he pondered William's question. Lillian cut a brief glance in William's direction to see if he was poking fun at her daddy...but he looked serious.

"Maybe some corn and potatoes. Those might be good crops to balance the soybeans. I know you have some cows. Have you considered adding more livestock?"

"We've considered it, but even with a few hired hands, we don't have the manpower to handle the business end of it. As it is, Pop and Amos do most of the work on the books." William chuckled. "And I don't think Amos and Mason are as big on office work as they thought they might be."

"I understand," her daddy said. "But it's necessary in any kind of business, including farming."

"Amos likes working outdoors, as do I, but Pop says it's much easier to find help for the crops than someone who'd want to sit indoors way out in the middle of nowhere."

"I'd hardly call your farm 'nowhere,' " Mama said. "It's a lovely place, from what I remember."

"You've been to the house?" William asked.

Mama blushed. "Well, yes, but only once. I was on a church

committee collecting quilts, and your mother offered to contribute some of hers."

"Mom and my grandma used to do quite a bit of quilting, until Grandma got sick. Then it seemed like all Mom ever did was wait on Grandma hand and foot until she passed away."

"I'm sorry," Mama said softly. She stood and skittered toward the stove. "Would you like more corn bread? I can whip up another batch in no time."

William held up his hands and shoved away from the table. "No thank you, Mrs. Pickard. The food was delicious, but I'm afraid I ate too much."

"You're a hardworking man, Mr. Tronnier. I would expect you to eat quite a bit." She lifted the basket of cookies and carried them over to the table. "How about a cookie? I'd planned to make some shortbread after dinner, but these cookies look much better."

"I ate a few too many cookies while Mom and Nelda were baking them, so I'll have to pass."

Lillian stood and started gathering plates. William hopped up to help.

"Why don't I help you with the dishes, Lillian, so your parents can relax?"

"No, you don't—" Mama began, before William gently placed his hands on her shoulders, turned her toward the living room, and guided her a few steps.

Lillian stifled a laugh at the expression on Mama's face. Daddy didn't waste any time getting up and hobbling out of the kitchen, leaving his daughter alone with their guest.

"So now what?" William asked as he carried some dishes to the sink.

"I can wash, and you can dry."

"No, that's not what I'm talking about. I want to know what I can do to make you want to spend more time with me."

"There really isn't much you can do."

"Why don't you like me?" William continued transporting dishes across the kitchen until the table was completely cleared. "Did I say something to upset you?"

"No, not really." Lillian had no idea how to explain something that should have been as obvious as the nose on her face.

"Surely you can give me a good reason why you don't want me around."

Lillian spun around and faced him directly. "Why do you *think* I don't want you around?"

"You don't like farmers?" He grabbed a towel and motioned for her to start washing. "Or you think I'm a boor?"

That was funny, but she didn't laugh. "Farmers are fine, and, no, you are not a boor."

"Then what is it? What did I do?" He chewed on his bottom lip for a few seconds. "Or what did I not do that I should have done?"

Now she burst out in laughter. "You haven't done…or *not* done anything."

"Then it doesn't make sense. I like you, and I bring you gifts. I give you rides when you're too tired to walk. If I haven't done anything wrong and there's nothing you want me to do that I haven't done…" He stopped and gave her a pretend hurt look.

Lillian tried as hard as she could to keep a straight face, but the conversation had taken such a silly twist and his face was so goofy that it wasn't possible. As soon as she burst into laughter, he joined in.

"At least you find me amusing," he said.

"Indeed I do."

"Laughter is a good thing between a man and a woman. I often witness Mom and Pop sharing a little private humor."

Lillian couldn't remember the last time she'd heard her parents amusing each other, but she didn't mention that. Instead, she kept the conversation on his parents. "How does your mother like being a farmer's wife?"

William shrugged. "I think she'd probably enjoy living in town, but Pop knows that, so he does everything he can to make her happy." He ran his towel over a clean dish. "Or at least as happy as he can, considering she doesn't get to see her friends as often as she'd like."

"Does she ever get involved in your family's business?"

"She tried doing the books, but Pop had to relieve her of that duty after she got the debit and credit columns confused one time too many." He stacked the last of the dry dishes. "Where do you want me to put these?"

Chapter Five

....

William stuck around and chatted with Daddy for less than an hour before he asked for his coat. Mama stood by the door, preventing Lillian from seeing him off.

After she closed the door, Mama turned to Lillian and shook her head. "I don't see anything good coming of this."

"I don't know what you're talking about," Daddy said. "He's a good boy. Smart too."

"He's not Lillian's type."

"Why don't we let Lillian and William decide that?" Daddy asked.

"What if they continue seeing each other and fall in love?"

"Aren't you jumping the gun, Helen? He just came over for supper. Besides, we raised a smart daughter, so I'm sure she can figure things out on her own."

Lillian wished her parents wouldn't discuss her as though she weren't there. "Y'all don't have to worry about anything," Lillian piped in. "I'm too busy working and helping out around here to fall in love with anyone."

Her parents exchanged a pained look before Daddy turned back to her. "Lillian, honey, we want you to find someone to love one of these days. But I do agree with your mama that whoever the man winds up being should be closer to...well, more similar to..." His voice trailed off as he turned to Mama for help.

"What your father is trying to say is that we don't want you getting hurt or involved with someone who might turn you into some hoity-toity person who'll be ashamed of us."

"I can't believe either of you would think so little of me. I would never do that."

"Maybe not, but we shouldn't have to keep reminding you that there are quite a few differences between the Tronniers and our family." Mama glanced at Daddy for reinforcement, and when he looked away, she continued. "Money does strange things to people."

"I think this conversation is pointless," Lillian said. "First of all, you are the one who invited him to supper. And second, I never said or did anything to give anyone the impression that something was going on between Will—Mr. Tronnier and me."

* * * * *

The next morning, Lillian trudged to work after a long, sleepless night of remembering her evening with William. She had to admit, he was charming. And handsome. When his hand grazed hers as she handed him the dishes, her stomach had fluttered. But the last thing she needed was to lose her heart to someone she couldn't have.

Mr. Joachim was at the Five and Dime when she arrived, and the instant she walked in, he started talking. "William Tronnier stopped by yesterday right before closing. He asked about you."

Alarms sounded in Lillian's head. She didn't want her boss to think that something was going on between her and William. "Did he—did he say anything?"

"He just asked if you were still here." Mr. Joachim chuckled. "The man must have quite a lot on his mind. He almost forgot to get what he came for."

Lillian relaxed. William obviously hadn't let on that he was pursuing her. Mr. Joachim scurried around the counter and stood with his hands on his hips as he surveyed the store.

"Christmas comes mighty fast. It'll be here before ya know it. Let's put a few things up here. We can decorate in stages." He took off for the back room, leaving Lillian alone at the front of the store.

Until last year, decorations had gone up the day before Thanksgiving so they'd be in place for the day after, when some of their customers liked to start their Christmas shopping. But Mr. Joachim had been making trips to New York City, where people did things differently. In many cases Lillian welcomed the changes, but this was one she didn't agree with.

Mr. Joachim reappeared with a cardboard box. "We can start by stringing some lights in the window. My wife is making garlands and bows too."

Rather than voice her opinion, Lillian simply nodded. She didn't have the energy to tell him what she thought, knowing that he wouldn't pay a bit of attention.

Since there were no customers in the store, the two of them framed the window with Christmas lights right away. At least she'd been able to talk Mr. Joachim out of lighting the real candles he'd used before she started working for him, reminding him that a fire could destroy his business and leave him with nothing.

After they finished clipping the last wire into place, he stood back and nodded. "Looks good for now. Why don't you grab a pack of colored paper and cut out some letters to spell 'Merry Christmas,' between customers? We can tape those to the window."

"Can't that wait at least another month?" she asked.

He frowned. "I s'pose. I just don't want to lose any business this season."

A customer arrived, so after a brief greeting Mr. Joachim scooted to the back of the store, leaving Lillian to do the selling. She brought a handbasket to the customer and offered her assistance. While the first customer was shopping, a couple more came in. Lillian loved being busy.

Business was steady throughout the day, with only a few lulls. Still, she found a chance to eat the lunch she kept tucked beneath the counter. Most days Mr. Joachim took over so she could eat in the office and take a break, but today he had to attend a meeting to greet some of the new business owners in town.

That afternoon, Lillian waited on a couple of groups of kids from the boarding school, sawmill workers after their shifts ended, a family who was changing trains and had an overnight stay in Cary, and her pastor's wife.

"It sure was nice to see someone new at church on Sunday," Mary Beth Butler said. "I hear he's one of the Tronnier boys."

So people had been talking. "Yes, ma'am, he is."

"Will he be coming back? Pastor and I would love to see him again."

"I–I'm not sure." Lillian hadn't even known he was coming last time, so she certainly wouldn't know what he planned for the future.

"Are the two of you seeing each other?"

"No." Lillian surprised herself with such an abrupt reply, and she forced a smile. "I mean, I barely know him. We met last Christmas and…" She had no idea what else to say.

Mrs. Butler offered an understanding grin as she touched Lillian on the arm. "I see. No one knows what the future holds, though, so we can keep praying for God's will."

"Yes, ma'am, that's what I like to do."

"Good." Mrs. Butler sashayed past the counter and made her way down the aisle of cleaning products. "Gussie asked me to pick up a new broom and some scouring pads. Would you mind showing me where they are? I don't buy them very often, and I can see that you have rearranged the store."

Lillian found what Mrs. Butler needed and carried the items to the front for her. "Is there anything else I can help you with?"

"No, I—" The sound of the bell on the door stopped her, and both Lillian and Mrs. Butler looked up.

William Tronnier came walking in and grinned at the women.

"Hi there, Lillian." He nodded toward Mrs. Butler. "And how do you do, Mrs. Butler? Your husband preached a mighty fine sermon on Sunday."

"Thank you, young man. We would like to have you back soon. Miss Pickard and I were just talking—"

Lillian cleared her throat. "Mrs. Butler, would you like to see some of the new night cream we just got in? Some of the customers who have tried it say it makes their skin feel really soft the next morning."

Mrs. Butler slowly nodded with a knowing look in her eyes. "That sounds very nice, Lillian. Yes, I would like to buy some, and then I'd better be getting on my way."

William stood off to the side of the counter while Lillian rang up Mrs. Butler's order. After she said her good-byes, he tipped his head and wished her a good evening.

Then he spun around and looked directly at Lillian. "Sorry if I interrupted something. I just wanted to stop by and tell you how much I enjoyed supper last night."

"Mama's a very good cook." Lillian left out the fact that Mama rarely had much to work with and that she'd spent most of the week's allowance on that one meal.

"Good. Then she might enjoy some of the bounty my pop sent. He had a bunch of produce left over from the harvest, and since we hate to have it go to waste, he suggested bringing it to you as a thank-you for being such great hosts."

"You don't have to do that, William."

He stepped closer to her and held her gaze, making her knees feel as if they might give way at any moment. "I realize I don't have to do anything, Lillian, but I want to. It's a gift."

"Yes, but—"

"Since it's out in the car and you're still working, why don't I just deliver it to your house?"

Lillian swallowed hard. "Mama would like that."

"Maybe I can have you over to our house sometime. Mama likes to think she's a good cook, but she mostly just helps Nelda, who tells her what to do."

Before Lillian had a chance to say anything, William wished her a good day and left the store. She watched him get into his automobile and take off toward her house.

A few more customers came in before closing time, so Lillian didn't have much time to think about William's visit. Five minutes after she flipped the sign to CLOSED, she locked up and headed home.

As soon as she walked through the door, her mama greeted her with a lingering hug. "Lillian, come and see all the food the Tronnier family gave us. I'll have to can some of the vegetables or they'll go bad. We can't let it spoil."

Lillian followed Mama into the kitchen and stopped short. The counters on both sides of the stove were covered with boxes of vegetables. She turned to the right and saw that an entire corner of the small kitchen had crates filled with tomatoes, peppers, corn, squash, and okra.

"He didn't tell me he was bringing this much," Lillian said as she stood there in awe. "He just said he had a bunch of produce left from the harvest."

"Well, this is certainly a bunch." Mama laughed. "Maybe we should have him over more often."

Lillian hadn't seen Mama this happy in a while. "I'm glad you have plenty of food to cook. That should take away some of the worry for a little bit."

"Yes, the Lord was good when He brought Mr. Tronnier into our lives." She moved one of the crates off the counter before turning around and facing Lillian. "I still don't understand why he's giving you so much attention."

Rather than let on that she was hurt, Lillian shrugged. "You're right. There's no reason for him to bother with someone like me." Inwardly she seethed. It wasn't her fault she'd been born into a family that required her to work so they could eat.

"Don't get all worked up over this, Lillian. You know exactly what I'm talking about. People with means generally stick with their own. We're working-class folk, and rarely do we move out of that."

Lillian lifted her hands and shook her head. "I know, I know."

"I don't want you getting hurt just because some man chooses to have a little fun at your expense." Her tone changed. "As much food as this is to us, it probably doesn't even make a dent in the Tronniers' pantry."

Later that night, Lillian lay in bed and pondered the conversation. Her mother could be right, but William sure did go to an awful lot of trouble to see her. And the gifts he gave… Maybe the cost didn't mean anything, but he still had to put forth effort to bring everything. Then there was the matter of his church visit. Why would someone do that if he wanted to simply have a little fun with her?

* * * * *

"Did they like the vegetables?" Pop asked when William arrived back at the farm.

"Mrs. Pickard did."

Pop stepped off the ladder where he'd been standing while repairing the side of the barn. "Did you see Lillian?"

"I stopped off at the Five and Dime on the way to her house, but she was busy and I didn't want to bother her."

With a chuckle, Pop brushed his hands together to get rid of the dust. "I'm sure you bothered her plenty. If she has any idea how smitten you are, I'm sure she's thinking about you quite a bit."

"Am I that transparent?" William felt heat rush into his face as Pop continued studying him.

"Afraid so. That girl has you all in a dither."

"I'm not sure what to do next."

"No one ever is, son. Women have kept men guessing since the beginning of time."

"What did you do to win Mom's heart?"

"Pretty much what you're doing. Her parents didn't trust me. They thought I was trying to buy her love."

Apprehension gripped William. "You don't think… I mean, I have been bringing her quite a few gifts. What if…" He rubbed his chin as he thought about his actions from a different perspective. "Maybe that's what I'm doing wrong. Should I back off for a while?"

"I wish I could tell you," Pop replied. "I'm the last person to give advice. Maybe your mother will know."

"I can't ask her questions like this."

"Why not? She's a woman, so she's more likely to know what goes on in another woman's mind."

Pop had a good point. "Maybe I'll talk to her later."

"Good. Now why don't you give me a hand with this so I can be done with it? I want to secure both barns in case we decide to bring in some more goats." He paused. "We also need to work on your house. I thought we could finish framing it out sometime during the next week or so."

"Don't you think getting more goats might be a bit risky, Pop? And the house can wait. We don't have enough hands on the farm as it is."

"Amos wants to spend more time out here, and I'll do what

I can to help. You've done more than your share of work around this place."

"With all of us working out of the office, who'll take care of the business?"

Pop shook his head and placed a hand on William's shoulder. "You need to stop worrying about matters you can't control. I've been praying for some answers, and I have no doubt that the Lord will provide when He's good and ready."

They worked on reinforcing the side of the barn for the next hour and then they went to the house they'd started building for William. It didn't take long to finish the frame. After William hammered the last nail, Pop started walking toward the house and gestured for William to follow.

"C'mon, son, it's starting to get mighty cold out. We'll have to knock off a little earlier as winter gets closer."

As they walked to the house, William decided to bring up hiring some workers. "Maybe we can put a poster up at the rail station and see if anyone is looking for work."

"That's an idea," Pop said. "Or we can talk to the pastor and ask if he knows anyone."

Mention of talking to the pastor gave William an idea. "Since about everyone I know from our church has employment or a business, perhaps I can talk to the Pickards' pastor too. He might know of some folks who need work."

Pop's eyes twinkled as he looked at William with pride. "What a great idea. I might also see about some of the men who used to work at the horse-and-buggy factory, since most of them have been furloughed. I hear their business has been flat lately."

"How many people do you reckon we'll need?"

"At least three or four. We can use a couple to help finish your house, and if we get more livestock, add a couple more."

"Don't forget, we need someone to do the office work." William deliberated for a few seconds. "Tell you what, Pop. I'll do whatever you need. Since you, Amos, and Mason have been stuck in the office for so long, I can take my turn. I've always been pretty good with numbers, and I know how to run the business side."

"Yep, son, you and Amos both get your ability to do numbers from me. I'm afraid Mason is more like your mom."

"Hey, what are y'all saying about me?" The voice coming from the shed near the house caught their attention.

"Oh, hey, Mason," Pop said. "We were just talking about how we need more men to run the farm and help finish building Will's house. It's tough enough as it is, and we're thinking about adding crops and livestock. And we'll need someone to run the business side."

Mason held up both hands and reared his head. "Don't look at me. Stick me back in that office and I might blow up the place."

"That's exactly why I'll take over so you and Amos can have some time working with your hands."

"Your mother and I are proud of you boys," Pop said as they got to the front porch steps. "After we finish William's house, we can start working on one for Amos."

Throughout supper, Mason, Amos, and William bantered. Occasionally Mom and Pop got a word in, but they let the boys chatter while they sat back and smiled. William noticed the occasional glimpses his parents exchanged, and he knew he wanted what they had—a love that transcended anything worldly.

Chapter Six

....

By the time Saturday rolled around, Lillian wondered if she'd ever see William again. He hadn't been to see her since earlier in the week when he'd brought the crates of vegetables.

"Thank the Lord for the Tronniers' generosity," Mama said as Lillian ate breakfast before leaving for work. "That meal I prepared for him set us back."

Lillian spread a small amount of jam on her toast and held it up for inspection before turning to face Mama. "You didn't have to go all out just because we had company."

"I don't want him to know how hard things are around here."

"It's not too difficult for anyone to figure out, Mama. I've been the only person in this house working since Daddy's accident."

Mama's jaw clenched, but she didn't say a word. Lillian didn't like upsetting her, but the truth couldn't be ignored. Plus she was tired. Working six days a week, nine to ten hours a day, and then coming home and doing chores would wear anyone out.

Mr. Joachim wasn't at the shop when she got there, so she had to unlock the door. She'd barely gotten all the lights turned on when she heard the bell. It was William.

"Don't you ever work?" she asked.

"I work plenty. I just wanted to stop by and see if you'd mind me coming over tonight."

Lillian remembered Mama's comment about how the meal had set them back. "Better not tonight."

William focused his gaze on her. "Mind if I ask why?"

She tried hard to be nonchalant. "It's just too soon. We've seen enough of each other this week."

"Oh," he said, nodding, "I get it. You want to space out our time together so we won't get tired of one another."

"It's not quite that complicated. I just don't think it's a good idea right now."

He pursed his lips as he backed toward the door. "In that case, I'd better head on back to the farm. We're looking for more help. If you know any strong men who need work, tell them we'd like to talk to them."

She glanced up and smiled at him but didn't say a word. After he left, she felt her shoulders sag. Whenever William showed up, her pulse quickened. And the instant he was out of sight, she felt out of sorts.

The day seemed to drag, but closing time finally came. Mr. Joachim left a few more decorations for her to put up, so she did that before leaving.

Mama and Daddy were quiet during dinner, which relieved Lillian. She didn't feel like making small talk. Ever since seeing William that morning, her head had been swirling with all kinds of thoughts and emotions.

Before she headed off to bed that night, Mama reminded her that it was her turn to be a greeter at church the next morning. "I'll leave a little early," Lillian said. "Don't worry about making breakfast for me in the morning."

* * * * *

The night chill still hung in the air as Lillian set off for church. She shoved her hands deeper into her coat pockets. She'd bought this coat last year with part of the Christmas bonus Mr. Joachim had given her, but she'd given her mama and daddy the rest of the money and then didn't have enough left for gloves. Perhaps Mr. Joachim would be generous again this year.

The other greeters were already there when Lillian walked up the church steps. After putting her coat away, she found a spot near the front door but out of the way of the draft as it opened.

Early birds who wanted a choice of seats arrived first; then a steady flow of people kept Lillian busy smiling, offering greetings, and shaking hands. She knew most of the people who came through the doors, but there were always a few she'd never seen before—boarders from Cary High School or new families who'd arrived in Cary for better opportunities and a fresh start in life.

The sound of William's voice stilled her even before she saw his face. As she slowly allowed her gaze to rise and meet his, her mouth went dry.

"Good morning, Lillian." He reached for her hand.

Her voice stuck in her throat, so she settled on a smile as she slowly shook his hand. The hum of voices around Lillian reminded her that they weren't alone, so she let go of William's hand, swallowed hard, and managed a weak, "Good to see you, Mr. Tronnier."

"Mind if I sit with you?" he asked.

"Sure, that's fine," she replied.

After he made his way into the sanctuary, Lillian tried to prepare herself for sitting next to William during the church service. She mentally gave herself a lecture about staying focused on the Word and not on the man beside her.

By the time she sat down between William and Mama, her brain was exhausted. Mama cast a curious glance her way, but she just smiled and turned to face the pastor.

After church, William gave her family a ride home in his

automobile. "Mom and Pop wanted to know if you would like to join us for Thanksgiving," he said as he helped them out of the automobile.

Stunned, Lillian turned to face Mama, who looked just as shocked. "Thanksgiving?" Mama managed to say. "That's weeks away."

"I know, but we wanted to ask before you had a chance to make other plans."

Mama turned to Daddy, who shook his head before looking back at William. "I'm sorry, but we already have plans. Tell your parents we appreciate their goodwill."

The look of disappointment on William's face tweaked Lillian's heart, but she reminded herself that Daddy was probably right. The invitation was more an act of charity than anything else.

"Perhaps some other time, then," he said at the door.

"Yes," Mama said. "Thank you for the ride, Mr. Tronnier. And please don't think you have to do this every Sunday. We've always managed quite well on our own."

Lillian knew this was Mama's way of dismissing William. She wished Mama would be more subtle.

"Would you like to come in?" Lillian asked, half hoping he wouldn't but half wishing he'd ignore the glares from Mama.

He glanced from her parents to her and shook his head, a dejected look on his face. "No, I'm afraid this isn't a good time for a visit. See you soon, though."

She stood at the door and watched William get back into his automobile and pull away before going inside. Mama and Daddy sat in the living room, obviously waiting for her.

"Sit down, Lillian," Daddy said. "We need to talk about your relationship with Mr. Tronnier before it gets out of hand."

Lillian sat, folded her hands in her lap, and fixed her gaze on them. "There is no relationship, Daddy."

Mama spoke next. "Lillian, we both understand what you're

feeling. Mr. Tronnier is a very handsome young man, and he's giving you more attention than you've ever gotten from a boy. However, we can't help but continue to question his motives."

Unexpected tears stung the backs of Lillian's eyes. She knew exactly what Mama was saying, but she was tired of hearing over and over how she wasn't suited for William.

"He obviously wants something and…" Mama's voice trailed off as she looked over at Daddy, whose jaw was set in determination.

She wanted to bolt from the room, but she knew Mama would follow, so she remained in her seat. Daddy spoke next.

"Lillian, we think you have a lot to offer a man. But William Tronnier is wrong for you." He glanced at Mama before continuing. "Working-class families rarely mix well with those who…" He frowned as he tried to come up with the right words.

Lillian took advantage of the lull. "He works quite hard. In case you haven't noticed, he's generally dressed in farm clothes."

"But he can stop working at any time and it wouldn't make any difference in the way he lives." Daddy's words were tinged with resentment.

"You don't know that," Lillian retorted with an edge of sarcasm.

Mama stood and planted her hands on her hips. "Don't ever speak to your daddy like that. He is only trying to protect you."

Daddy pulled up to a standing position and steadied himself by holding onto the back of the sofa. "I don't want to tell you who you can or can't see, but I can tell you what I think, Lillian."

"I thought you liked William."

Mama and Daddy gave each other the look that was becoming more frequent, and Daddy spoke up. "We think he is very nice when he's here, but that doesn't change the fact that you come from very different families, which is why we're concerned about his motives."

It always came back to that motive thing. There was no way Lillian could argue with something that wasn't tangible, so she didn't even try.

"I'll go get dinner started," she said as she got up and headed toward the kitchen.

* * * * *

William was baffled by the change in Lillian's parents' demeanor. They had been so friendly until today, and now they blatantly pushed him away. He reflected on everything he'd said, and he couldn't think of a single offensive thing.

All the way home, he pondered the problem and tried to consider every angle, but when he pulled up in front of the house, he still hadn't come to a conclusion. No one in his family was home, so he figured they must still be at church. Nelda was leaned over the oven door when he walked into the kitchen. She stood up when she heard him come in.

"Hi, Mr. William. I'm making your favorite dessert."

"Pound cake?"

She grinned and nodded, her eyes sparkling with delight. William always suspected he was Nelda's favorite of the Tronnier clan, but he would never take advantage of it.

"Sounds scrumptious. What's for dinner?"

"Country ham, fried okra, and sweet potatoes."

The sound of a horse and buggy let them know that the family had arrived home from church. William went out to greet them.

"How was church with Miss Pickard's family?" Mom asked.

William shook his head. "Church was fine, but something happened later that has me puzzled. I need some advice."

Mom hugged him and hung onto his arm as she looked at him with the eyes of a loving, concerned mother. "I'm sure we'll have plenty of advice as soon as we know what you need."

Pop chuckled. "Your mother doesn't mince words, does she?"

"Admit it, James. That's what you love about me, isn't it?"

"Yup. The direct approach grabbed me right here." He tapped his chest. "And it hasn't let go." He gestured for William to go inside, and he followed, still talking. "Did you have a chance to ask the pastor if anyone needed work?"

William nodded. "He said he'd speak to a few people who haven't been able to find a job."

"Good. I'm glad you got the ball rolling."

"I'm somewhat concerned about that, though," William said. "With all the new businesses opening up in town, I think something must be wrong with someone who can't get a job."

"Perhaps the jobs in town aren't a good fit for some. Not everyone wants to be a sales clerk."

"Maybe."

Pop narrowed his eyes and studied him for a few seconds. "So what happened with Lillian, son? You're acting different. Did she give you the cold shoulder?"

Chapter Seven

Over the next couple of weeks, Lillian jumped every time she heard the bell on the door at the Five and Dime. As each day passed, she found herself missing William's impromptu visits more and more.

Thanksgiving was now less than a week away and she still hadn't heard from him. She got home from work on Friday night and headed straight for her room to lie down and close her eyes.

A few minutes later, a knock sounded on her door. "Lillian, what is wrong with you? Supper is ready. I've had it waiting for you, so come out and join us."

"I'm not hungry, Mama. You and Daddy go on ahead and eat without me."

"We will do no such thing. Stop behaving this way and be part of the family."

Lillian got up and took a long look in the mirror. Her face was drawn and drab. Her hair had flattened on one side, so she fluffed it with her fingers. "Give me a few minutes. I'll be out there shortly."

"Don't wait too long. Your daddy's hungry."

Lillian tensed. Her mama was demanding, and her daddy was hungry. What about her? Didn't her feelings matter?

The instant that thought popped into her mind, she squeezed her eyes shut. *Lord, forgive me for being so selfish, but I can't get rid of these feelings. You know what I want, but apparently it isn't good for me—at least not in Mama's and Daddy's minds.*

When she finished her prayer, she knew she had to go to the supper table or she'd have to answer questions she didn't want to deal with later. The soft mumbling of conversation quieted as she entered the kitchen.

Daddy forced a smile. "How's my beautiful daughter?"

Mama didn't give Lillian a chance to respond. "It's about time you got over your sulking, Lillian. This is a difficult time in a girl's life. You have to keep your wits about you, or you'll wind up getting terribly hurt over some man who is playing with your affections."

"Not now, Helen," Daddy said before turning to Lillian. "I'll go ahead and say the blessing, and then you can tell us about your day."

They joined hands for the blessing then passed the bowl of butter beans and the basket of biscuits. A small vegetable platter with a sliced tomato, scallions, and cucumbers graced the center of the table.

There wasn't much to say about her day, since it wasn't any different from the day before. "We were busy from opening till closing."

"Mary Beth Butler stopped by this afternoon and mentioned that you've already started decorating for Christmas," Daddy said, obviously trying to make conversation. "Isn't it a little early?"

"I think so, but Mr. Joachim has other ideas. He has me putting up a new decoration everyday."

"He must know something we don't, then," Daddy said. "That's why he's a successful proprietor and I'm not."

"If you had a store, you'd be very successful, Frank."

Lillian saw the spark of adoration in her mother's eyes. At least her parents still loved each other, after all they'd been through.

"But I don't. I'm just glad Joachim knows what he's doing. I heard he's considering hiring some people to help out for the Christmas season."

"That's what he says. Do you know anyone who might be interested?" Lillian asked, although she knew her parents didn't get out much. She was just trying to keep the conversation from getting too personal. "There are quite a few jobs in town going unfilled."

"Maybe I should consider getting a job," Daddy said.

"You can't," Mama blurted. "That leg would give you fits if you had to stand all day."

"Maybe I can sit a little. We sure could use the money."

"Daddy, Mama's right. Most of the jobs out there don't give anyone much time for sitting." Lillian thought about how exhausted she was every day—and she had two perfectly good legs.

"We need to do something, or we won't have the money for Christmas this year," Daddy said sadly.

"Don't worry about getting me anything," Lillian said. "I don't need a thing."

"You could use some gloves," Mama said. "And I was thinking you'd look cute in one of those new bob haircuts."

"The problem with that is, my hair will keep growing and I'd have to keep going back to the beauty shop."

"True," Mama agreed.

"Your hair is pretty just like it is," Daddy said. "I don't want you chasing after some trend and copying everyone else. One of the things I always liked about your mama was she didn't try to do what all the other girls did. She's one of a kind."

Lillian glanced at her mother, who patted the side of her salt-and-pepper bun. When she let her hair down, it practically reached her waist, and Lillian was pretty sure her mother would have loved to get it trimmed into a more stylish shape. But a trip to the beauty shop was a luxury they hadn't been able to afford for years. They had to settle for occasional trims in the backyard when the weather was nice.

After dinner, Mama shooed Lillian away and said she'd clean the kitchen. Lillian wanted to go for a walk, but the temperature outside had plummeted so she retreated to her bedroom and tried to read a book. But she had a difficult time concentrating.

* * * * *

On Monday afternoon, after completing his farm duties, William drove into town to make a deposit at the bank and to drop off some paperwork. Staying away from Lillian for the past couple of weeks had been one of the most challenging things William had ever done. Most of the time he had the automobile, since his brothers still preferred horses for transportation. Pop drove occasionally, but he'd been so busy with the farm, he rarely had time to drive anywhere. Instead, he sent William on errands to town. And each time William drove past Joachim's Five and Dime, he slowed down, hoping to catch a glimpse of Lillian through the window.

Pastor Butler had sent some men who were looking for work out to the farm, and Pop had hired a couple of them. They were trying to do as much as they could before the weather got too cold. Once the first snow came, most of the outdoor work came to a standstill until early spring, but there was still plenty of work that needed to be done on William's house and in the barns.

After he completed his errands, William decided to swing past the Five and Dime. Just as he'd rounded the corner, he spotted Lillian leaving the store. She glanced up, hesitated for a second, and turned toward her house. He was fairly certain she'd seen him, but she obviously didn't want to talk.

Mr. Joachim stood at the door watching, so William decided to get out. As he walked up to the front door, the store owner opened it for him.

"What was that all about?" he asked. "Is something going on between you and Lillian?"

William could only wish for something...anything...to be going on. "Afraid not, but it's not because I'm not trying."

"What seems to be the problem?"

"Seems she's not interested." William pressed to think of something else to talk about, so he decided to ask about the store. "If you're not closed, I'd like to pick up some personal items."

"We have five minutes till closing, so come on in and get whatever you need."

Ten minutes later, William walked out of Joachim's Five and Dime with a bag of items he didn't need. But that was okay. While in the store, he'd found out that Mr. Joachim was concerned about the Pickards not having enough food for Thanksgiving. He went home with a heavy heart, concerned about their family.

When he told Mom about it, she shook her head in disbelief. "We cannot let that happen. We have more than enough food, so I think we should make up a nice basket for them."

"I don't want to overstep and injure anyone's pride by forcing our charity on them," William said.

Mom pursed her lips as she pondered what to do. Then her face lit up. "I have a brilliant idea. Let's make up food baskets for all the people we do business with in town. That way we can show our appreciation to everyone and no one will feel like we're turning them into a charity case."

William laughed as he hugged Mom. "You are the best."

"No, you are," she teased back. "Now let's figure out a way to do this. You'll have to deliver everything on Wednesday, so I s'pose we'd better clear this with your father."

During dinner, William waited for the right moment to bring up the food baskets. Pop glanced at Mom, who nodded.

"You two really cooked up something crazy this time," he said. "But if it makes you happy, then go right ahead. What do you need from me?"

Mom tapped her chin with the tip of her finger. "About a dozen hens and some straw. I'll get Nelda to help me make some simple baskets tomorrow."

Pop chuckled. "I'll have the hens ready to be dressed. Amos, can you gather some vegetables to add?"

"Of course. I bet everyone would love one of Nelda's pies to go with it."

"Whoa." Pop lifted his hands. "Nelda is only one woman, and your mom already has her making baskets."

"What are y'all saying about me?" Nelda asked from the dining room doorway. "I keep hearing my name."

Mom told Nelda their plans, and Nelda clapped her hands together. "I love this! Tell you what. I'll bring my oldest daughter to work with me tomorrow, and she can help. She's a good little pie maker."

Warmth flooded William as he realized what had just happened. One person's need became an opportunity to bring a lot of people together who loved each other. He hadn't been around Nelda's daughter much, but he knew Mom adored her.

By the time they finished dinner, everyone in the family had a task to do to get the gift baskets ready. William helped clear the table before stepping outside with the men.

* * * * *

On Wednesday, William carefully placed the filled baskets in the automobile. Mom gave him explicit instructions on not swerving too quickly and being extra careful when making turns. He finally pulled away and made his way to town. The aroma wafting from the pies made his mouth water. He sure hoped the women had made enough for his family's meal tomorrow.

His first stop was the bank. He carried three baskets inside and distributed them to the people his family worked with.

Next he went to the drug store and delivered a basket. The pharmacist handed him a jar filled with peppermints to take home to his family.

He stopped at the parsonage where Pastor and Mrs. Butler lived. They were thrilled to receive such a wonderful gift, and they volunteered to share some of the food with less-fortunate members of their congregation.

He made his way through town and ended his gift-giving excursion at Joachim's Five and Dime. He carefully lifted the last two baskets from the seat and carried them to the front door. Mr. Joachim saw him through the window and opened the door for him.

"What's this?"

"Since tomorrow's Thanksgiving, my family wanted to give thanks to all the fine people in Cary. Here's one for you and one for Miss Pickard."

"That's mighty nice of your family, but I'm afraid Miss Pickard has left for the day. Her mama wasn't feeling well this morning, so I sent Lillian home early."

William nodded toward one of the baskets as he lifted the other to take it to the Pickards' house. "Then enjoy your basket. I'll take Lillian's to her home."

Mr. Joachim leaned over his basket and started rummaging through it. "Your family is quite generous. I can't say anyone has ever done anything like this before. Let me get something for you. Stay right here for a moment. I'll be right back."

"That's not necessary," William said.

"Don't deny me the pleasure. It's something I want to do."

William left the store a few minutes later with a jar filled with maple candy, Pop's favorite. As he drove to the Pickards' house, he prayed that their pride wouldn't prevent them from accepting his family's gift. If she'd gotten it at work, she would have seen that she wasn't the only person receiving such a gift.

After pulling up in front of her house, he grabbed the basket, prayed for the right words, then strode up to the front door.

Lillian answered the door and glanced down at the basket with an expression he couldn't read. One thing he could see, though, was the weary droop of her shoulders.

"My family wanted to express our gratitude for everyone's service and support in town, so Mom and Nelda made up some gift baskets. I brought one for you and one for Mr. Joachim, but he said you came home early." William stopped when he realized he was talking too much. "Here." He thrust the basket toward her.

"Would you like to come in?" she asked as she took a step back. She didn't take the basket, so he felt that he had no choice but to follow her inside.

"Who's there, Lillian?" Mr. Pickard hollered.

"Mr. Tronnier. He brought us something."

Mr. Pickard limped into the living room, a scowl on his face. William suspected it must be quite difficult to have such an infirmity that affected everything in his life.

"We don't need charity."

"Oh, it's not charity," William said. Then he explained how much his family appreciated the support of the people in town and how they'd made up a bunch of baskets.

"In that case…," Mr. Pickard said with a dubious look still on his face, as he stepped up to the table where William had placed the basket. "Whatcha got in there?" He started to pull back the gingham cover, but Lillian grabbed the basket and took it to the kitchen.

"We can go through it later," she said when she came back out. "Thank you, Mr. Tronnier. Would you like some hot cocoa? I was just making some for Mama."

"No thank you. Not today anyway. I need to get back home before it gets dark."

After he left the Pickards' house, William felt the tension release from his shoulders. He was glad Lillian had accepted the gift, but her prideful expression let him know she was on to him.

Chapter Eight

Lillian couldn't believe how much food was in the basket. There was enough for Thanksgiving dinner and several days afterward. She'd already told Mama that they probably wouldn't have any meat for the big meal. Now they'd eat like royalty.

"What's all the ruckus I've been hearing?"

"Ruckus? William stopped by and delivered this, but he didn't stay long. I'm sorry if we woke you."

Mama pulled her robe more tightly around her as she crossed the kitchen to see what William had brought. She lifted the gingham cloth and stared at the contents.

Mama arched an eyebrow. "A hen?"

"I'd better get it on ice." Lillian lifted the hen and carried it to the icebox.

"Ooh, there's a ham in here too."

Lillian couldn't remember the last time they'd had so much meat in the house. "Looks like we'll have a bountiful Thanksgiving after all."

A smile tweaked Mama's lips. "For a family of means, the Tronniers seem to be very generous people."

"Yes, they do, don't they?" She turned to face Mama. "How are you feeling?"

"Much better. The nap did me some good."

Lillian was certain the basket of food sitting on the table had helped Mama's mood too, but she didn't mention it.

* * * * *

"Lord, bless this food and keep us humble as we enjoy the bounty You have provided. Amen."

After Pop finished his prayer, a chorus of amens followed. William loved it when his entire family came together—brothers, sisters, brothers-in-law, nieces, and nephews all sitting at the same table. Mom occasionally commented that if anyone else got married or had another child, she'd have to knock down a wall and get a bigger table. William had no doubt that nothing would please her more.

The only thing that would make the day complete would be if he could see Lillian. He'd fallen in love with her over the past couple of months. The first time they ever talked, she'd intrigued him with stories about work, her family, and how she enjoyed celebrating Christmas. However, it appeared that she wasn't quite in a celebratory mood this season.

Mom and Pop had agreed not to discuss the gift baskets during dinner because they didn't want to sound boastful. "You've been mighty quiet, William," Mom said as the conversation slowed.

He smiled. "With this group, it's hard to get a word in."

Pop lifted his eyebrows. "You've never had trouble doing that before. I suspect I know what's going on."

William suspected his father did know, but he didn't want to discuss it now. "This food is excellent, Mom. I'd like seconds of the squash casserole."

Her eyes lit up. "Really? That's the only thing I made all by myself. Nelda didn't even have to tell me what to do."

William knew that, but he didn't let on. "You did an excellent job with it."

That seemed to appease his mother and take the focus off his silence. He was able to enjoy the remainder of the meal without anyone commenting on how little he spoke.

After everyone finished dessert, William hung around with Mom and his sisters, Loretta and Virginia. "Why don't you join the men in the living room?" Mom asked.

"I'd like to help you all, if you don't mind."

Virginia snorted. "I don't know what has happened to you, Will, but I like it."

Mom patted William on the cheek as she passed him to get another load of dishes off the table. "He's always been such a good boy. He'll make a fine husband someday."

"Oh, that reminds me," Loretta said. "I've heard that you've been visiting that Pickard girl. She's cute in sort of an old-fashioned way."

Now William regretted his decision to help out. He opened his mouth to explain, but Mom piped up instead. "Lillian Pickard is a lovely girl. Old-fashioned isn't always a bad thing, you know."

"Of course we know, Mom," Loretta said. "I was simply making an observation."

William couldn't let go of Mom's comment. "When did you see Lillian, Mom?"

Mom's face turned a dark shade of pink. "Well, I just happened to be in town one day, and I needed some cold cream, and…" She cast a look of helplessness toward William. "Okay, I was curious, so I stopped in at Joachim's Five and Dime."

"Did you tell her who you were?" William asked, annoyed but somewhat amused.

"Of course not. Why would I?"

Loretta scowled at Mom. "I hope you didn't ruin anything for William. If she ever finds out—"

"If she ever finds out, I'm sure she'll understand," William said. "She has parents, too, ya know."

"Of course she does. I never said she didn't." Loretta pouted. "Forgive me for trying to stick up for you."

William put down the gravy boat he had in his hands and closed the distance to his sister. He put an arm around her neck and ruffled her hair with his other hand. "I appreciate everything you do, sis. You and Virginia are the best sisters a guy could have."

That seemed to satisfy Loretta. She pulled away and straightened her hair. "So what's going on between you and the Pickard girl?"

"I wish I knew. I like her quite a bit, and I'm pretty sure she likes me. But something is holding her back...maybe pride?"

"Of course," Mom said. "You can't imagine how uncomfortable it is to wonder where your next meal is coming from while you watch others throw perfectly good food to the dogs."

"You would be the one to know," William said. He'd heard the story many times about how his grandfather had died, leaving his wife and children destitute. If it weren't for Pop's parents hiring his grandmother to help out with domestic duties, there was no telling where they would have wound up. And he probably wouldn't even be here.

Mom changed the subject, but he could tell it was still on her mind as she passed him carrying dishes to the kitchen. He also saw that she had the look she always had when crafting a plan. And nothing would stop her once she got something in her head.

After all the dishes had been cleared and William did everything his mother and sisters would let him do, he started toward the living room, where he could hear the men talking. Loretta called out to him, so he turned around to see what she wanted.

"William, if there's anything I can do to help you with Miss Pickard, please don't hesitate to ask. There's nothing better than being with the person you love."

His heart was touched by his sister's gesture. "Thank you, Loretta, but I'm leaving this in God's hands."

"I just wanted to make the offer." She turned and went back into the kitchen.

* * * * *

"If you just happen to see Mr. Tronnier, don't forget to thank him for all the delicious food." Mama sighed. "That ham was heavenly."

"Of course I'll thank him." Lillian also planned to find out whether the Tronniers truly did give out other gift baskets.

The day was particularly cold for the time of year, so she wore layers over her dress and topped them with Mama's coat, which was warmer than her own. The wind was brisk, so she wrapped her wool knit scarf around as much of her face as she could without rendering herself incapable of seeing where she was going.

She'd gotten to the corner where she had to turn toward the store when she spotted the Tronniers' automobile coming toward her. It was apparent that William didn't recognize her when he drove right past without so much as a wave. He appeared to be on a mission, his gaze fixed straight ahead and both hands at the top of his steering wheel. Then another automobile passed and startled her. Progress had obviously not skipped Cary.

When Lillian walked into the already-opened Five and Dime, Mr. Joachim was uncharacteristically jolly. "A bit cold but a beautiful morning," he said in greeting. "How was your family's Thanksgiving?"

"Very nice," she said as she removed her scarf. "And yours?"

"We had a delightful day. Between the meal my wife had planned and the food from the Tronniers' gift basket, we'll have enough to eat for a week."

That answered one question. "When did Mr. Tronnier bring you your basket?"

Still smiling, Mr. Joachim replied, "Right before he went to your house. He was hoping to save the trip and deliver both at the same time. By the way, how is your mama?"

"Much better. I think she was just overworked."

Mr. Joachim's smile faded a bit as he studied Lillian. "How are you feeling? I've had you working pretty hard lately too."

"Oh, I'm just fine." Lillian didn't need Mr. Joachim to worry about her being able to do the job. This would be a terrible time to lose her income—not that there was any good time. She needed to act more energetic.

"Let me know if you get tired, Lillian. I know how difficult this season can be for retail clerks." His expression didn't seem threatening; instead it appeared to be more filled with concern. But she still wasn't taking any chances.

"Are we putting up more decorations this weekend?" she asked.

"Oh my, you are enthusiastic, aren't you? I got the impression that you didn't want to decorate any more."

The bell on the door jingled, so they dropped the conversation for the time being. Mr. Joachim skittered back to his office, while Lillian tended to the flow of customers. Most people came in for standard items, but a few customers were shopping early for Christmas gifts.

As she was about to close the shop, Mr. Joachim approached her. "I'm going to stay open an extra hour every day, including Saturday, until Christmas Eve. I'd planned to hire someone to help out during the extra hours, but so far no one has come in looking for a job."

A sense of dread washed over Lillian. She couldn't let him know how difficult her life already was, so she simply nodded and said, "I'd be happy to work the extra hours, but if you want me to, I can help you find someone."

"Why don't you do both?" he asked. "I'll pay you a bonus for the extra time."

"I'll start by putting an ad in the window."

"Only if you have time to interview people. I didn't do that because I don't want to bother."

He expected more from her than he should, but she nodded. "I'll do whatever I need to do."

"I might not tell you this enough, Lillian, but I appreciate having you here. You're reliable, and I never have to worry about your walking out."

His compliment shocked her. "Why, th–thank you, Mr. Joachim."

"I'm the one who should be thanking you." The warmth in his smile touched her heart.

The first thing Lillian did the next morning was make a HELP WANTED sign. Within five minutes of sticking it in the window, an applicant appeared.

"I'll need Saturdays and Wednesdays off," the middle-aged woman said. "I can't stay past dark, and I am unable to lift anything."

"I see," Lillian said as she tried hard not to frown. "When *can* you work, and what can you do?"

The woman's face scrunched as she leveled Lillian with a disapproving glare. "Don't get sarcastic with me, young lady."

"I—I wasn't." Lillian hoped this wouldn't be her only applicant. "I was just trying to find out what hours you would be available."

"Most days, no nights."

"During the holidays, we are staying open until seven during the week and Saturday until six. We really need someone who is flexible and can come in any time we're open," Lillian explained.

"You're young. You can work the late hours. I have responsibilities at home, but we could use some extra money."

Lillian wouldn't know what to do with extra money, since every dime of her income was needed for essentials. She tried her best not to let the woman see her exasperation.

"Well? Do I get the job or not?"

"I just started interviewing, but I should know something soon. Please check back on Tuesday."

The woman tossed her scarf over her shoulder and huffed. "I'm not sure if I'll be able to do that. One of my friends is hosting a tea that afternoon, and I promised I'd help her set up."

That pretty much sealed Lillian's notion that this woman wouldn't work out, no matter what. "Then check back whenever you're available."

After the woman left, Lillian realized that the store was already crowded. Mr. Joachim had gone behind the counter and started ringing up a customer. He cut a glance in her direction, so she went over to relieve him. He didn't waste any time scurrying to his office.

They were busy for the remainder of the morning. By the end of the day, she'd interviewed a total of three people, and the only one who seemed like a good candidate was Rose, a woman in her early twenties—a year younger than Lillian—and she was able to work whatever hours Lillian needed her. Lillian's only concern was that Rose had left her job at a drugstore in Raleigh a couple of months ago, and she was evasive when asked why.

"Can you come back on Monday morning?" Lillian asked. "I need to discuss all the applicants with my boss."

Rose nervously nodded. "I'll come in first thing Monday morning." She turned toward the door to leave but stopped. "I'm a very good salesperson. Most customers like me."

Lillian smiled. "I'm sure they do. You seem very nice."

After Rose left, Lillian reflected on the interview. Everything about Rose seemed perfect for the job—her willingness to work whatever hours she was needed, her pleasant personality, and the fact that she showed up at the right time. But there was something Lillian couldn't put her finger on that bothered her.

She presented Rose's application to Mr. Joachim at the end of the day. He looked it over and nodded. "Looks good. When does she start?"

Lillian started to tell him about her feeling, but she stopped herself. It was probably just silly nerves. Her lack of experience with this sort of thing likely just made her jittery.

"She's coming in on Monday morning to find out whether or not she got the job," Lillian said.

"Good. When she comes in, we can start her right away, if she doesn't have any other commitments."

Since she couldn't think of a way to find out what happened with Rose's last job, she had no choice but to take a chance. None of the other applicants came close to fitting what they needed in the store.

At the end of the day, Lillian and Mr. Joachim closed the store together. "You put in a good day's work, Lillian." He slipped her an envelope. "Here's a little something extra for everything you've done."

She wanted to rip into the envelope to see what was in it, but she didn't want to appear crass, so she tucked it into her coat pocket. "Thank you."

He smiled and patted her shoulder. "See you on Monday." Then he turned toward his house and left her standing there alone.

Lillian stood and stared after her boss, thinking about how he'd recently softened his demeanor with her. He used to be stern, but now he treated her with a gentleness that made her wonder what had happened.

Finally, she turned and started walking home. She jumped when she heard the sound of an automobile coming from behind. Her heart hammered as she thought it might be William, but when the rattling noise passed her, she felt let down. It was one of the other automobiles that had begun to appear in town.

Feeling dejected, she continued her walk home. But when she got within sight of her family's tiny house, she saw an automobile parked in front. There was no doubt it was William's vehicle. And it took every ounce of self-restraint not to run the rest of the way.

Chapter Nine

. . . .

William had driven by Joachim's Five and Dime a number of times throughout the late afternoon. The last time he'd spotted Lillian, she was chatting with another woman, so he didn't stop. Not wanting to bother her, he decided to wait for her at her house. It was risky since her parents had turned cold toward him, but maybe he could find out what was going on without her there.

Her mother had answered the door. He could tell she wasn't thrilled by him being there, but since the temperature outside had dropped significantly, she let him in.

"We appreciate the gift basket you brought," Mrs. Pickard had said. "Don't think you have to continue bringing us food."

"That was something my family wanted to do," he said. "Mom and Nelda, the woman who helps Mom around the house, enjoyed making the baskets. I think it was more fun for them than anything."

Mrs. Pickard forced a smile and nodded. "It is always fun to give to others if you have something to offer."

Lillian's father was sitting in a chair in the corner of the room, bundled up in blankets and reading a book beneath a dim light. He glanced up when William walked in.

William started talking about the weather, which led to farming. When William brought up the fact that his father was expanding some of his crops and livestock holdings, Lillian's father's eyes lit up. He'd finally hit on something they could discuss without the conversation being so one-sided.

It didn't take long to figure out that Mr. Pickard was actually very good with numbers and seemed to have a pretty good head for business. As they discussed specifics about the farm, Mr. Pickard had some excellent suggestions on ordering seed.

"Too bad I didn't invest in some land when I was younger," Mr. Pickard said. "If I had, I wouldn't be sitting here right now, and my daughter wouldn't be out there in the cold, hard-working world."

"She's good at what she does," William said. "And I think Mr. Joachim treats her well."

A rattle of the front doorknob caught their attention. He turned his head just in time to meet Lillian's gaze as she stepped inside.

"Close the door, Lillian," Mrs. Pickard ordered. "You're letting all the cold air in."

Lillian did as she was told. The warmth of seeing her superseded the chill in the tiny house.

William watched as she shrugged out of her scarf and coat. Her hands were red and chapped from the bitter cold. She should be wearing gloves, but he suspected she didn't have any. If he didn't think it would injure her pride, he would bring her some. His mom certainly had enough to spare.

"How was your day at work?" he asked. "Is business picking up?"

"It always does right after Thanksgiving." She crossed the room and stood next to her dad. His heart melted as she placed her hand on the man's shoulder, leaned over, and asked, "How's your leg feeling?"

Mr. Pickard shrugged. "It hurt earlier, but ever since Mr. Tronnier and I started talking, I've forgotten about it."

Lillian looked up and met William's gaze. "I s'pose I owe you my gratitude for whatever you're saying to take Daddy's mind off his pain."

"It's not me so much as the subject," William said. "Your father has an excellent mind for business."

Mr. Pickard straightened in the chair and pushed one of the

blankets to the side. "I've always had an interest in business, but the opportunity to do anything about it has never come up."

"Perhaps one day it will," William offered.

Mr. Pickard chuckled good-naturedly. "I'm afraid it might be too late for me, but I can at least talk about it."

Lillian cast a curious glance between her father and William. He wanted to ask what she was thinking, but Mr. Pickard spoke before he had a chance.

"Did you find someone to help out in the store?" he asked.

"I think so. She's coming in on Monday, and Mr. Joachim has given me permission to offer her the job." Her lips spread into a slight grin as she added, "I'm even going to have some supervisory responsibilities."

William delighted in her obvious joy. It didn't appear to take much to make Lillian happy—unlike some women he'd known.

"You'll be very good at it too, I'm sure," he said.

Even in the dim lighting he could see her blush. She tucked a stray strand of hair behind her ear in a nervous gesture and glanced over at her father. William turned toward Mr. Pickard and saw that he was thoughtfully watching them.

"Would you like to go for a ride in my automobile?" William asked.

Lillian started to shake her head, but her father spoke up. "That sounds like an excellent idea. Your mama is cooking supper, though, so don't stay gone too long."

"But…" Lillian glanced at her father then looked back into William's eyes. "Yes, that would be very nice, if you can have me back home soon. I'd better talk to Mama first, though."

"No, I'll tell her," Mr. Pickard said as he slowly stood from the chair. William started to reach out to help him but thought better of it. "Go on, you two. Get out of here before I change my mind."

William extended his elbow. "Shall we?"

"We might be going in your automobile, but I'll still need my coat. It's not like you can have a roaring fire in there."

William chuckled. "You're right. I wouldn't want you to freeze to death. There's also a blanket on the seat; Mom insists I take it with me at all times."

* * * * *

Lillian was so happy that she was downright giddy. She couldn't remember ever having such a wonderful time. All her exhaustion seemed to fade the moment she stepped foot inside her house and saw William.

No matter how much she tried to deny it, she liked him way more than she knew was good for her in the long run. But right now, sitting beside him in the automobile, riding through the streets of Cary, she felt as though she didn't have a thing to worry about. The future would take care of itself.

Finally, after covering most of downtown and crossing back over the railroad tracks, William pulled up in front of her house. He didn't waste any time getting out and coming around to help her to the ground.

"Thank you for obliging me," he said as they walked toward the house. "I'll see you to your door; then I'd best be getting home."

"I enjoyed it," she said, doing everything she could to keep her voice from sounding as breathless as she felt.

Lillian had barely opened the door when her mother came toward her, shaking her head. "You are playing with fire, young lady. When your father told me where you went, I told him that was a huge mistake."

"Maybe so, Mama, but it's mine to make. I like William. I tried not to, but I can't help it. He's so nice."

Mama placed her hands on Lillian's shoulders and looked her in the eyes, her face inches from Lillian's. "That's what boys like William

Tronnier do. They cross the railroad tracks to this side of town to have a little fun, but then when it comes time to settle down with one woman, they go back to their own side and find someone more suited to their station in life."

Lillian knew Mama was right about most cases, but maybe not this time. William had to be different. He certainly seemed to be.

"Go wash your hands and come to the kitchen for supper. Your daddy has already sat down at the table."

Washing her hands gave her an opportunity to mentally prepare for any questions her parents might ask. By the time she got to the table, Mama had calmed down considerably, and Daddy had a pleased look on his face.

"So how was the ride?" Daddy asked, a twinkle in his eyes.

"Very nice." Lillian glanced down at her empty plate before allowing herself to look back up at Mama.

"Like I said when you first got home, this is a dangerous situation. Don't get used to having all this attention from a man you have no business seeing."

Daddy reached for Mama's hand. "Let Lillian enjoy her moment, Helen. It's not like she's wanting to run off with the boy."

Mama opened her mouth but closed it before anything came out. Lillian let out a sigh of relief as she reached for the bowl of beans.

The next morning, Lillian and her parents arrived at church at the regular time. She kept watching the door, hoping to see William. Mama occasionally gave her a look of disapproval.

"Don't get your hopes up, Lillian," she whispered. "Remember what I said, or you'll get hurt."

Lillian didn't respond. Instead, she forced herself to turn her attention to the message in the sermon.

Lillian wanted to throw herself across her bed and sob after they got home from church. She didn't have a good reason, but the disappointment of not seeing William clouded everything around her. Daddy kept winking at her, and that only made it worse.

She helped Mama put together their big meal of the day in the early afternoon. Afterward, she took advantage of a brief warming spell and went for a walk. She heard the occasional sound of an automobile, but each time she looked, she was disappointed to see that it wasn't William. This was one day she was glad to be finished with.

On Monday morning, she popped out of bed before her alarm clock went off. Mama hadn't gotten up yet, and since there was no reason to wake her, Lillian went about her business of getting ready in the silence of the sleeping household.

She managed to get all the way to the door to leave when she heard Mama calling after her. "Why are you leaving so early? The store doesn't open for another hour yet."

"I want to get ready for our new employee," Lillian replied. "If you don't have to be up, why don't you go back to bed?"

Mama looked at her with sleepy eyes. "Good idea. I didn't sleep well last night because your daddy was snoring so loud."

"I'll be home a little later every evening until after Christmas, so don't hold supper for me. I can eat whatever is left when I get home."

She walked out the door and pulled it shut behind her. The store was already unlocked when she arrived.

Mr. Joachim had pulled out another dozen or so boxes and strewn them across the floor, blocking the way to the cash register. He glanced up from the wires he was trying to untangle. "Oh, good. I'm glad you came in early. Here, give me a hand with this. I want to finish getting all these decorations up before we open for customers."

Instead of preparing what to say to Rose, Lillian spent the next hour decorating the store. They managed to finish everything on time, though, and that gave her some relief. Mr. Joachim took a step back, surveyed everything as he brushed his hands together, and nodded. "Looks very festive, doesn't it?"

"Yes," she agreed. "Very festive."

The bell on the door jingled. She glanced over her shoulder and saw Rose come in. "You said to come back on Monday morning, so here I am. I hope you have some good news for me."

Mr. Joachim held his hand toward Lillian, gesturing for her to speak. She nodded, walked toward Rose, and extended her hand. "Yes, we have some very good news. We'd like to hire you to work during the Christmas season."

Rose broke into a smile. "That is such a relief. I need this job."

"You do realize it's temporary, right?" Mr. Joachim said. "We're doing a booming business now, but it will slow way down after Christmas."

"Yes, sir," Rose said with a sweet smile.

"Can you start today?" Lillian asked.

"Absolutely, yes!"

Mr. Joachim beamed. "Good. Now why don't you ladies discuss the job while I go do some paperwork?"

Lillian watched him as he headed back to his office. She'd noticed that he spent less and less time on the sales floor, and she often wondered if he didn't enjoy waiting on customers. But he'd inherited the store from his father and grandfather, so perhaps he would have rather done something else.

After he was out of listening range, Rose turned to Lillian. "Okay, now why don't I help the customers while you ring them up?" She scanned the floor. "We must get those boxes out of here. They look absolutely ghastly. While you're doing that, I'll tidy up around the cash register and make it look a little nicer."

Lillian was stunned and started to do what she was told, but then she stopped. Rose had barely been hired, and here she was bossing Lillian around as though she owned the place.

"No, Rose. I don't know how you did things at your last job back in Raleigh, but you need to learn how we do things here."

Rose's forehead scrunched, and she folded her arms. "I just wanted to help make this place look nice."

"After you learn your job, you can share your ideas. But in the meantime, you'll need to do what's needed around here."

"Just tell me what to do," Rose said in a tone of exasperation. "Even if it doesn't make any sense, I'll do it just to keep you from getting mad."

"I'm not mad," Lillian said. "Let's get through the day, and we can discuss everything after we close the store."

"Oh, I can't stay after we close." Rose thought for a few seconds. "By the way, I might need to leave early today. Mother doesn't know where I am, so I'll have to come up with a reason why I won't be home every day."

"You didn't tell your mother you applied for this job?" Lillian asked incredulously.

Rose shook her head. "She'd be appalled at the very thought of her only daughter working at a five and dime." She lifted her hand and giggled behind it. "And if she knew I was taking the train to work, she'd probably put a padlock on my bedroom door to keep me there."

"Where does she think you are when you're not home all day?"

"Oh, just gallivanting around, doing the things girls my age do."

Chapter Ten

Lillian was about to comment when someone came into the store. As she helped the customer, she wished she'd had more time to talk to Rose before hiring her. Fortunately, Rose didn't hold onto her notion of being the boss after Lillian had set her straight.

Mr. Joachim seemed to be pleased with Rose. He came out of his office at various times throughout the day and observed. Rose didn't disappoint him, either. When she saw him watching, she turned on the charm and made the customers feel as though they were in an exclusive boutique rather than the Five and Dime.

He cornered Lillian when she went to the back to get stock to replenish the shelves. "Maybe we'll consider keeping her on after Christmas," he said. "She's really livened up the place."

Lillian didn't let on that Rose's parents wouldn't have approved of the job. She wished she knew why Rose was there.

Toward the end of the afternoon, William stopped by. Lillian didn't even try to hide her joy at seeing him.

"What can I do for you?" Rose said from behind Lillian. "Would you like to see a nice shave set?"

"He's a friend," Lillian said.

An odd expression covered William's face. "Rose McNault? What are you doing here?"

She tilted her head back and laughed. "Killing time. What are you doing here, William Tronnier?"

"I stopped by to see Miss Pickard."

"Oh you did, did you?" Rose turned to the side and looked back at William coquettishly. "Sort of how you used to stop by and see me when I worked in Raleigh?" She let out an ear-piercing laugh. "Oh, I get it. You're having a little fun on the other side of the tracks. My brothers did that before they settled down."

Lillian felt as though the earth had opened up and swallowed her. She looked at William, whose chin had dropped, and then back to Rose, who held his gaze with her own flirty eyes.

As difficult as it was, Lillian forced herself to take a step toward the back of the store. "Um…I need to go see about something. I'll be right back."

She walked away as quickly as she could. Mr. Joachim stepped out of his office, but she wouldn't look him in the eye. She could tell he started to follow her but stopped.

As soon as she was out of sight, she leaned against the wall. Mama had been right. She had no business even thinking that William Tronnier was interested in her. She sniffled back the tears, cleared her throat, and took several deep breaths.

The pain of her discovery turned to anger. How dare he treat her so disrespectfully? Lillian pulled herself together, squared her shoulders, and gave herself a lecture. *This is not the end of the world. It's best to find out now and be done with someone who only wanted to pretend.*

When she was certain she could face William and Rose without crumbling, she marched right back out to the sales floor. He was gone, but Rose stood behind the counter with a smug look on her face.

"That was a pleasant surprise," Rose said, her voice laced with sarcasm. "I didn't realize you and William were such good friends."

"We're not." Lillian couldn't keep the edge from her voice. "We're merely acquaintances."

"Oh?" Rose ran her hand along the edge of the counter, studied her hand, and flicked away the dust with the other hand. "I thought maybe…well, it was just a silly notion. Anyway, I need to leave soon. What time should I be here tomorrow?"

"We open at nine. I like to get here early."

Rose patted her bobbed hair and pouted her brightly glossed red lips as she headed toward the door. "I'll be here around nine. See ya."

Lillian wondered if she'd made the biggest mistake of her life by hiring Rose. But then if she hadn't, she wouldn't know about William. Lillian cringed as she thought about how she'd been played a fool.

She wiped off the cash register and dusted the countertop before gathering her personal belongings and going home. Mr. Joachim stayed behind and told her he'd lock up. William wasn't anywhere around—not even in front of her house, where she'd half expected to see him.

Mama had prepared a nice little meat loaf and a compote with some fruit she'd purchased with the extra money Mr. Joachim had given Lillian. Although having meat on the table more than a couple of nights a week was good, Lillian thought it might be nice to spend a little on herself. She could use a pair of gloves, and maybe one of these days she might even consider going to the beauty salon. The one time she'd gone there was when Daddy was still working and she wasn't old enough to appreciate it.

Daddy was cranky, which kept Mama occupied, and Lillian wasn't terribly upset about it. She didn't have all the attention on her, so she could eat in peace and then retire to her room after the dishes were done.

She lay in bed staring up at the ceiling with only the light of the half-moon filtered through the sheer draperies. Her initial resistance to William came from a gut feeling that she didn't belong with someone like him. Mama and Daddy had warned her, but William's charm had broken through her shell and Daddy's. She needed to listen to Mama and not even think of straying from what she knew was good for her: working hard and not thinking about romance.

As she dozed off, images of William swirled in her head, with Rose standing at his side laughing and teasing her. "You'll never be good enough for a man like William," came Rose's taunts. Lillian awoke with a crick in her neck and a sense of dread about facing Rose at the store.

Lillian arrived at the store at a quarter to nine. Mr. Joachim was right behind her, humming a familiar tune and smiling. "Nice morning for this time of year, isn't it, Miss Pickard?"

"Very nice," she said, trying hard to act more cheerful than she felt.

He instantly stopped humming, scrunched his forehead, and leaned toward her. "Are you not feeling well? I've heard there's something going around."

"I'm feeling just fine," Lillian said. "I just know we're going to be very busy today, so I have to set everything up. Would you like me to put one of the display racks on the sidewalk, since the sun is shining and it's not too cold?"

"Rose said she didn't like that display," Mr. Joachim said. "So I'm thinking we might find another way to get people into the store."

"Well, I like it." Lillian grabbed both sides of the rack that rested against the wall next to the front door. "So I think I'll put it out there, if you don't mind."

He jumped back. "Okay, if that's what you think we should do." He started for his office and then stopped and turned around. "Please send Rose back to my office when she gets in. Tell her I have something to discuss with her."

"Yes, sir."

Rose was five minutes late, and she didn't even bother with an excuse. Instead, she lifted her head, looked directly at Lillian, and asked if she needed help bringing in that "hideous-looking" display. "I think it cheapens the look of the store," she explained.

"Well, this *is* a five and dime," Lillian retorted. "It's not exactly a specialty boutique." Lillian cleared her throat. "Oh, by the way, Mr.

Joachim would like to see you. He said to tell you to go back to his office when you got here."

"Be a dear and go tell him I'm busy right now. I'll see him a little bit later."

Lillian stopped in her tracks, spun around, and glared at Rose. "I don't know who you think you are, but Mr. Joachim is the owner of this store. He is the one who gives us our pay at the end of the week. I will *not* go tell him you're too busy to see him."

"Wow, you sure are testy this morning. I thought you'd be a sweet girl to work with, but you've actually turned out to be quite difficult." She frowned and contorted her face. "Okay, I'll go see what he wants."

Lillian had no idea what Mr. Joachim would want to see Rose about, since he'd given her the task of training. The only thing she knew was that he really seemed to like Rose, and he'd been in a particularly good mood until he realized Lillian wasn't. Uh-oh. What if she'd made him mad and he wanted to discuss it with Rose?

Lillian felt as if all the blood had drained from her body. She stood still, willing her body not to react like it was.

Then Rose came storming out of Mr. Joachim's office, ranting about no one appreciating her good taste. Instead of stopping by the cash-register counter, she continued until she was out the door, letting it slam behind her.

What had just happened?

Lillian leaned forward to see if Mr. Joachim's office door was still open. Not only was his door open, but he was on his way to the front of the store with a smug look on his face.

"Tell you what, Lillian. Next time we hire someone, let me take care of it. I don't want to take a chance and have that happen again."

"Wh–what just happened?"

"You don't know?" he asked.

She shook her head. "I have no idea."

"First off, I don't want to see my prized employee butting heads with the new person."

"I'm sorry," Lillian said. "That was partly my fault—"

"No, you were right," he interrupted. "That young woman is no lady. She doesn't have an ounce of respect for authority, and she doesn't seem to know the difference between right and wrong. I don't mind giving a young person direction, but I don't want to hire someone then turn around and have to act like a parent."

"Oh." Lillian felt terrible about her decision to hire Rose. "I'm very sorry I made such a horrible mistake."

"It's not your fault, Lillian," he said, his voice tender and kind. "You have such a strong work ethic, and you're so honest that you don't expect this kind of behavior from others. I've known people ten years younger than Rose who've acted more mature. Do you know who her parents are?"

Lillian shook her head. "How would I know?"

He chuckled. "I'm surprised she didn't tell you. Her daddy owns about ten percent of Raleigh, including the second-largest bank. He's considering buying some of the businesses here in Cary."

That confused Lillian. Why would Rose go to the trouble of coming to Cary and getting a job at the Five and Dime? Mr. Joachim continued. "I found out yesterday evening when William stopped by after you left."

"William came by the store?"

"Yes, he said he was looking for you, and since you often stick around after closing, he thought he might find you here. He wanted to talk to you when Rose wasn't nearby."

"Oh." Lillian hung her head. Now it was confirmed; William was embarrassed to be seen with her, and he didn't want Rose to know.

"William is a very honorable young man. He didn't want to snitch, but I managed to find out what I needed about Rose. And what he didn't tell me, I found out from a business acquaintance in

Raleigh. Apparently, she lost her last job because she refused to do the work. I'm not sure why she came here looking for work, but William seems to think it has something to do with defying her parents, who have always kept tight reins on her…and possibly creating a path of destruction before they come here."

Whatever the case, it was obvious that William still didn't want Rose to know he was coming to see the girl from the wrong side of the tracks. Lillian might not be experienced with men, but she wasn't stupid or desperate either.

Mr. Joachim leaned over and caught her gaze. "I'm sorry I wasn't more involved in helping you with the hiring. Don't think I'm blaming you for anything regarding Rose. There wasn't any way for you to know. On the surface, she seemed like a good choice, but people like her can fool anyone."

Lillian nodded. "I need to get to work now."

"Since we're probably going to be busy, I'll help out until we find someone with your sign in the window." He smiled. "By the way, I appreciate your diligence in everything."

As expected, the store became busy and remained that way for most of the day. Lillian rarely had time to reflect on anything that had happened until the last customer left.

"Good job, Lillian," Mr. Joachim said as he reached into his pocket and pulled out an envelope. "Here's a little extra for all your hard work."

"Thank you," she said.

"I want you to buy yourself something nice," he said. "There should be enough in there to give your mama the household money and have some left over for you."

All the way home, she thought about what she'd do with her personal money. Gloves would be nice, but then so would a stylish haircut. Since she wasn't sure how much money was in the envelope, she knew she shouldn't be daydreaming about it.

When she arrived home, Mama was in the kitchen and Daddy was asleep and snoring in his chair, an open book face down on his chest. After a brief pause, she scurried to her room, closed the door, and opened the envelope.

Mr. Joachim wasn't kidding. There was more than enough to give Mama the household money for a week and keep something for herself. In fact, she could purchase the gloves *and* get a haircut.

She tucked a little bit of the money into her pocketbook and stuffed the rest of it back into the envelope. As she passed the mirror, she glanced at it and smiled. It wouldn't be long before she had a completely different, more modern look.

Mama looked over her shoulder when Lillian came into the kitchen. "How was your day with the new girl?"

"She didn't work out."

"Too bad. Was Mr. Joachim upset with you for hiring her?"

"No," Lillian replied. "In fact, he gave me a bonus for having to work so hard."

Mama spun around with an eager expression. "A bonus?"

"Here," Lillian said as she handed Mama the envelope. "We should be able to eat well for a while."

Mama took the envelope and thumbed through it. She opened her mouth to speak, but the sound of someone knocking on the front door stopped her.

Chapter Eleven

....

Daddy got to the door before Lillian or her mama. William stood on the other side with an expectant look on his face.

"I'm sorry to bother you, but may I see Lillian?" William's gaze shifted from Daddy's to hers. "Lillian?"

She folded her arms and stared at him for a few seconds before nodding. "I suppose there's no harm in talking to you. Let me get my coat, and we can go outside."

"Lillian!" Mama frowned at her. "You'll catch your death of cold. Invite Mr. Tronnier inside."

"That's okay, Mrs. Pickard," William said. "My coat is warm, and besides, I'm not all that cold-natured."

Lillian didn't waste any time grabbing her coat and heading for the door. William followed her down the walk. "Want to go for a drive?"

"No, I think it's best if we talk here." She cleared her throat and gathered her thoughts. "William, I don't know what kind of game you're playing, but I want you to leave me out of it."

"Game?" He tilted his head and frowned. "What makes you think I'm playing a game?"

"You're obviously visiting more than one girl at work, and you and I both know I'm not exactly in your social—"

A light of dawning appeared on his face. "Hold on there, Lillian. If you're talking about what happened with Rose, I can explain."

Lillian held up her hands. "You don't have to explain a thing. It's all very clear."

"No, it's not clear at all. The way Rose made things appear isn't accurate."

"Did you visit her where she worked in Raleigh?"

"Yes, but…" He rubbed his chin with a gloved hand. "What all did she tell you?"

"I don't think it matters. But what does matter is that I'm busy with work and I can't afford to lose my job. My parents count on me."

"I realize that."

"Mr. Joachim has asked me to work longer hours, which means I have very little time to socialize."

"He's also planning to bring someone else in to work for him, so that should help."

Lillian nodded. "I'm sure it will help, but the store will be open longer and I'll need to be there."

Frustration showed in William's eyes. "Lillian, I like you very much. In fact, I think I might…well, I care for you more than I have any other woman."

Lillian wished she could believe him. "That's very sweet, but you need to find someone else."

He started to touch her cheek but pulled back before he made contact. "I don't want anyone else."

The sound of the door opening got their attention. "Lillian, are you still out there? Supper is ready."

Lillian turned back to face William. "I need to go in now."

"May we resume this conversation again soon? I would really like to talk to you."

"We'll see." Lillian took a step backward toward the house. "But I don't think there's much left to say." With that, she turned around and didn't look back.

* * * * *

William stared at the closed front door. He loved Lillian, and his heart ached for her. Pop had always said that when a man truly loved a woman, he would do anything to protect her. Now William knew exactly what Pop was talking about.

On his way back to the farm, he pondered his next move. His mission to make Lillian see his true feelings and to do whatever it took to win her heart would be a difficult task, but he didn't care. Having Lillian in his life was worth it.

As he sat at the table with Mom, Pop, and his brothers, he noticed them casting curious looks his way then exchanging glances with each other. He didn't say anything until Mom cornered him in the kitchen when he got up to help with dessert.

"What happened today, Will?"

He shrugged and forced a grin. "Nothing you can do anything about."

"Let me just ask you one thing." She lifted an eyebrow and held his gaze. "Is it business or personal?"

"Personal."

"Girl problems?"

William laughed. "You said you were only going to ask me one thing."

"Who can count when it comes to love?"

"And who said anything about love?" William asked.

She rolled her eyes and shook her head. "You are so much like your father sometimes."

"And you adore my father, so that's a good thing."

"We'd better get this dessert to the guys before they come after us."

"After you, Mom."

William noticed the way his brothers looked back and forth between him and their mother, but no one said a word. Pop didn't look at either of them, which was just as telling. They'd obviously discussed him when he was in the kitchen with Mom.

After everyone finished dessert, Mason stood. "I need to head on home since we have an early start in the morning."

"It's not like you have that far to go," Mom argued. "Why don't you stick around and have some coffee?"

Mason glanced at William and then at Amos before shaking his head. "I'll be here for breakfast."

William and Amos shooed Mom out of the kitchen so they could finish cleaning up. As soon as she was gone, Amos turned to William. "So are you gonna tell me what's bothering you, or is this when I have to pry it out of you?"

"I don't know what to do about Lillian."

"We all figured as much. So what's the problem?"

"Lots of things." He held up his fingers and touched each one as he listed her objections. "She's too busy. She thinks we're too different. She's upset about something Rose said…."

"All those are minor obstacles, from what I can tell."

"Maybe minor to you, but she thinks they're major, and there isn't much I can do about it."

"C'mon, Will. You've never given up that easily before."

"Who says I'm giving up? I'm just taking a step back and planning a strategy."

Amos chuckled. "That's the Will I know."

"So let's get this job done."

* * * * *

Lillian arrived at the shop early the next morning to move some of the stock around. Mr. Joachim liked fresh presentations to add visual interest to the merchandise, and it gave her something to get her mind off William.

When Mr. Joachim walked in the door, he took an appreciative look around. "Great job, Lillian. You'll be happy to know that I'll be interviewing someone looking for seasonal work. She is a scholarship boarding student at Cary High School, and she needs the money for incidentals. The principal of the school highly recommends her."

"I hope she's good, then."

"We'll have to see. After I talk to her, you can have a chat if you want."

Lillian started to say that wouldn't be necessary, but she stopped herself. It would be nice to at least meet the person she'd be training. "I'd like that."

Customers started coming in, so both of them became extremely busy until things died down around lunchtime. Mr. Joachim glanced at his watch. "She should be here any minute now. Send her back when she arrives." He started toward the back then stopped. "Oh, by the way, her name is Anne Jamison."

After he went to his office, Lillian took advantage of the lull and wiped off the counter. A container of talcum powder had developed a leak, and dust had settled around the cash register. When the bell jingled, Lillian glanced up at the door and saw a young woman walk in. A look of guarded fear was on her face.

"Are you Anne?"

The girl's eyes widened as she nodded. Lillian's heart went out to the girl, who had probably never held a job before. "Is Mr. Joachim available?"

"Yes," Lillian said. "Follow me."

After she delivered Anne to Mr. Joachim, Lillian found herself eager to talk to the girl who reminded her of herself, the first time she'd interviewed for a job—this job. Maybe she could help to put Anne's mind at ease.

Finally Mr. Joachim appeared. "I'll take over out here while you talk to Anne. She's a rather timid girl, so I'm not sure how she'll do with customers."

"I'll speak with her." Lillian scurried back to Mr. Joachim's office.

Anne sat in the folding chair, her white gloved hands in her lap and her legs crossed at the ankles. When she realized Lillian was there, her lips twitched into a nervous smile.

"So is this your first job?" Lillian asked.

"Yes, ma'am."

Lillian smiled. "This is my first job too. I remember being scared to death when I first started, but I'm not anymore. When you work in a store like this, you pretty much just help people find what they came in for, and then you sell it to them. There are other duties as well, but none of it is difficult."

"How will I find everything?" Anne asked.

Lillian sat down and explained the general layout of the store. "At first, you might have to ask me, but it won't be long before you know where to find the merchandise. And since you'll be adding stock to the shelves when we run low, it'll be easy to remember."

"When will I know if I got the job?" Anne asked.

"I'm sure Mr. Joachim will tell you soon. He needs to hire someone to help out during the holidays."

Anne nodded. "That's what Mr. Parker at the school said."

"Do you have any more questions before I go get Mr. Joachim?"

"No, not right now."

"Okay, wait right here." Lillian left Anne in the office.

Mr. Joachim was finishing up with the only customer in the store. After she left, he turned to Lillian. "Well? What do you think? Should we hire her?"

"I think so. She seems very nice, and I'm sure I can teach her what she needs to know."

"All right, then, why don't you go tell her she has a job? And if she wants to start now, we can put her to work."

When Lillian delivered the news, Anne instantly looked scared.

Then her features softened. "I can start now. Mr. Parker told me this might happen."

"Come on. Let me show you around before we get too busy."

The rest of the day, Lillian let Anne follow her around the store. After showing her how the cash register worked, she even let Anne ring up several small orders. Each time, Anne appeared more confident.

"So how do you like the job so far?" Lillian asked. "Is it as bad as you thought?"

"No, it's not bad at all," Anne said. "I enjoy working the cash register."

After they flipped the sign on the door from Open to Closed, Mr. Joachim discussed Anne's hours with Lillian. "Since you're in school during the morning, I'll expect you to work until closing during the week. On Saturdays, you can come in at the same time as Lillian."

Based on Anne's expression, Lillian could tell she was mentally calculating how much she'd be working. "Is that too many hours for you?" she asked.

"No, ma'am. I need as many hours as I can get if I want to buy Christmas presents for everyone."

Lillian glanced over at their boss, whose eyes had misted. She knew he had a soft spot for people who needed him.

Anne glanced over at the door, and her eyes widened. Lillian turned around and saw William standing there, looking in.

"Don't worry about him," Lillian said as Mr. Joachim went to open the door. "He's a good friend."

Mr. Joachim spoke to William for a moment, and he nodded. Then the men joined Lillian and Anne. "He's agreed to take Anne back to the school when he's in town."

Lillian looked up at William, who was smiling down at the girl. "Are you ready to leave now?"

Anne still looked frightened, so Lillian took her by the arm and looked at William. "Would you mind taking me home too? We can drop Anne off at the school first."

* * * * *

William couldn't believe his good fortune. He'd stopped by the Five and Dime with a sliver of hope that Lillian would talk to him, and now she was asking for a ride.

"Of course I don't mind. In fact, it's my pleasure."

Mr. Joachim said his farewells to the rest and then retreated to his office to tally the day's receipts. Lillian and Anne got their coats and followed William to his automobile.

"I've never ridden in one of these before," Anne said as she reluctantly got inside.

"You're in for a treat, then," Lillian told her.

After they took Anne back to the school, William turned to face Lillian. "So how did I do?"

"How did you do what?" Lillian asked.

"With your new friend Anne? Do you think she'll ever allow me to take her back to school again?"

Lillian allowed herself to laugh. "I'm sure she'll be more than happy not to have to walk."

William frowned. "It worries me that a young girl will have to walk this far everyday."

"It's only a quarter of a mile."

"I know, but it gets dark early, and there's no telling—" He stopped abruptly and slowed down the automobile. "Why are you grinning?"

Lillian shrugged. "I think it's sweet that you're so concerned for Anne, even though you've barely met her."

"I can't imagine any decent man not being concerned about the welfare of a young, innocent girl."

Lillian felt a twinge in her chest. William did have a decent side, even if he was toying with her heart.

A few minutes later, he pulled up in front of Lillian's house. "Thanks for the ride."

"Thank you for riding with me," William replied.

Lillian allowed herself to hold his gaze for a couple of seconds. "That was a very sweet thing you did for Anne. Have a safe trip home."

She ran for the front door before giving him a chance to say anything. Once she got inside, she leaned over and glanced through the window in time to see him pull away.

"Did William just bring you home?" Mama asked.

"Yes." She took a deep breath before turning around. "We started a new girl from the high school, and William offered her a ride. She doesn't know him, so I went with them."

Mama narrowed her gaze and set her jaw. "Don't forget—"

"Don't worry."

"Lillian! Don't speak to your mama like that."

"Daddy, this whole thing between William and me has been so misconstrued. He's a very sweet man with a charitable nature. He's the type who rescues injured birds...."

"And women he wants to notice him?" Mama added.

Lillian folded her arms. "I don't think he has a bit of trouble getting women to notice him."

"Some of the women from my weekly Bible class told me about the girl from Raleigh. Rose McNault, I believe, is her name?"

"What about Rose?" Lillian hung her coat on the rack by the door.

"Rose has been talking to some people in town about how William can't be trusted. Apparently they had a spat, and now he's gotten her fired from a couple of jobs."

"Mama, Rose is the woman who worked at Joachim's for less than a day."

"Just be careful, Lillian," Daddy warned. "Too many girls' heads have been turned by the wrong men who tell them what they want to hear."

"I know, Daddy."

Chapter Twelve

....

Every afternoon for the remainder of the week, William stopped by Joachim's to take Anne and Lillian home. Friday night, he brought up the subject of what had happened to Rose. Lillian said she didn't want to discuss her, but William continued.

"I stopped by the store where she worked, and next thing I knew, she was telling everyone she and I were an item," he explained. "That wasn't the truth. One afternoon when I went by to pick up something for Mom, she cornered me. I told her I had to go, and she followed me without letting the owner know she was leaving."

"So that's how she lost her job?"

William nodded. "That combined with a few other things. You have to trust me when I tell you I've never been interested in Rose."

Since Lillian had gotten a taste of how Rose operated, she believed William. "I'm sorry I thought the worst."

He smiled. "And I'm sorry I didn't explain sooner."

On Saturday, he got out of the automobile and walked Lillian to her door. Before she opened it, he took her by the arm, turned her to face him, and asked if she'd like to come out to his family's farm after church on Sunday. Her heart hammered when she met his gaze, so she glanced down at the ground to catch her breath before looking back at him.

"That's sweet of you to ask, William, but I don't think it's such a good idea."

"And why not? Do you have something against my family?"

She gasped. "No, of course I don't. Why would you even say such a thing?"

He shrugged. "Every time I mention my family, you get a distasteful look on your face."

"I'm sorry if that's how it appears. I have nothing against your family."

"That's not the way it appears to me. I've met your parents, and I can see where you get your strength."

Lillian realized she'd passed judgment on William, which was one of the things she hated about the different social classes. "I'm sorry if I seemed to be judgmental."

"I bet you'd love my folks if you gave them half a chance." He took her hand and held it between both of his. "What can I do to get you to come to my farm?"

"I'll go." Lillian knew what her parents would say—that she was setting herself up for heartache—but William did have a point. "I'm really sorry if I came across as judgmental against your family."

William's smile was wider than she'd ever seen it. "I'll let my parents know. Mom and Nelda will want to cook something special, and Pop will probably spend a little time cleaning up."

"They don't have to do that," she argued.

"Oh, but they'll want to. I need to warn you about my brothers, though. Mason and Amos will try to outdo each other to get your attention, so brace yourself for some terrible jokes."

Lillian laughed. "I have brothers, so I understand."

His forehead puckered. "Why do I never see your brothers? Do they live around here?"

"No, Seth moved to Detroit after he got married, and Tyler went in the other direction—to New York."

"Oh." William made a comical face. "I'm afraid Mom would bust our chops if any of us even hinted at moving away. My two sisters live in Durham, so we don't see as much of them as my parents would like.

You'd think they lived on the other side of the universe, hearing Mom talk about them."

"I'd like to see my brothers more," Lillian admitted, "but they had to go where the work was."

"That's one of the best things about having a farm," William admitted. "There's always work to do."

"I can't imagine either of my brothers farming. It must be something you have to be born with. Both of my parents grew up on farms, but Daddy thought he'd do better working at the sawmill." A lump formed in her throat at that, so she cleared it. "And now he can't do that job anymore."

* * * * *

William saw how quickly her mood changed when she mentioned her brothers. It must be hard having family members so far away.

"So how about I come to your church and we leave from there?" he asked.

She slowly nodded. "I'll have to talk to Mama and Daddy."

"Will that be a problem?" When Lillian looked back at him, realization suddenly hit him. "Your parents don't want you seeing me, do they?"

"It's not that they don't want me seeing you. It's just that…well, you know how we come from such different backgrounds and all… and they think I'll get hurt if…well…" She looked down and started kicking the toe of her shoe on the ground.

He tucked a finger beneath her chin and tilted her head to face him. "Why do they think you'll get hurt?"

She blinked and swallowed hard. "I should never have told you that."

"I would like to know why your parents feel this way."

The door opened, and Mrs. Pickard stuck her head out. "Come on inside, Lillian. It's too cold to be standing outside." She glanced at William but didn't smile. "Good evening, Mr. Tronnier."

"Hi, Mrs. Pickard. We were just finishing up. She'll be inside in a moment."

"Don't take too long."

As soon as Mrs. Pickard closed the door, William faced Lillian again. "I'll see you at church."

She nodded.

"Would you like me to talk to your parents about coming to my house?"

Without hesitation, she shook her head. "No, I'd better discuss this with them alone."

"If you need me to, I can talk to them tomorrow."

"Good night, William." She held his gaze and offered him a smile before reaching for the doorknob and turning it.

He waited until she was safely inside before leaving. Although he had plenty to look forward to with Lillian coming home with him, he felt a heavy burden in his chest. Now he needed to figure out how to convince her parents that he had honorable intentions.

Mom and Pop were delighted about Lillian coming home with him after church. He hesitated to tell them about her parents' feelings toward him, but he came to the conclusion that they might have some perspective—so immediately after supper, after his brothers left the table, he spoke up.

"Mom. Pop. We need to talk."

"Sure, son," Pop said. "What's going on?"

"Let me start from the beginning." William explained everything. "She's not only interesting, but she's smart, strong, and loyal to a fault," he added.

Pop chuckled and placed his hand on Mom's. "Just like your mother."

"Lillian loves the Lord, and she takes her responsibilities at home and at work very seriously." William paused before adding, "So much so that she doesn't allow herself to let loose."

"Are you in love with this girl, son?" Pop asked.

"Yes, Pop, I am. Very much so."

"That's what I thought."

Mom's eyes misted, so she dabbed them with a tissue she pulled from her pocket. "I am so happy for you, William. There's nothing better than love."

"Except when I'm the only one who is in love."

Pop leaned forward. "Have you told her how you feel?"

"No, sir."

"Has she said she doesn't love you?"

"Well…" William fidgeted for a moment. "Not exactly."

"Then how do you know you're the only one who's in love?"

"I s'pose I don't."

Mom clasped her hands together. "I look forward to having her here tomorrow. I can't wait to show her around. Do you know if she likes to cook?"

"She cooks, but I don't know if she likes it," William replied.

"Given her circumstances, she probably doesn't have time to think about what she likes or doesn't like," Mom said. "I know I didn't—at least until I had the freedom of being able to make some choices for myself, thanks to your father."

William watched his parents exchange a loving look. That was exactly what he wanted—a wife who adored him and one he couldn't wait to see every evening.

"Maybe I can have her to myself for a while—that is, if you don't mind," Mom said. "I'll let her know that my upbringing isn't that different from hers. Perhaps that will set her mind at ease."

Pop nodded. "Excellent idea, as long as it doesn't appear that we're trying to sell her on our son. That's his job."

"William said she's a smart woman, so I'm sure she knows he's a good catch."

"Mom." William laughed. "Don't all mothers feel that way about their sons?"

* * * * *

Butterflies threatened to take over Lillian's insides as she and her parents approached the church. They hadn't been happy about her going to visit William's family, but finally her daddy said it might be a good way to see for herself that she wouldn't fit into William's life. Mama didn't agree, but she relented.

William stood by the corner of the church, waiting for her. His eyes lit up as he met her gaze.

"I have to admit, he looks mighty handsome," Mama whispered.

"And he's obviously happy to see you." Daddy's voice cracked. "I think he's probably a nice enough man, if it weren't for…well, you know."

After greetings were exchanged, the four of them went inside the church and sat down. A few heads turned, as they had the first time William sat with them, but Lillian kept her attention on the pastor. When the sermon was over, they all walked out together.

"Would you like a ride home?" William asked her parents.

"You don't need to go to the trouble," Mama said. "It's out of your way."

"That doesn't matter. I don't want you walking home in the cold."

Lillian felt stiff and formal with the four of them in the automobile. After her parents got out, William waited until they were inside before driving off.

"My family is looking forward to getting to know you," William said. "Especially Mom. She can't wait to show you her kitchen and sewing room."

"She has a separate room for sewing?" Lillian asked. Mama generally sat at the kitchen table to do her mending.

William nodded. "It used to be Mason's bedroom, but as soon as he moved out, in went her sewing stuff. And there's quite a bit of it. Pop and I marvel at how much there is. He said if he had known she had so many sewing notions, he would have built her a sewing room years ago."

"Must be nice to have that luxury." Lillian repositioned herself and folded her arms.

They rode for several minutes in silence, until William turned off the main road and onto one leading to a house in the distance.

"Is that your house?" she asked.

"That's my parents' house. You can't see it from here, but we're building a house for me on another section of the property." He told her about how they'd done the same thing for Mason a few years ago and how after they finished William's house, they'd start one for Amos.

"It's nice that all of you are able to stay in this area. Mama and Daddy were heartbroken that Seth and Tyler moved away."

"We are fortunate. Farming is the type of business that requires quite a few different skills. That's why we've had Amos and Mason taking turns working with Pop in the office. Unfortunately, they're not cut out to work with numbers, so I'll take a turn for a while—at least until Pop figures out what to do."

"Do you like being in an office?" Lillian asked.

He shook his head. "I hate it, but it's only fair."

"Daddy always said he would have enjoyed being a banker or a businessman if the opportunity had been available to him. He even tried to get a job at the bank in Cary, but they turned him down due to not having any experience."

"That's insane," William said. "How do they expect him to get experience if they don't give him an opportunity?"

Lillian shrugged. "That's exactly what Mama and Daddy said."

"Did he not like his job at the sawmill?"

"He didn't dislike it, but after he started there, I heard he never felt that was what he was called to do."

William tsked. "It's a shame when someone can't at least try something." As they pulled up to the front of the house, he turned to her. "Ready for a tour?" The house was massive—even more than she'd realized from a distance.

She scanned everything before her then turned to William. "As ready as I'll ever be. But I have to admit I'm nervous."

"So am I."

They got out of the car, and he took her by the hand and led her to the front porch. Before they reached the first step, four people walked through the front door.

"That's my mom," William whispered, "my pop, and my brothers."

"Welcome," Mrs. Tronnier said. "Come on in where it's warm."

Lillian instantly felt the love in the Tronnier family as they ushered her and William inside. She hadn't expected such genuine warmth.

"Nelda made me leave the kitchen," Mrs. Tronnier said. "The last time she put me in charge of the biscuits, they came out as flat as pancakes."

"Tell her about the time you burned the pies," Amos said.

Mrs. Tronnier gave him a look of mock anger. "I don't want to scare the girl away before she gets to know how lovely I can be."

In spite of her nerves, Lillian couldn't help but laugh. She could see where William got his charm and wonderful disposition.

"Mom, why don't you show her your sewing room?" William said.

"Would you like to see it?" his mother asked.

Lillian nodded. "I'd love to see it."

"Then come on." Mrs. Tronnier made a shooing gesture toward the men. "You guys can go do something manly while I show Lillian my favorite room in the house."

As Lillian followed William's mother upstairs to the sewing room, she was taken by how chatty the woman was—not what she'd expected. She often touched Lillian and occasionally gave her a squeeze on the hand or shoulder.

"So, what do you think?" she asked after she flung open the door.

Lillian glanced around at a room filled with fabric swatches, a dress form, a couple of long tables, and a sewing machine. "It's wonderful." Mama would love a room like this.

"I used to dream of having a place to sew—more than that, even, a room where I could get away by myself," Mrs. Tronnier said. "Back before I met James, I never imagined I'd have anything like this." Her smile faded. "My family was so poor, we never even knew if we'd have a place to live half the time."

Lillian blinked. "Really?"

Mrs. Tronnier nodded. "It was terrible. I tried to get work, but no one would hire me. In order to put food on the table, Mother took in other people's mending. I used to beg her to let me help. Of course, she never let me work on other people's clothes, but I mended many of my family's garments." She took Lillian's hand and squeezed it. "It made me feel good to be useful."

"If you don't mind my asking, how did you meet Mr. Tronnier?"

"His mother was one of the people who dropped off baskets of clothes to be mended. One afternoon, she asked James to deliver it because she had to be somewhere else. Mother wasn't home, so I took the basket from him. We talked for a few minutes, and I have to admit, I became smitten." A dreamy look washed over her face. "After that, he became the regular delivery person for his mother. I didn't realize then that he actually ripped holes in some of his favorite things just so he could see me."

Lillian laughed. "That is so romantic!"

"It would have been if Mama hadn't caught on. As soon as she realized we were using that as an excuse to see each other, she forbade me to see James."

"But why?"

Mrs. Tronnier tilted her head and smiled. "Mama was trying to protect me and prevent me from getting hurt. She couldn't see that James and I truly loved each other, something that crossed all lines of what others might consider improper."

"How...how did you and Mr. Tronnier work through this?"

After a long sigh, Mrs. Tronnier closed the door to the sewing room and motioned for Lillian to sit in the chair beside a table. Then she sat in the adjacent chair. "I would have given up, but my husband doesn't know how to let things go. He persisted and continued to come around until finally Mama relented and let me see him."

Lillian pondered the situation and realized how similar it was to her own—only perhaps a bit worse. "What did your mother say when you wanted to marry Mr. Tronnier?"

"After she got over the shock, Mother was very happy for us because James insisted she come live with us. I have to admit I saw a different side of her when she wasn't quite so desperately trying to make ends meet."

"I can understand," Lillian said.

Mrs. Tronnier's expression softened a bit. "James doted on her and made sure she never went without anything she needed. She loved being a grandmother, and she did everything she could to help out." Mrs. Tronnier paused before adding, "And now she's in heaven with the Lord. The end of her life was much more pleasant than the early years, and fortunately, she passed away peacefully in her sleep."

"That is a beautiful story, Mrs. Tronnier."

Chapter Thirteen

....

"What do you think the women are up to?" Pop asked.

William tried not to show his nervousness. "No telling. You know how Mom can be."

"Yeah, that woman can talk the ears off a donkey." He chuckled. "But she's harmless and lovable."

"I'm sure they're getting along just fine."

"Are you talking about us?"

William glanced toward the sound of his mother's voice. "Can't deny we were." He extended his hand toward Lillian, and she tentatively came toward him. "So what do you think about Mom's sewing room?"

"It's wonderful."

"I thought you'd like it." William pulled Lillian closer to his side as he addressed his mother. "Nelda asked if y'all were almost ready for dinner."

Mom started for the kitchen. "I'll go help her get everything on the table."

"I can help too," Lillian said as she started to pull away.

"No," Mom said. "You're a first-time guest in our home, so you stay right here."

William leaned over and whispered, "Next time you can help if you really want to. I think Nelda would prefer that everyone stay out of the kitchen, but Mom can be stubborn when she sets her mind to something."

A few minutes later, everyone sat around the large dining room table. Pop reached for the hands of those on either side of him.

"I'll say the blessing so we can dig into this delicious feast."

William bowed his head as Pop began the blessing, but he lifted one eyelid halfway through to take a glimpse of Lillian. He was relieved to see that she appeared much less nervous than she had when they first arrived.

The second everyone said, "Amen," the men grabbed the bowls in front of them and started scooping food onto their plates.

"Calm down, guys," Mom said. "Let's not scare our guest by making her think we're a bunch of savage animals."

Mason howled. "She might as well find out what a bunch of hungry men look like, if she's going to keep coming around."

William looked at Lillian to see if she caught the last part of Mason's comment. "That's okay," she said. "I have brothers. They've been gone awhile, but I do remember them at the dinner table."

Mom scooped a serving of corn onto her plate. "Our daughters used to fuss at the boys for eating all the food before they got any."

"We left plenty," Amos said. "See? You can't even see the bottom of the bowl."

William loved the banter at the dinner table. Even if he didn't, it was good for Lillian to see what it was like when the Tronnier family sat down together. And from the look on her face, she was enjoying every minute of it.

Nelda came out periodically to make sure they had plenty of rolls and corn bread. After everyone finished eating, she announced that she'd made rice pudding and pumpkin pie. All the men wanted some of both, but Mom and Lillian said they'd like a small amount of rice pudding. He'd noticed some similarities between Mom and Lillian before, but now he realized there were quite a few.

After dessert, William offered to help, but Mason and Amos

practically shoved him and Lillian out the door. "We've got cleanup duty covered this time. When we bring a girl home, you can take over for us."

Lillian giggled as she followed William out the door. Once they got to the front room, he asked if she'd like a tour of the farm.

"I'd love one," she said.

"Walk, automobile, or horse?"

"Let's walk," she said as she rubbed her tummy. "It'll help digest our food."

Once they got outside, William asked what she thought of his family. "I know they can be overbearing sometimes, but everything they do is out of love."

"They seem so…so normal."

William roared. "Why wouldn't they be?"

Lillian pursed her lips as they walked a few feet; then she stopped and turned toward him. "No reason. It's just that I've never been around anyone like your family before."

"Is that a good or bad thing?"

"They are wonderful, William. Your mother is very sweet and makes me feel like I fit in."

"Why wouldn't you fit in?"

Lillian hung her head and shrugged.

"I think I can handle whatever it is, if you'll explain it to me."

"Your family obviously doesn't have to worry about where the next meal comes from. You even have an automobile. That's not something we'll ever have."

"How do you know?" William asked.

She shook her head. "How can that happen when we barely make ends meet?"

"Lillian," he said softly, "please come here." He reached out both hands.

At first she barely looked at him, but, finally, she sighed and took a step toward him. He pulled her into his arms.

"I care about you very much, Lillian. In fact, I think I have fallen in love with you."

He felt her body tense. "William, I—"

"You don't have to say anything. I just thought you should know how I feel." He paused for a moment. "I take that back. I want to know how you feel."

She licked her lips and shifted in his arms. He watched her and waited, holding his breath at first then slowly taking a breath.

"I think I might be falling in love with you too."

Her words hit him so hard that a small breeze would have knocked him over. "What did you say?"

Lillian's eyelashes fluttered as she looked at him and blinked. "You didn't hear me?"

"I think I did, but I want to make sure." William felt like dancing across the field, but he stayed in that spot, looking into her eyes, hoping she'd repeat the words he'd just heard.

"This is hard for me," she whispered. "I'm not used to any of this."

"Please tell me what you said one more time. I want to commit your words…your voice…everything about this moment to memory."

"William, I can't allow myself to feel this way."

"Why not, Lillian? I love you, and if you love me, then it's a beautiful thing."

"No." She stepped back and pushed him away. "It's not a beautiful thing. I still have to take care of my family, and loving you will only make life difficult."

"We'll figure out something," he argued.

"I'm not about to put that kind of burden on someone else."

"If that someone else loves you, it's a blessing, not a burden."

Lillian pursed her lips and slowly shook her head. "Let's go back inside so I can say good-bye and thank your family."

William couldn't help but wonder what he could have said or done differently. He loved Lillian now more than he did during dinner, and he had no reason to believe he wouldn't love her more as time went on.

Mom was waiting for them when they got back to the house. "Nelda baked some cookies, and I made some hot chocolate."

"I'll take the hot chocolate," Lillian said. "But I'm still too full from dinner to eat cookies."

"William?" Mom asked. "How about you? Cookies and hot chocolate?"

"Yes, of course. Both."

After they finished their hot chocolate, Lillian told his parents good-bye. His brothers had already left to see something Mason was putting in his house, so Lillian asked his parents to tell them she was happy to have met them.

As she got into the automobile, William tried to think of something to bring back the magic from earlier that afternoon, but nothing came to mind. He drove back to town with silence hovering between them.

He pulled up in front of her house and stopped the engine. "I had a wonderful time, Lillian. Would you like—?"

"We need to spend some time away from each other and think about things for a while," she said.

* * * * *

Lillian was glad when Monday morning arrived. Yesterday afternoon when she got home, her parents had exchanged plenty of glances, but she didn't say much other than the fact that William's family was very nice and that she enjoyed the dinner their cook had prepared.

After eating a biscuit and small sliver of ham for breakfast, Lillian set out for work. She was eager to be in her regular weekly routine to keep her mind off her feelings for William.

She walked into the Five and Dime and heard the strains of Christmas music playing on Mr. Joachim's phonograph. The record was scratched, but it still added a festive touch to the store.

Lillian had always enjoyed the festivities of the Christmas season—from the church activities and music to the busy shoppers rushing about to pick up gifts for loved ones and friends. Mama and Daddy rarely gave more than a few words and kisses to each other, but ever since she'd had a job, she'd brought a gift home for each of them. Mama generally hung a stocking for her and filled it with fruit and nuts.

"I have something for you, Lillian," Mr. Joachim said as he came up to the front of the store. "I'd planned to save this until Christmas Eve, but I think you can use it early." He pulled a messily wrapped parcel from his jacket pocket and handed it to her with an expectant look on his face.

"Thank you," she said as she took it.

"Open it now."

She tore the paper and pulled out the gift. "Gloves! I love them!" She swallowed hard to hold back her emotions. "These are exactly what I need."

Mr. Joachim's face turned bright red. "I thought they might help keep you warm on cold nights when you have to walk home."

Lillian put them on and held out her hands. They were a tad too big, but they fit what she felt in her heart. "They're perfect."

Until this year, she hadn't given Mr. Joachim much thought, other than when she referred to him as her boss. But something had changed, and she realized it was her, not him. She'd matured enough to see herself as an adult.

She carefully pulled off the gloves and shoved them into her coat pockets. "I'll enjoy wearing them tonight, that's for sure. I heard it might snow."

"Even if it doesn't snow, it'll be cold."

A customer walked in, and for the remainder of the morning, Lillian was busy. Mr. Joachim had to come out of the office a couple of times to help with the crowd. By the time Anne arrived, they were happy to have a third person in the store.

"This place is hopping," Anne said. "What would you like me to do?"

"If you don't mind running the cash register while I help people find what they're looking for, that would be a big help. Mr. Joachim needs to restock some of the shelves."

"I don't mind at all." Anne instantly did as she was told.

The rest of the day ran smoothly, and the customers all left happy. By the time Mr. Joachim flipped the sign on the door, Lillian was ready to be done with the day.

"Great job, ladies," he said. "If business keeps up like this, you'll both get bonuses."

Anne's eyebrows shot up. "Bonuses, as in more money?"

Mr. Joachim chuckled. "That's what I'm talking about."

Anne started to speak, but something outside caught her attention and she leaned forward, staring. "Is that...?" She squinted.

Lillian turned around and spotted William's automobile parked outside, with him leaning against it. "That's William Tronnier."

"I bet he came to take you ladies home," Mr. Joachim said. "Have a good evening. See you both tomorrow."

Since Anne and William now knew each other, Lillian said she'd walk home. But they both seemed appalled by the very thought, and since she didn't want to make an issue of it, she accepted William's offer of a ride as long as they dropped her off first. William looked hurt, but he did as she asked.

Lillian walked through the door of her home and showed Mama and Daddy her new gloves from Mr. Joachim. Mama seemed impressed, but Daddy appeared to have something else on his mind. Lillian helped with dinner then retired to her room to read.

As she turned the pages, she heard the murmuring of her parents' conversation. Mama sounded irritated about something. It probably had something to do with William, but since Lillian had put the skids on that relationship, it wouldn't be an issue.

* * * * *

Business was slow at the Five and Dime the next morning, but that wasn't unusual for a Tuesday. Lillian knew it would pick up later in the day, after the high schoolers got out of school.

When the bell on the door jingled, Lillian looked up to greet the customer. Rose came walking into the store dressed to the nines, her head held in a high, jaunty manner as though she were in charge.

"Did you need something, Rose?" Lillian didn't bother coming out from behind the counter.

"I just wanted to tell you how amusing you are. William and I laughed about it all evening after he dropped Anne off at school."

"What are you talking about?" Lillian asked. She gripped the edge of the counter so tightly that the wood cut into the palm of her hand.

"You obviously haven't spoken to him since last night." Rose covered her mouth and pretended to hide her laughter. "He just feels sorry for you because you're so poor."

"Is that what he said?" Anger welled inside Lillian.

"Well, not exactly in so many words. He just said…well, never mind. I only stopped in to pick up some bath salts."

Lillian told Rose where the bath salts were located. After Rose brought them to the counter, paid, and walked out of the store, Lillian let out a low growling sound. If she hadn't already told William they couldn't be together, she would now.

She seethed and fumed until Anne arrived. "What happened to you?" Anne asked.

"Nothing. Tell me if you see William. I need to talk to him as soon as possible."

Anne pointed toward the street. "He's over at the bank right now. Why don't you ask Mr. Joachim if you can take a break since we're not busy?"

Lillian looked at her for a moment, narrowing her eyes. "Are you ready to be left alone on the floor?"

"Of course. I can handle things as long as it's not too crowded."

Lillian ran to the office and got permission from Mr. Joachim to leave for a few minutes. "Is everything all right? You're not sick, are you?"

"No, sir. I just need to chat with Mr. Tronnier, and Anne said he's down the street at the bank."

"By all means, go talk to him. I'll keep an eye on the floor, and if Anne gets busy while you're gone, I'll give her a hand. Take as much time as you need."

Lillian thanked him, grabbed her coat, and pulled it on as she scurried toward the door. She'd barely made it outside when William came walking up the sidewalk toward Joachim's.

"I was just coming to see you," he said. "We need to talk."

"Stop," she ordered. "We don't need to talk, but I do need to tell you one thing. I will not stand for you being all nice and acting like you care about me and then running to Rose McNault and making me look pitiful and desperate."

"What?" Sincere indignation covered his face.

"She told me y'all were laughing about me last night."

"Come on, Lillian, you know she's a liar."

"Did you see her last night?" Lillian folded her arms and tilted her head, all the while staring him in the eye.

"Well, yes, but only because she flagged me down after I dropped off Anne."

"Where was she?"

"Here in Cary. She asked me if I minded taking her home since she missed the train."

"Did you take her home?"

William hung his head. "Yes, I did. I probably shouldn't have, but I didn't want that on my conscience."

Lillian felt some of her anger fade as she realized that Rose had played another of her games. And she regretted confronting William.

"Look, Lillian, I meant every single word I said to you on Sunday. I care about you more than you can imagine, and I thought my heart would explode with joy when you said you loved me too."

She closed her eyes, inhaled deeply, and slowly let out her breath before looking back at William. "I'm sorry, William. I should know better than to accuse you of anything Rose says."

"In that case, would you mind if I stop by your house later tonight?"

Lillian smiled. "How about another night later in the week? I'd like to talk to my parents first."

He hesitated then nodded. "Okay. How about Thursday?"

* * * * *

William wasn't sure, but he didn't think Lillian had any idea that he and his pop had been talking to her dad about the business. A few things Lillian mentioned had sparked an idea, and after discussing it with Pop, they went into town one day and dropped in to discuss the details with Mr. Pickard. At first, he shook his head and said he didn't want handouts from the rich, but they convinced him to listen to what they had to say before making a decision.

Since William was already in town, he decided to stop off at the Pickard home and see how Lillian's parents were doing. Mrs. Pickard answered the door and let him in.

"My husband told me what you and your father want to do. I don't know if that's such a good idea."

William looked her squarely in the eyes. "I'm in love with your daughter, Mrs. Pickard, and I have a tremendous amount of respect for you and your husband for raising such a smart woman. He seems to have a good business mind, and Pop and I would like to give him a break."

She reared back and blinked a couple of times. "Well…yes, my husband is a very smart man, but do you really think—?"

"Helen, I'll talk to him." Mr. Pickard came out from one of the back rooms of the house, limping but moving forward with purpose. "Good afternoon, Mr. Tronnier. I've been thinking about this opportunity with your family business."

* * * * *

The entire way home from work, Lillian tried to think of a good way to tell her parents that William was coming over on Thursday. She'd look for a break in conversation, but if it didn't come, she'd wait until tomorrow.

Mama had dinner ready, and Daddy was already sitting at the table waiting for her to get home. "Take off your coat and sit down, Lillian. I'm starving."

She was shocked at his firm but assured tone, so she did as she was told without saying a word. It had been a long time since Daddy had spoken to her like this. She glanced over at Mama, who wouldn't look her in the eye. Something was going on.

Throughout dinner, Daddy chatted about the weather, business, and other topics he used to enjoy. Lillian listened as she wondered about the change.

As she stood up to help clear the table, Daddy cleared his throat and pointed to the chair. "Sit back down, Lillian."

She quickly sat.

"William Tronnier is coming over tomorrow, and I'd like you to be nice to him while he's here."

"Tomorrow? I thought he was coming on Thursday."

Daddy nodded. "He asked if he could come on Thursday, and I said why wait."

"Oh."

Lillian glanced back and forth at her parents and caught them exchanging their own private look. Finally, Mama told her to help clean the house so she wouldn't have so much to do the next day to get ready for company.

Mama didn't talk much as they swept and dusted. After Lillian went to her room, she sat on the edge of her bed and stared at the wall. As she got older, life seemed to get stranger.

Chapter Fourteen
....

William picked Lillian and Anne up from work the next day. Without anyone saying a word, he drove straight to the school and dropped Anne off then turned the car toward the Pickard house. Before William got out, he turned to face her, took her hand, and said, "I love you, Lillian Pickard, and that will never change."

Her heart hammered, but she didn't say a word until they were halfway to the door. Finally she blurted, "I feel the same way, but we both need to get over it because it simply won't do either of us any good not to."

He grinned. "I'm not easily dissuaded. You should know that by now."

The house was filled with the fragrant aroma of baked chicken and apple pie. By now, it wasn't a surprise to have such a lavish meal waiting for them.

After Daddy said grace, everyone started eating right away. Having William at the table had taken away Lillian's appetite, but she didn't mind. She'd have a snack later.

Conversation seemed a little more jovial than usual and appeared to have some underlying current that Lillian couldn't quite put her finger on. Mama's smiles were extra wide for William, and Daddy was much more relaxed than she would have expected. After dinner, instead of asking if he could be alone with Lillian, William sat in the living room with all three of the Pickards.

They chatted about trivial things for about an hour until William yawned and said he needed to get home. Lillian walked him to the door. He touched her cheek, said he'd see her soon, and left. She turned around and saw that her parents were already engrossed in conversation, so she went to her room.

The next couple of weeks were similar. William stopped by, had dinner, chatted with the family, and went home. She thought it was odd, but the familiarity was growing on her, and she liked it.

"Have you gotten anything for your parents for Christmas yet?" Mr. Joachim said. "It's less than two days away."

"I know. I'd thought about getting Mama some powder, but she doesn't have much use for it."

"How about one of those vanity sets?" he asked. "I know it's probably more than you wanted to spend, but with your employee discount and…" He dug into his pocket and pulled out a thick envelope. "Here, with this you can afford it. Go ahead and open it."

She took the envelope and opened it in front of him. "Mr. Joachim, this is much more than I ever expected. You don't have to—"

"I know I don't have to, but you've worked here a very long time, and it's time to show my appreciation."

"Thank you."

"So if you get the vanity set for your mama, how about the shaving kit for your daddy? I think he'll like the one with the pecan wood handle."

Lillian took his advice and purchased the lavish gifts for her parents. And just in case she might see William, she picked up a new winter scarf for him. Mr. Joachim nodded and said that color was perfect for William.

Christmas Eve was extremely busy at the store, which suited Lillian just fine. She hadn't seen William in several days, and she needed to take her mind off worrying that he'd lost interest. Mama teased her and said she was upset when he gave her too much attention and worried when he didn't give her enough. Lillian was confused by Mama's apparent change of heart.

The store closed early on Christmas Eve. Lillian looked both ways, hoping William would come puttering up in his automobile to take her home, but she was disappointed. He was nowhere in sight.

When Lillian arrived home, she noticed a different mood between her parents. Mama appeared nervous, and Daddy wouldn't look her in the eye. And when she went into the kitchen, she spotted a massive batch of shortbread cookies cooling on the counter.

"Do you mind if we just have sandwiches tonight for supper?" Mama asked. "One of the ladies from church brought over some ham, so I thought we could eat that and potato salad, if you don't mind making it."

"Of course I don't mind," Lillian said as she put on her apron.

Mama left her alone in the kitchen, something she rarely did. When the potato salad was finished, Lillian went to get her parents, who sat very close together on the sofa. They jumped at the sound of her entering the room.

"What is going on around here?" Lillian asked.

Mama stifled a giggle as she shook her head. "Why would you ask such a silly question? Your father and I were just discussing something...." She cast a glance over at Daddy. "Something very private."

Lillian felt the tension in her face as she glared at her parents. Who were these people? "Let's eat. I don't want to miss church."

The remainder of the evening was just as strange. Mama and Daddy insisted she go caroling with some of the families from church while they went on home. It was obvious they wanted to be alone. Daddy appeared more confident lately, and her parents seemed to be happier overall.

She hovered toward the back of the group as they strolled up and down the streets of Cary, singing Christmas carols. When they got close to her house, she let a couple people know she was finished for the night. By the time she got home, all the lights were out and her parents were in bed, so she tiptoed through the house and went to her own room.

For a long time, she lay in bed thinking about how strange her parents were acting and pondered what was going on. She finally fell asleep, only to be awakened by the sound of Mama pounding on her door.

"Don't sleep all day, Lillian. It's Christmas."

Lillian sat up in bed, rubbed her eyes, and got up. "Okay, I'll be right out. Why don't you go back to bed, Mama, and I'll fix breakfast?"

Mama giggled. Lillian tilted her head, scrunched her face, and wondered again what was happening to her parents. Until recently, Lillian had never heard her mama giggle.

She got dressed and went out to see about Mama and Daddy, but they were already ready for the day. They sure did seem awfully nervous and fidgety, though.

"Lillian, why don't you go outside and see how cold it is?" Daddy said.

She stood by the window. "I can tell you right now, it's mighty cold. I can feel it from here."

Mama looked at Daddy then at her. "Would you mind checking to see if that ribbon I tied on the post outside is still there?"

"Why wouldn't it be?"

"Well, you know how windy it's been this winter…." Mama looked at Daddy, who shrugged. They were obviously trying everything they could to get her to go outside. The last time they had acted so strangely on a Christmas morning, they had something special for her.

Lillian held up her hands. "Okay, let me get my coat, and I'll go check on the ribbon."

"Good girl," Daddy said. *Did he just cover up a chuckle? Very strange.*

After she had her coat on, Lillian opened the door, took a step outside, and glanced up in time to see William coming down the street in his automobile. That was odd.

Lillian found the post with the ribbon and saw that it hadn't moved. Then she waited for William to pull up in front of the house.

He cranked down the window, and before she had a chance to say a word, he hollered, "Hey, gorgeous! Merry Christmas! Need a ride?"

"What is going on, William?"

"Hop in and I'll tell you." He patted the seat next to him.

"Okay, but let me go tell my parents."

"Oh, you don't have to." He nodded toward the house behind her. "Here they come now."

"Get in, Lillian. It's freezing out here, and we don't have all day." Mama helped Daddy into the backseat of William's car and fussed at her. "Hurry up. You're such a slowpoke."

Lillian got in and gave William a curious stare. He didn't look directly at her, but a grin played on his lips. He drove without talking, and Mama and Daddy didn't say a word from the backseat.

The suspense was driving her nuts. "Where are we going?" she asked as they neared the edge of town.

"Oh, didn't I tell you?" Mama said from the backseat. "Margaret Tronnier invited us to Christmas brunch. Isn't that sweet?"

Lillian's eyes widened. "Yes, that's very sweet." She folded her arms and thought for a moment. "So when did we get the invitation, and why am I just now finding out about it?"

William patted her hand. "Shh. Don't worry about the details. Just sit back and enjoy the Lord's birthday."

The drive was mostly silent, with a few comments from Mama about how pretty the countryside was this time of year. A combination of excitement and trepidation welled in Lillian's chest.

After they arrived at the farm, William helped all of them out of the automobile. That was when Lillian noticed the tin in Mama's hands. She nodded toward it and gave Mama a questioning look.

"You don't think I'd come here empty-handed, do you? I'm bringing shortbread."

Mrs. Tronnier greeted them at the door, took Mama by the arm, and led her through the house. Everyone else followed.

"Where's that sewing room I've heard about?" Mama asked.

"Would you like to see it?" Mrs. Tronnier said. "Nelda said it will be a few minutes before it's time to eat."

Lillian started to follow them, but William gently guided her to the parlor. She glanced over her shoulder and saw that Mr. Tronnier and William's brothers were chatting with Daddy. This whole situation seemed very cozy and…well, odd.

"I don't understand all this," Lillian said when they were alone.

William laughed. "You will soon." His expression softened to one of tenderness. "I just want you to know how much you mean to me, Lillian."

The warmth in his eyes melted her heart. "Thank you for making my parents so happy. It's such a sweet thing to do."

"Are you happy?" he asked.

She looked into his eyes and nodded. He lowered his head and dropped a soft kiss on her lips. Her tummy fluttered.

"Let's go check out the dining room. Mom pulled out all the stops for today's brunch. You should have seen her running around this morning, making sure everything was just right."

As they stood at the door of the dining room, Lillian stared in disbelief. The chairs had been covered in all white, with gold-colored bows tied at the backs. An immense green bowl filled with gold-and-red balls graced the center of the table that had been covered with layers of white-and-gold fabric. Gold-rimmed fine china was flanked by sparkling crystal and gold-dipped silverware.

"Your mother did all this for us?"

"Yes," William said. "She wanted to make a good impression."

Lillian had never seen anything so beautiful in real life. She glanced up at William. "Mama will love this."

"I hope so." William kissed the top of Lillian's head and led her away from the dining room. "Let's go see what's taking everyone so long."

Mama and Mrs. Tronnier were coming down the stairs, chattering as though they'd known each other for years. Daddy and Mr. Tronnier were deep in conversation in the foyer. Lillian had never seen either of her parents so engaged with others before.

"Amazing they get along so well, isn't it?" William said.

Lillian was speechless. She could only nod.

Nelda came out of the kitchen and gestured to Mrs. Tronnier, who announced, "Brunch will be served soon. Let's everyone have a seat in the dining room."

Mama made all the right sounds when she saw the decorations. Mrs. Tronnier showed everyone where to sit.

As if on cue, Nelda and a couple of teenage children began serving the meal. Occasionally, Lillian stole a glance at her parents and was amazed by how comfortable they both seemed. As the conversation continued, she realized how familiar the two sets of parents were with each other—particularly Daddy and Mr. Tronnier. The discussion turned to business, and that was when she realized they'd been planning something for a while. They'd finished the last of the meal when Daddy commented on the farm's balance sheet.

"What is going on here?" she whispered to William.

"Just a second." William tapped his water glass to get everyone's attention. "I think it's time to make an announcement. Pop, would you do the honors?"

Mr. Tronnier looked around the table as he spoke then settled his gaze on Lillian. "We've recently decided to increase the size of our livestock holdings and variety of crops. The only thing that made it difficult was the lack of manpower—particularly on the business side. My sons and I are in agreement that we need someone to do the ordering and keep up with the accounting. When I learned about your father's acute business mind, I decided to offer him a job handling the office affairs of the Tronnier farm." He paused and winked at Lillian. "My son is happy about this because it means he has an excuse to see his sweetheart."

Lillian's instant joy for Daddy quickly faded when she considered how far the farm was from town. "Daddy, how are you planning to get here everyday?"

Daddy started to speak, but William held up his hands. "That was one of the first things we thought of. My brothers and I are working on a cottage for your parents."

Lillian sat back in her chair. What did all this mean? She still had her job at Joachim's. William had said the cottage was for her parents, so where did that leave her?

Before she had a chance to ask those questions, William blurted, "I might like to marry Lillian one of these days, and if she says yes, we'll be nearby in our own house."

Mrs. Tronnier narrowed her gaze at her son. "William, that's not the way—"

Her husband interrupted her. "Didn't you pay any attention to what I told you, son?"

The room started to swirl with all the voices blaring. Daddy's stare held her attention. "Lillian, are you going to follow your heart this time, or do you plan on remaining stubborn and be a nuisance to your mama and me for the rest of our lives?"

Everyone burst out in laughter. Lillian even thought the situation was funny, so she giggled.

"Well?" Daddy said. "We're waiting."

"Um…I don't know…maybe…" She looked at William and smiled. Her face flamed.

Silence momentarily filled the room; then William's brothers broke into nervous laughter—until their mother gave them a look. Mama's grin was wider than Lillian ever remembered.

William stood and cleared his throat. "Since we're finished, why don't we take a tour of the property so we can show off the houses we've been working on?"

Everyone got up and went to get their coats. Mr. Tronnier led the way, with Daddy limping along behind him. Mama and Mrs. Tronnier followed, still chatting like old friends. William took Lillian by the hand and gestured for his brothers to go ahead of them.

They walked over toward a clearing of trees on the edge of the back lawn. William pointed to a shell of a cottage that appeared to be quite a bit larger than the house the Pickards rented in town. "We'll finish the cottage first so you can move right in," William explained. "Pop hired a few extra workers to complete the construction, so it shouldn't be too much longer. Mom wants Mrs. Pickard to help decorate it since she's the one who'll be living there."

Lillian saw that Mama had misty eyes and a broad smile. A lump formed in her throat.

Daddy nodded. "I think it's a good idea to be close to my work."

Mr. Tronnier explained that William would go into town to pick him up until the cottage was ready for them to move in to. "We need you to start right after the New Year begins."

Everyone began talking again. William tugged at Lillian and whispered, "I want to show you something."

This whole thing felt like a dream to Lillian. She followed William as he practically ran to a slightly smaller version of the main house.

"What do you think?" He pointed to the house.

"It's beautiful. Is this yours?"

Instead of answering her question, he pulled her toward the house. "Let's go inside. I want to show you around."

They walked through the door and into the foyer. He led her along, pointing out the rooms as they went. Lillian was amazed by the organization of the downstairs with the library and casual gathering room on one side of the hallway and the parlor and dining room on the other. The kitchen spanned the entire back of the house, with the cooking station on one end and a large eating area on the other.

"There are four bedrooms upstairs," he said. "I wasn't sure how many we'd need, so I decided to start with four." His hand began to shake. "Lillian…"

She turned to face him, and her breath caught in her throat. The combination of tenderness and longing in his expression grabbed her heart and squeezed.

William continued holding onto her hand as he slowly lowered to one knee. "I love you with all my heart, Lillian, and I want this to be our home." He shifted a bit and reached into his pocket then spread out her left hand. "If you will accept this ring, I'll be the happiest man in the world."

"But I thought…" She stared at the solitaire diamond ring. "Are you—?"

"I'm asking you to be my wife—to share the rest of our lives together."

Lillian held his gaze for a couple of seconds then nodded. "Yes, William, I will marry you."

He closed his eyes and smiled before placing the ring on her finger. Then he jumped up, flung his arms around her, and swung her in a circle. "You have just made me one very happy man."

Lillian held out her left hand and stared at the sparkling diamond. "This is beautiful, William. Thank you so much."

William chuckled. "You might not be thanking me after I tell you what you need to do next."

She frowned at him. "I have to do something?"

With a nod, he replied, "Yes, now you need to get to work

decorating this place. I can build a house, but you don't want to let me loose with the décor."

Lillian laughed. "I'll be glad to."

"C'mon, let's go let everyone know you said yes."

As soon as they reached the porch, William lifted her hand and announced, "She said yes!"

Everyone cheered. Lillian looked out over the people standing before her, and she had no doubt that the Lord had blessed her with a family filled with people who would always be there for her and William.

Pickard-Tronnier Shortbread
(or Shortbread Cookies)

....

2 cups sifted flour

1 teaspoon cornstarch

1 cup softened butter

1/2 cup sugar

1 teaspoon vanilla (optional)

Directions:

1 Mix the flour and cornstarch in a medium bowl.

2 In a large bowl, mix softened butter with sugar and vanilla (optional) until creamy.

3 Add the flour mixture to the butter and sugar.

4 Press the mixture into an 8x8-inch cake pan. (See below if you are making cookies.)

5 Bake in a 325-degree oven for approximately 30 minutes.

6 Cool slightly but cut into 2-inch squares while still warm.

Directions for cookies:

1 Follow steps 1–3 in the directions above.

2 Use a teaspoon to scoop the batter, roll it into balls, and flatten each one on a cookie sheet.

3 Bake for approximately 15 to 20 minutes until brown around the edges.

4 Cool before removing from the pan.

About the Author

....

 Debby Mayne grew up in a military family, which meant moving every few years throughout her childhood. She has worked as managing editor of a national health magazine, a product information writer for a TV retailer, a creative writing instructor, and a copyeditor and proofreader for several book publishers. Debby currently enjoys writing Christian fiction, which allows her the freedom to tell stories without restraining her convictions. She has published more than thirty books and novellas, including *Love Finds You in Treasure Island, Florida*, and approximately four hundred short stories and articles. She was a contributing author to the popular devotional for busy women, *Be Still...and Let Your Nail Polish Dry*, and she and Trish Perry both contributed to the follow-up devotional, *Delight Yourself in the Lord...Even on Bad Hair Days*.

Debby and her husband, Wally, have two adult daughters, a son-in-law, and a granddaughter. They make their home on Florida's west coast with their cat, Misty.

Read more about Debby at www.debbymayne.com.

'Tis the Season

BY TRISH PERRY

And in him you too are being built together
to become a dwelling in which God lives by his Spirit.
EPHESIANS 2:22 NIV

Chapter One

....

Early March, modern day

"Have I ever told you why I stole you away from Armand, Nikki?"

Nicole Tronnier dusted a trace of flour off the tip of her nose and gave old Mr. Fennicle a smile. "Of course you have, Harvey. I amazed you with my culinary prowess and sparkling personality."

She placed a basket of warm rosemary biscuits near his plate. The pumpkin-potato puree and veggie medley looked perfect next to his rack of lamb, if she did say so herself. The rich winter colors were almost as important to her as the fragrance and taste of the food she served. "If anyone deserves the very best personal chef in North Carolina, it's an absolutely spoiled multimillionaire like you."

She saw him fight against the twitch of a smile.

"I resent your insinuation about me, young lady."

"I call 'em as I see 'em, Harvey."

"I'm an absolutely spoiled *billionaire*, at the very least. And that's not why I lured you away. I've always been very fond of Armand and his fine restaurant. It's one of the reasons I opened a plant in Charlotte, so I could visit him and still make money. Pilfering his star chef gave me no pleasure, and I could have found an equally gifted chef elsewhere, I'm certain."

"But?" She crossed her arms. She adored this old man, and it had taken so little time to settle into fond banter with him once she joined the staff of his spacious Cary, North Carolina, mansion almost a year ago.

He closed his eyes and swallowed his bite of lamb, ecstasy in his expression. "Perfect." He breathed a satisfied sigh. "But I saw you do something that put you over the top, in my book. I don't suppose you even know what that was."

"I gave you an extra-large slice of my mango-coconut terrine for dessert. Was that it?"

"Didn't hurt, but no. Do you remember that odd fellow who made off with a dish full of food the day I met you?"

She frowned. "Odd fellow. No. What do you mean he made off with—oh, you mean the homeless guy in the fake waiter suit." She chuckled at the memory.

"I was outside in my limo when that happened," Harvey said. "I hadn't yet entered the restaurant and was on the phone with one of my more boring advisors. I saw that fellow rush out of the restaurant, glancing back, forth, and behind. He was protecting that plate of food as if eagles would swoop down and carry it off."

"Poor guy," Nikki said. "I think he just wandered in off the street, fully intending to beg—from our customers or from the restaurant, I don't know for sure. But he was in that old black suit, and a customer handed her dish to him to bring it back to the kitchen for reheating or something. She thought he was a waiter. And he thought he hit the jackpot."

Harvey laughed. "When you stormed out the front door after him and nearly tripped over him, sitting there—"

"You never told me you saw all that, Harvey!"

"I did indeed."

"Yeah, I remember it now. It was just like you said. He was so hungry he didn't even run beyond the front stoop. Broke my heart." She shrugged. "I had to redo the customer's order anyway. No sense in wasting food."

"I saw you pat his head, Nikki. Not only did you let him eat, you weren't afraid to touch him."

She sighed. "And *that's* why you hired me?"

He focused on cutting his lamb. "Says a lot about a person, the things they'll do when they think no one else is watching. If I'm going to have someone join my live-in staff, I want to make sure she's made of the right stuff, not just able to *make* the right stuff."

"Yep." She nodded. "I'm pretty special, all right."

Harvey's personal assistant, Laura, walked into the dining room. "Excuse me, Mr. Fennicle."

"Laura, please." He tilted his head. "Call me Harvey. I've told you about that."

She simply smiled. Nikki knew Laura would never loosen up enough to accommodate Harvey's request. She had replaced his previous assistant who'd retired months ago, and she was still loath to so much as chat over a cup of coffee. After Nikki's years of active social life in college and then working in bustling kitchens full of chatty coworkers, the lack of sisterly camaraderie was sometimes lonely.

"Elliot Kincaid in New York is calling," Laura said to Harvey. "What would you like me to—?"

"Thanks, yes. Please tell him I'll call him in about a half hour. And could you bring me those papers he sent down yesterday? I'll look them over while I eat. Did you get dinner?"

"Yes, thank you." She smiled formally at Nikki. "Very nice, Nikki. Thank you."

"My pleasure."

Although the woman hadn't yet proven easy to cozy up to, Nikki still had hope. She watched Laura's prim steps carry her out of the room and then returned her attention to Harvey. "Okay, I'll leave you to it, then. Do you need anything else?"

"Only the fountain of youth, dear."

She squeezed his shoulder and almost gave him a kiss on his feathery-haired head. "I'll check on you in a little while. I have something special for your dessert."

She returned to the kitchen and started tidying up. Harvey's panna cotta was ready in the refrigerator. She only needed to drizzle the rose syrup over it before she served it to him. He loved trying new flavors, and this would be exactly that. Her old boss, Armand Gaudet, had introduced her to Italian rose syrup while she apprenticed under him in Charlotte.

Not for the first time, Nikki felt the tiniest twinge of guilt about leaving Armand, even though he had been completely gracious when Harvey offered her this job. There had simply been too many "God things" involved for her to ignore the opportunity.

Although she had moved away from Cary years ago in order to attend college and then train under Armand, she was definitely a family girl. She loved the city but missed her hometown. The three-hour drive between Charlotte and Cary made visiting her parents, sister, and old friends prohibitive. So for the location alone, she gave Harvey's offer serious consideration as soon as he made it.

But there was another reason she couldn't refuse the offer to work as personal chef to the eccentric Harvey Fennicle. He had doubled her income with a stroke of his pen on her employment contract. Nikki wasn't money-hungry, but as long as she could remember, she had saved for a specific goal in mind. Now she might actually reach that goal.

Her family's old home here in Cary—the home her great-grandfather William Tronnier and his brothers built for William and his new bride, Lillian—had been on the market for a year or more. Neither her parents nor her grandparents had maintained ownership of the Tronnier home, seeking instead to buy more modern homes for themselves and their families.

But Nikki's fondest early childhood memories were wrapped up in that home. As a little girl, she'd thought Granny Lillian and Grampa William would always be around. And she'd thought the family would spend every holiday, especially Christmas morning, celebrating in their home. She wanted to bring those memories back into her family's lives and futures.

The house was still beautiful but needed considerable refurbishing. Until Harvey Fennicle came into her life, Nikki had little hope of saving enough to purchase and remodel the home. Now she was close to having saved a sizable down payment. It wouldn't be long before she could make an offer to the current owner. The house had been vacant for quite a while. Nikki had confidence in her chances.

She couldn't think of anything or anyone that would stand in her way now.

Chapter Two

....

Drew Cornell seldom awoke in a bad mood, especially on Saturday mornings. Regardless of how hard or how late he had worked the night before, he typically couldn't keep from giving in to optimism within moments after waking. His golden retriever Freddie saw to that, padding dutifully from the plush living-room carpet into Drew's bedroom the moment the alarm rang each morning.

The two of them had fallen into the kind of rhythm only a lifelong bachelor and his trusty best friend could after years of companionship. Five years, to be exact. Even the move to Cary nine months ago and the need to orient themselves to this small rental apartment hadn't disrupted their routine for long. For his part, Freddie carried Drew's running shoes in his mouth, dropped them at the side of the bed, and greeted Drew with his panting grin each day.

But this morning Drew was unable to welcome Freddie with the enthusiasm he usually demonstrated. Still facedown on the bed, he groaned and blindly reached his hand out to find the top of Freddie's head and give it a cursory rub.

"Ugh. Okay. Be with you in a minute, pal." At least those were the words he spoke into the mattress. He assumed Freddie would grasp his meaning despite the fuzzy enunciation.

Not only had he lost sleep worrying about his dad's latest health scare, but he had spent more than an hour on the phone in the middle of the night, comforting his old girlfriend in California. Isabelle had already dated, fallen for, and been dumped by a new man since Drew moved to Cary this past year, and she tended to forget about the three-hour time difference when she leaned on Drew for a consoling ear. He didn't have the heart to remind her when she called, crying, at three in the morning, that he needed to be up at six to start his day, even this weekend.

So he listened and tried to encourage her without slipping into telling her what she ought to do. Back when they dated, she'd taught him that was a big no-no with women. Just lend an ear or a shoulder, she had told him, and try to sympathize. For that pointer alone, he would always be grateful, even though the strategy seemed to drag problems on longer than necessary, as far as he was concerned.

Freddie pressed his cold nose up against Drew's arm, which dangled over the edge of the bed. Drew pulled it in and pushed himself up.

"Right." He sat up and rubbed his eyes. The dog tilted his head as if awaiting an explanation for this delay. His tail worked like a metronome.

Drew chuckled. "Okay, buddy. I guess skipping this morning's run is out of the question."

The moment he stood, the dog's excitement kicked into gear. He dashed out of the bedroom as if his paws were on fire. Drew barely had time to brush his teeth and throw on his T-shirt and sweats before Freddie returned and sat at his feet, his leash in his mouth.

* * * * *

"Let's try a change of scenery here, boy." He tugged at the dog's leash when the sidewalk forked in two directions. One side led to the park and the other to the mixed-use section of the residential community, where shops and small office buildings were clustered.

Their typical route took them through the park, but Drew needed caffeine earlier than usual today. The air was cold, and that had helped at first. But now that he had worked up a sweat and the cool air was more comforting than bracing, he was going to need something stronger. They'd stop at the coffee shop and take a more leisurely stroll home. He hadn't missed a day's run yet this week. He could afford to slack off on his return for one morning.

It was early enough that few shops or offices had even opened yet. But he could smell the heavenly fragrance from the Coffee Bean before he even rounded the corner.

When he did round the corner, however, a flash of fur whizzed past him so quickly that he almost tripped over it. His lack of sleep kicked in, and he grumbled about the near accident. People needed to hang onto their dogs better than that.

He halted abruptly, but Freddie had other plans. The retriever took off after the other dog, and Drew didn't have a firm enough hold on the leash to stop him.

"Freddie! No!"

Before he even started running after him, a young woman ran past him, clearly in pursuit of the smaller dog.

"If your dog hurts mine—" She didn't finish her threat. She had already passed him.

He laughed, incredulous. "If my dog hurts hers? Freddie! No!" He broke into a run when he saw all three of them disappear into the park.

By the time he caught up to them, the lightning-quick fur ball had come to a halt at the base of an old oak tree. He was a tough little red-haired cuss—a terrier—with short legs and a big-dog attitude. He alternated between barking at whatever had run up the tree and barking at Freddie, whose own pattern mirrored his exactly. The two of them didn't seem to know which crisis was more important, their prey or each other. So they divided their energies accordingly.

The woman squatted next to the terrier and fiddled with the leash before picking up the dog and holding him as if she were about to run for a touchdown.

"Enough, Riley! That's *enough* out of you. Calm down." She glanced at Freddie and raised her voice. "You too. Shush!" She wore a frown when she turned around, obviously seeking the dog's errant owner. She met eyes with Drew. "Oh." That was it. Just "Oh." But the word was full of annoyance.

Freddie continued to instigate barks here and there, and Riley couldn't resist echoing him.

"Freddie." Drew said it calmly. Now that he was this close in proximity to his dog, that was all he chose to say to assure him that all bark-worthy circumstances were under control.

The young woman nodded at him. "Well, Freddie, I would say nice to meet you, but I hadn't planned on working up a sweat this morning, so I cannot tell a lie."

"No, the dog is Freddie. I wasn't introducing myself."

He saw a flash of embarrassment in her expression. Again, she simply said, "Oh."

Now that her frown was gone, there was no mistaking how pretty she was. Small, feminine, and clearly full of energy and sass. With her eyes downcast like that, her eyelashes looked as full and dark as her hair.

"I *would* have introduced myself," Drew said, "but I was preoccupied with making sure my dog wasn't attacking your precious little Poopsie there."

She glanced up, but he continued before she could speak.

"And then there was your whole working-up-a-sweat thing." With a quick wave of his index finger, he indicated that he was talking about her appearance, which was, in fact, lovely. "Pretty horrible."

Her brown eyes widened before she seemed to figure out that he was teasing her. Even then, she struggled at making eye contact with him, as if she were shy or unwilling to loosen up.

Just as he was about to say his name, she spoke to the ground.

"Excuse me. I'm late." And she took off, back toward the shops, her grip around Riley firm.

Within moments it dawned on him. This was the first time since he had moved out here to the East Coast that any woman had brought out his playful side. He had been so busy with work, he had dated very little. And those few dates had been with friends of his coworkers and hadn't worked out well at all.

Regardless of getting shut down just now—if, in fact, that was what had just happened—he had a feeling about Riley's owner.

He was about to grab Freddie's leash to try to catch up with her when a certain idiot squirrel decided that the silence at the bottom of the tree meant the coast was clear. When he took off, so did Freddie.

"Freddie! Are you kidding me? Freddie!" Drew ran after him, getting the run he had decided to skip and losing the girl he had decided to pursue.

All in all, a pretty disappointing morning.

Chapter Three

....

By the time Nikki got back to Harvey's home with Riley, she had pushed her thoughts about the cheeky cute guy right out of her mind. Almost, anyway. She did catch herself replaying what he said before she wimped away from him in the park.

She set Riley down in the foyer, and Harvey's housekeeper, Jackie, broke into her thoughts. "You all right, Nikki?"

"Nothing!" *Nothing?* What did *that* mean? "Uh, I mean, yeah, I'm fine, Jackie. Nothing's wrong."

Jackie ran a dust cloth around the rim of the umbrella stand while she studied Nikki. "You look flushed."

"That little stinker Riley ran after a squirrel. I had to chase him down in the park."

"You didn't have him leashed? You're a far braver soul than I."

Nikki held up the broken leash. "The clasp broke when he ran. I tried to fix it, but he was acting so dodgy that it seemed smarter to just grab him and carry him home."

Jackie took the broken leash from her. She slipped her reading glasses from her apron and gave it a close look. "I'll have Edward take a crack at fixing it. Thanks for taking Riley out for me."

"My pleasure." She hung her jacket in the closet. "Is Harvey up and about yet? I should get started on his breakfast."

"Only just up, I think. Edward has gone to lay out his clothes—said Harvey wanted to meet with his accountants a bit later this morning."

Nikki nodded and looked around the foyer. "Riley?"

"He's already run up to Harvey's room." Jackie jerked her thumb toward the stairs. "Must check in with the master, you know."

Nikki headed for the kitchen. She had promised Harvey those cornmeal crepes he loved so much, so she needed to get to work.

* * * * *

Forty minutes later, she greeted him in the dining room and got the appreciative reception she had expected.

"Nikki, you're a living doll to remember how much I love these crepes. Same filling as before?"

"Yep. Scrambled eggs and Manchego cheese. I didn't want to mess with something you enjoyed so much before. Although I did use chorizo sausage today. It's a little spicier than what I gave you earlier. But I have some of the milder kind and can have that together in no time if—"

"No, no, this looks and smells perfect. I like how you broaden my culinary horizons."

She laughed. "Harvey, you may have retained your waistline over the years, but something tells me you've been around the culinary block a few times."

With a brisk tap on the wall, Harvey's grandson Nathan—an attractive man only a few years older than Nikki—came around the corner. "Morning, Grandpa! Oh, Nikki. I didn't realize you were here. Morning." He pushed his glasses up the bridge of his nose and flashed her a comfortable smile, which she returned.

"Good morning, Nathan."

Harvey set down his coffee cup. "Wonderful morning! And where's my brilliant great-grandson? You didn't leave him home with his mother, I hope?"

"No, he's actually on the phone with her, outside on the porch. He'll come inside in a minute. Sharon's Pittsburgh meeting ran late and then they got that snow, so her flight home was postponed. Paul really needs this bit of Mom time, although he'll never admit it."

Nikki's heart melted a little over that entire comment. If God blessed her with children in the future, she hoped to never have a job steal her time with them. And she loved that Paul, ten years old, needed to touch base with Mom and that Nathan recognized that need. They were a charming little family.

She stepped toward the kitchen and spoke over her shoulder. "Can I get you some breakfast, Nathan?"

"No, but thanks. Paul and I had a quick bite together before we came over. Grandpa, I thought maybe we could take you to the movies with us. That new spy thriller opened today."

Harvey rested his knife and fork against his plate. "I have a meeting with my accountants."

"On Saturday? Come on, Grandpa, you need to relax on the weekends."

"It shouldn't take long. If you can wait till early this afternoon, I'd love to join you."

They were still discussing their plans as Nikki returned to the kitchen.

Harvey's wife Louise had died the year before Nikki came to work for him. Whenever he mentioned her, his expression always turned bittersweet, as if a specific, nostalgic moment with her had come to mind. Nikki was glad he had such a loving and attentive family. Between their visits and his continued involvement in business and Cary's social events, he never seemed terribly lonely or depressed. Nikki had a touch of the rescuer in her, so she appreciated the fact that Harvey didn't seem to need rescuing.

She had barely started cleaning up the kitchen when her cell phone rang.

"Nikki? It's Estelle Garber from Financial Consultants. You have a minute?"

"Yeah. Hi, Estelle. I'm working, but I have a minute. What are you doing at work on a Saturday? Everything okay with my account?"

"Your account is fine. Terrific, in fact—which is why I'm calling. I'm working from home. Just doing a little catch-up, you know, and I wanted to talk with you about the goals we established when you first moved back to Cary. How about meeting me for lunch today?"

Nikki glanced at the door to the dining room. Her Saturdays and Sundays tended to be fairly free, especially if Harvey planned to be away.

"Hang on a minute, Estelle."

She pushed open the door and found Harvey on his own again, finishing up his crepes and scanning the morning newspaper.

"Excuse me. Harvey?"

He broke into a smile the moment he saw her. With a jaunty thumbs-up, he put down his fork and lifted his napkin to his mouth. "Excellent as always, Nikki. You're a gem."

"The feeling's mutual." She laughed softly. "Say, Harvey, I heard you were going to a meeting and then maybe a movie. Right?"

"Right."

"So you wouldn't mind if I saw to some personal business today, would you?"

He lifted his eyebrows. "A young man?"

Now she laughed outright. "I swear, you're as bad as my mother. No. I happen to be a very important person just like you, and my accountant wants to meet with *me* today too."

He nodded. "We *are* very important, you and I, aren't we? I say take the rest of the day off, my dear. I'm sure I'll have lunch out and will get dinner with Nathan and his family after we watch the movie."

"Thanks, Harvey. You're the best."

"Yes, I believe I am."

Nikki glanced at her watch and returned to the kitchen. "Estelle, when and where do you need me?"

"Come on over to my house. I'll give you lunch, if you don't mind slumming it, food-wise."

"Oh, nonsense. You know I'm not a food snob. Peanut butter and jelly will suit me just fine."

"Even I can do better than that. See you here around twelve thirty?"

"I'll be there."

* * * * *

"Come on in here and let me fatten you up, girl." Estelle opened her front door before Nikki could knock. "I always thought chefs were supposed to be robust and rotund."

Nikki waved off the comment. "I have a fast metabolism. My mom keeps warning me that it will all change in my fifties. So far so good, though." She sniffed at the warm, garlicky fragrance coming from the kitchen. "Smells good in here. What are you treating me to?"

"Nothing but the best for my vigilant investor. Macaroni and cheese with kosher-beef hot dogs cut up in it. Cucumber sticks. Apple slices. Same thing I made for my son before he ran next door to play."

Nikki grinned. "That sounds perfect."

"You did say you actually enjoyed the pedestrian fare from time to time, so I figured this could be one of those times. I'll take you out to lunch another day. Or *you* might want to take *me,* after what I have to share with you today."

Nikki rubbed her hands together. "Goody. That sounds promising."

They sat in Estelle's sunny breakfast nook and enjoyed lunch and each other's company. Estelle was one of the first people Nikki had gotten to know when she moved back to Cary. Estelle had helped Nikki's younger sister Hannah with her budgeting and investing while Nikki was away at college and working for Armand in Charlotte. Hannah was only twenty-five, four years younger than Nikki, but she had done far better with her income than Nikki had, thanks to Estelle's guidance.

Now Nikki earned twice as much as she had before coming to work for Harvey, and she leaned on Estelle's financial advice religiously. She was saving more responsibly and felt more hopeful about her future security and goals.

"All right, so take a look at these figures," Estelle said after she swallowed a mouthful of macaroni. She spread several papers out on the table and described in simple terms what she had been doing with the money Nikki had entrusted to her over the past year.

"Well, I like the look of that bar graph, anyway," Nikki said. "But you didn't call me over here just to show off how well you've invested my income, did you? You look like the kid who got the last cookie from the tin. What's up?"

Estelle wiggled her eyebrows and pulled out another sheet of paper. "This is a list of your various investment goals. I put this together when we first discussed what you wanted to do with your money. You see, here, we're meeting your ongoing goal of an automatic monthly deposit into these three mutual funds. And here, we've already met your goal of saving eight months' worth of living expenses, just in case Harvey kicks you to the curb."

"Estelle! I knew both of those things. Stop toying with me, you sadist."

Estelle sat back in her chair and crossed her hands over her stomach. "You told me you always wished you could buy the house—"

"The house my Grampa William built for Granny Lillian." A rush of warmth ran up Nikki's body. This was exactly what she'd hoped. Her grandparents had sold the house immediately after Granny Lillian died. And her own parents had never seemed interested in it either. But to Nikki, the warm memories of that lovely home were the very stuff of her happy childhood. "Estelle, are you telling me—?"

"You've scrimped and saved and lived for a year with little privacy or freedom, boarding with your employer—an old, eccentric fellow, albeit a sweet one. And for your diligence, hard work, and whopping-good paycheck, you are now in a very nice position. You need to continue your scrimping for, say, one more month to get there. But for the most part, you, my darling, are ready to make an offer on that house."

Chapter Four

....

The next day Drew stood in the crowded, noisy fellowship hall of Cary Community Church and sought a familiar face. Phillip Nester's face, to be exact. His coworker had promised that he and his family would attend the ten-thirty service, and Drew had made plans to sit with them.

After nine months in the area, Drew had yet to put much effort into finding a home church. But judging by how long his engineering project was taking, it was clear he was going to be here another year at least. He decided he needed to work harder at meeting some fellow Christians in town.

"Drew!" Phillip's pleasant baritone cut through the preservice chatter.

Drew turned and grinned. Phillip's wife and two teenaged daughters stood beside the bear of a man. They were exactly as Phillip had described them—short, cute, and all smiles. The foursome approached and welcomed him as if he were a relative they didn't get to see often enough.

"Let's get on into the sanctuary." Phillip cocked his head toward his wife. "Gigi here is a big worship-music fan. If she misses any of the songs, I'll hear about it all afternoon."

"Oh, stop." Gigi smacked at her husband's arm, but she didn't hang around to argue. She led the way into the service, and the rest of them followed.

"Did you get those load figures straightened out on the anchor building?" Phillip spoke softly enough that, had their building project not been on Drew's mind already, he might not have heard the question correctly.

"Yeah." He responded just as quietly. "But I'm going to meet with the construction manager tomorrow morning to make sure we're all on the same page."

As they entered their row, Gigi shot Phillip a pleading glance. "Please, honey, no shoptalk for an hour, okay? Let's give Drew a chance to experience the entire service."

Phillip looked at Drew and shrugged. "My wife has excellent judgment."

"And hearing," Drew said. He gave Gigi a wink when she smirked at him.

The music was exactly what Drew needed. The church he'd attended back in San Diego had musicians and singers as good as anyone he had heard on Christian radio, so he found it hard to match in other churches he tried. But this was an excellent group of men and women. Their upbeat songs were as inspiring as their more contemplative ones.

And the pastor was both entertaining and smart. He taught about the importance of strong emotional relationships, whether formed by blood or by choice. He quoted from the book of Ruth, focusing on her adamant statement of loyalty to her mother-in-law Naomi, " 'Where you go I will go, and where you stay I will stay.' "

Drew took a quick glimpse of Phillip and his tight little family. Phillip seemed to be about the same age as Drew, around thirty-five. And look what he had already. It wasn't that Drew avoided strong emotional relationships. They simply hadn't happened yet—not the romantic ones, anyway. Sure, he had good buddies from UCLA and various engineering positions afterward, and he was close with his parents. His father's heart attack last month had driven home how hard it was to be so far from everyone in California. So he had a firm grasp on that kind of bond.

But he had to admit, when he'd gotten the offer to consult on the building of an office complex here in Cary, he hadn't worried much about what would happen between his girlfriend Isabelle and him.

They'd dated for nearly a year and hadn't really progressed to the point that either of them would miss the other terribly. They had become good friends. Nothing more. Their parting was practically businesslike.

Drew worried that maybe he lacked the ability to fall for a girl any harder than that.

When the pastor led the congregation in prayer, Drew went rogue and prayed on his own.

Lord, You've blessed me big-time with my family, my friends, my career, my health, and so many other things. My dog. My awesome dog. But if I'm messed up—I mean, if the reason I haven't fallen in love yet is because I'm coldhearted or too wrapped up in myself—could You light a fire under me or something? I don't want to end up a wealthy, lonely old man. I mean, I wouldn't mind the wealthy part. Not that I only care about money—

His prayer abruptly ended when everyone around him said, "Amen." He said it too. He figured the Lord understood the heart of his poorly worded request.

"So, what did you think?" Phillip stood, and his family followed suit.

Drew closed his Bible and tucked it under his arm as they all filed out of their row. "Loved it. Pastor's cool. Music's great."

"Yeah, we're really happy with the church. I think you'd fit right in. It's a really good 'family' kind of environment. I'm afraid I can't claim they have a terribly active singles' group, though." Phillip put his arm around Gigi's shoulders when they reached the aisle. "Am I right, honey? There don't seem to be all that many singles here."

Before Gigi had a chance to answer, Drew caught sight of two young women about to leave the sanctuary through another set of doors. After the initial spark of attraction that one of them triggered, he realized he recognized her. Both women were beautiful and had long, dark hair and slim builds. But the shorter of the two—where had he seen her before?

Gigi broke into his thoughts. "I think *those* two ladies are single."

Drew looked away from the women and at Gigi's appraising scrutiny. He chuckled and lifted his chin toward her. "Good judgment, great hearing, and sharp eyes."

"Well, I have to say, you have good taste." She laced her arm through his and guided him out of the sanctuary, as if they might catch up to the women out in the fellowship hall. "I don't know those young ladies personally, but I've seen them here for at least as long as we've been coming. The tall one, anyway. The shorter one showed up sometime this year. Sisters, you think? I have absolutely no qualms about meeting them at this very minute, if you're so inclined."

And then he remembered. The woman in the park. Running after her yappy dog. Yes, she had been a spunky one, he remembered that. And she was a Christian, apparently. That fact made him smile.

"Ah, you seem so inclined," Gigi said. They had reached the fellowship hall, and she tugged him in the direction of the other set of doors.

"No, no, I don't think so." Drew didn't feel prepared to meet her cold like this. He didn't tend to shyness, but they hadn't parted on the most impressive terms the first time they'd crossed paths. He preferred not coming across as a stuttering oaf the second time around. "If they're regulars here, there will be other chances. I'd rather think about it first."

"Gigi, unhand the poor guy." Phillip gently pulled his wife away. "Sorry, man. My wife is the consummate romantic."

"You betcha." She clearly felt no need to apologize, and she patted her hand on her husband's chest. "And don't you love that about me? You *know* you do." Still, she gave Drew an endearing smile. "I'm sure you can handle meeting them on your own if you decide to. You don't need me. But you just let me know if you want me to act as your buffer, and I'll be your gal. I've never met a stranger."

"I can see that." Drew returned her smile. "And I might actually take you up on your offer. See you all next week?"

Gigi nodded. "Same time, same station."

"And I'll see you at the site tomorrow," Phillip said.

Drew gave him a quick handshake before he left the building. He couldn't help himself, though, once he saw Phillip and Gigi turn away to talk with other congregants. He scanned the crowd inside and the people spilling out of the building with him. And there she was, walking with the taller woman, headed toward the other end of the parking lot. The taller woman said something and laughed and the smaller one shook her head, as if her sister's comment were incorrigible. At least he assumed that was her sister. They were so similar, but his girl was definitely more...just more. He couldn't place it, but there was something captivating about her.

His girl. What was he thinking? With that frame of thought, he was certain he would have made an awkward impression on her today. He was glad she hadn't seen him.

Chapter Five

Nikki had seen him. She'd pretended otherwise. But Hannah hadn't been fooled.

They arrived at church early enough that they were able to find seats fairly close to the front of the church, where Nikki preferred to sit. So she didn't notice that Freddie's owner had come into the church until they all slowly filed out of the sanctuary. She couldn't believe she remembered the dog's name, more than a week after he chased Riley into the park.

As she and Hannah walked toward the sanctuary's exit, she looked away, heat running up her neck, the moment she spotted him and sensed he was about to look at her. She wasn't completely sure why she reacted that way, but Hannah happened to look at her, ready to comment about something, and she noticed.

"What's wrong?" Hannah frowned. "Did something just happen?"

"No." Nikki heard an almost defensive tone to her quick reply. "Why would you say that? Nothing happened."

"Because I know your nervous look." Hannah pointed at Nikki's face. "And that's it."

"Oh, don't be ridiculous." She straightened and lifted her chin.

Hannah gasped. "And that's your pretty stance."

"My what?"

"Your pretty stance. Come on, we both do it, so don't even bother to deny it. It's a guy." Hannah immediately surveyed the crowd of people leaving the sanctuary.

"I hate it when you do that." Nikki nudged her sister with her elbow. "Stop!"

Hannah laughed. "When I do what? Read you like a book? Where is he? Tell me, and I'll stop looking for him."

Nikki nearly dug her nails into Hannah's arm. "All *right*. He's on the other side, in the aisle, with that really big guy and his—"

"Ooh la la!" Hannah's eyes widened.

"You said you'd stop looking for him!"

"Yes, but I'm not looking for him anymore. I'm looking *at* him. And I must say, hubba hubba."

They had reached the doorway into the fellowship hall, and Nikki tutted at Hannah and tried to turn her away. "Really, Hannah. Who says stuff like that anymore? 'Hubba hubba.' "

"I do. Grandma used to say that when she teased Grandpa, and I always thought it was adorable. And speaking of adorable, do you know that guy, or what? I've never seen you get all bothered like that about a stranger."

Nikki met eyes with a friend from an old Bible study class and waved before answering. She sighed. "His dog chased Riley when Riley was chasing a squirrel a week or so ago. Yeah, it was last Saturday, because that's the last time I walked Riley for Jackie."

"If anything, I would think you'd walk the little stinker more often now. So you met over dogs. And?"

"And nothing. We didn't really meet. I was a little snippy with him, and he was snippy back." Although, when she really thought about it, he wasn't *snippy* so much as *saucy*.

"Hmm. He doesn't look like the snippy type."

Nikki realized Hannah had found him again in the crowd. "Please stop, Hannah. He'll know I told you about him if he sees you checking him out like that."

Hannah looked back at her. "And what would be so horrible

about it if he knew you talked about him? You're single. It looks like he might be single. He's not with a woman. It's not as if you'd have to do a lot of reshuffling on the old dating calendar to make room for him. I believe you have copious openings, no?"

"Thanks so much for that word of encouragement."

"All I'm saying is, you need to get out of that old man's house once in a while and join the land of the living. I can't believe you're too shy to go say hi to the guy. It's like you've forgotten how to talk with people who weren't around during the Depression."

"Don't talk about Harvey that way. He's a sweetheart, and he's never required me to spend as much time at his home as I do."

"Fine, then. For whatever reason, you've become all about the job and not at all about your personal life. Let's get over there before Mr. Snippy leaves." Hannah grabbed her and pulled her along. "Come on! Look, he's leaving!"

Despite a subtle physical struggle, Nikki was unable to bring Hannah to a total stop, not without making a scene. "You are *insane*!" But she did manage to force her to leave the church through the doors on the other end of the fellowship hall, putting distance between them and "Mr. Snippy."

"That's enough now!" She spoke through tight lips, and Hannah stopped with her on the sidewalk outside. "Hannah, I made a bad impression the first time, if you must know."

"But you can fix that. If he sees you here, he'll probably cut you some slack, since you're a good Christian girl."

"A *pushy* Christian girl is more like it."

"No, I'm the pushy one. You're a sweetie pie. Please?" Hannah tilted her head and made a beseeching face that made Nikki laugh.

"Okay, look. If he's here next Sunday, I'll approach him and introduce myself. How about that?"

"Why wait a week?"

"Because it will give me time to think about a better approach than what I used before, which was pretty much just being a smart-mouth."

After a pause, Hannah sighed in resignation. "All right."

The two of them headed toward Hannah's car, and Hannah made one last comment.

"But, personally, I think you're at your most charming when you're a smart-mouth."

Nikki gave her a sideways glance, which made her laugh.

Even though Nikki shook her head about her sister, she loved that Hannah cared that much about her romantic happiness. It was simply easier for Hannah to get out there and date around. She had always been the one who invested less emotion in every nuance of a relationship. She flitted from one boyfriend to the next without either party getting too ruffled at the relationship's end.

Nikki had dated very little, but she took each experience seriously. Just as she did her job. And maybe every other aspect of her life. She wondered if that might be her problem.

Chapter Six

....

The following weekend Drew jogged down the sidewalk without having to make way for anyone. Freddie ran beside him, his tongue lolling to one side. For a Saturday morning, the shopping area was rather quiet. Drew had expected the early spring weather to bring people outdoors, especially after the rainy week they'd just experienced. Without breaking his stride he checked his watch and frowned. This was exactly the time he and Freddie came through here two weeks ago—when he nearly ran down that noisy little dog and his pretty owner. Maybe he should feel embarrassed for deliberately retracing his path...but he didn't.

He planned to attend church again the next day, but it would certainly be more comfortable to strike up a conversation out here in the open than among all those people in the fellowship hall of Cary Community Church. So he circled back around when he and Freddie reached the end of the shopping vicinity, and they retraced their steps again.

By the time they repeated the process a second time, he started to see faces he'd seen his first two times around. Now he *did* feel a little embarrassed, especially after one café owner, who had been setting up tables for outdoor dining, laughed and called out to him.

"If you're waiting for the shops to open, they're already open. Come have some breakfast!"

He smiled and waved. "No thanks. Just jogging through."

So now he had to actually jog *through* to avoid seeming a bit stalker-like. The tempting smell of bacon and something baked wafted outside from the café, but Drew hadn't brought money with him. He'd wait until he got home.

"Okay, Freddie, let's move on. I guess it's not happening today."

They ran past the shops and into the residential area. Everywhere Drew looked, he noticed new growth sprouting from the manicured landscapes. His spirits rose over the cheery freshness of the lush colors. He wasn't a huge fan of winter just yet. He had enjoyed the *look* of the perfect white snow covering everything, but not the necessary navigation of it. Still, if not for North Carolina's winter, he might not appreciate the spring renewal as much as he did this morning. He didn't experience this feeling so much in San Diego. He decided he would like living with the change of seasons.

The garden apartments gave way to town houses, and the town houses eventually gave way to lovely old single-family homes mixed with some more contemporary houses.

As an engineer, Drew had explored plenty of modern structures, but he didn't have a lot of experience with older buildings. He loved the unique style the older homes showed, each different from the other.

Eventually he passed one that seemed to call out to him. He studied it as he ran by, and then he kept thinking of it as he got farther away. He turned around and gave Freddie's collar a gentle tug.

"Come on, boy, let's head on back."

He approached the house from a different angle and noticed that there was a lot more house than had been obvious from the front. It looked as if new sections had been added over time to extend the depth in back. Sometimes that kind of addition was a nightmare, aesthetically, but this was tastefully done.

And now he knew why the house stood out in his mind, besides the fact that it was, in his opinion, absolutely inviting. There was a For Sale sign out front. The moment he spotted the sign, he got a rush of goose bumps—not something he was prone to.

He slowed down, and the moment he stopped, Freddie heeled at his side. The two of them studied the house together.

Drew loved the large, three-windowed dormer in the center of the roof, as well as the repeated dormer on the side. Black shutters accented the white house beautifully, and Drew suddenly imagined sitting in a comfortable rocking chair on that wraparound front porch, enjoying a balmy evening with his loved ones. Of course, he didn't *have* any loved ones—not here in Cary—but that could happen, in time.

He didn't want to bother the current residents, but he hoped to get at least a slightly better look, so he walked up the driveway. The closer he got, the more obvious it was that no one lived in the house at present. So he peered in through the windows. He couldn't get a strong feel for the conditions inside, but he could see a broad, open staircase and spacious rooms.

"Yep, Freddie. This one has my interest piqued."

For his part, Freddie had already spread out comfortably on the porch, as if he were meant to be there all along. Drew's chuckle made him raise and tilt his head, ready for further instructions.

They walked back to the FOR SALE sign, but Drew had nothing to write on or with. They backtracked to see the name of the cross street. He would get a Realtor to look into the place and get him the specifics. He hadn't consciously yearned for a home here in Cary, except for the fact that his rental apartment was especially cramped for Freddie. But now the idea of a home was enticing enough to distract him from a certain young lady for the duration of his run.

* * * * *

And the distraction continued into the week, which was fortunate, considering the fact that the sisters either skipped church the next day or went to a different service.

By Tuesday Drew's coworker Phillip had set him up with his Realtor, a brassy woman named Jolene. She met with Drew in her perfume-clouded office the day after he gave her the address.

"Okay, here's the story." She leaned back in her desk chair. "The house is eighty-five years old."

A short, breathy whistle escaped from Drew's lips before he spoke. "It sure doesn't look that old. I realize that not all eighty-five-year-old houses fall into disarray. Still…is it structurally sound?"

She nodded. "Built the way they used to, frankly, before they started with all the prefab and slapdash construction that goes on today. A tornado wouldn't take the place down."

"That's promising."

"But it needs work inside. There hasn't been a tenant for well over a year, because the entire thing really ought to be gutted and rebuilt. Or maybe not gutted, but definitely remodeled a lot. The market wants new, no fuss–no muss these days."

"Even that cool staircase? That has to come down? That's all I could really make out from the window—hey, can we go check it out?"

"Sure. Maybe the staircase is salvageable." She shrugged. "I'd want to have it looked at closely before letting you make an offer."

"What are they asking?"

"Three hundred thousand, but I think we can get it for far less, considering that there haven't been any offers at this price and there's so much work to be done inside." She tilted her head. "And that might be something you'll want to consider."

"Remodeling costs, you mean?"

"Yeah. Sometimes it *is* easier to just pay up front and get everything new."

He chuckled. "Didn't you just criticize the quality of the newer buildings?" She knew he was in Cary to engineer the construction of an office-building complex himself. His own building project was of the finest quality.

Jolene tapped the keyboard of her computer. "I wasn't talking about *all* the construction in the area. Just some. By the time you factor in the cost of remodeling this old beauty, you could have bought yourself something new *and* well-built."

Why did that not interest him?

"There's something about that particular house, though. As you said, it's an old beauty. When can we see it?"

She pushed away from her desk and grabbed her cell phone. "Let's go."

* * * * *

It was perfect. He knew it the moment he walked in. The staircase was even more stunning than he remembered, and it was plenty sturdy.

"Maybe it's already been replaced sometime in the past eighty-five years," Jolene said.

They slowly walked through the rooms on the main floor. In a flash, Drew could envision the house's potential. He pictured warm family gatherings, plenty of kids running around—with Freddie, of course—and dinners being served in the spacious dining room. At least, he assumed this was the dining room, since it had the wiring for a chandelier in the center of the ceiling and the kitchen was the next room over.

"Dining room." Jolene's announcement confirmed it. "Nice and big. Must have been built for a big family."

"Or an optimistic couple." Drew smiled at Jolene.

She laughed. "Could be."

"I see what you mean about the need for remodeling." He ran his hand over a mottled wall that would need to be replaced or taken down altogether. "I wonder if this is a support wall—I don't think it is. This room could be opened up even more." He walked deeper into the house. He nodded when he stepped into the kitchen. "Yeah, this would definitely have to be redone. I'm not much of a chef, but I'd want to update the layout and upgrade the appliances."

"We're talking about a considerable outlay of cash above and beyond the purchase price." Jolene spoke as she walked beyond the kitchen. The house was deep, as Drew had noticed on his jog. "But that fact will give us some good leverage when we negotiate with the seller."

Drew walked into the living room, the windows of which let in plenty of light. The entire house was positioned well, as far as that was concerned. He missed the California lightness of his old home. His rental apartment here was often depressingly dark. So the sunlight in this house added another mark in the "purchase" column.

They both stopped walking when a skittering noise came from the very back of the house.

Jolene frowned. "Now, I don't like the sound of that one bit."

Drew slipped off his shoes and moved quietly onward. He had taken only a few steps when Jolene yelled out behind him. "Watch out!"

A squirrel darted across his path, ran back again, and dashed out of the house through a broken pane in the room's glass door.

Even though he had been startled, he laughed. "It was just a squirrel."

"Just a squirrel? Do you keep squirrels in *your* home?"

He approached the broken pane. "We'll have to get this patched up right away."

Shaken as she was, Jolene calmed quickly. "We? You're already talking like you're the future homeowner."

"Maybe I am." He turned around and surveyed the room. What a terrific spot this would be for a home office, especially if he could open it up a bit more. "I'd love to get hold of the blueprints for the place, Jolene. I wonder if they're available."

"After eighty-five years?" She looked at him as if he had asked the impossible. "Not likely." She shrugged. "I don't know. There are a number of places we could look. The city keeps some of those records in their archives, but I don't know about that far back. And if it was built by the original owner, I think you're totally out of luck."

Drew didn't think luck had anything to do with this house or his having found it. The more he thought about the circumstances of his coming down this particular street last weekend, the more he felt a thrilling, possibly divine connection. He didn't quite understand what the connection was, but he knew he was going to lose sleep tonight thinking about this place, as if he were a kid and it was Christmas Eve.

Chapter Seven

....

The following Saturday afternoon, Nikki and the housekeeper worked together in Harvey's kitchen. Jackie tidied up the luncheon dishes while Nikki packed several containers of leftovers into the refrigerator.

"I think Harvey's guests really liked my chocolate soufflé. I expected to have some of that left, but it looks like they finished it off."

Jackie closed the dishwasher and dried off her hands. "They had some help with that. Little Paul and his parents got here just as the lunch meeting was ending. Harvey sent Paul off to the front porch with a bowlful of the stuff so Nathan and Sharon could chat with everyone."

"You think Nathan will run Harvey's...empire someday?"

Jackie shrugged. "Not my place to ponder, I suppose. But I think Nathan is more interested in Harvey's business—and Harvey—than his father is. Morgan Fennicle is a dear man, but he seems more interested in traveling and writing than running the—"

The swinging kitchen doors burst open.

"Hi, Nikki! Hi, Jackie!" Harvey's ten-year-old great-grandson ran in, breathing heavily and laughing with nearly maniacal delight, closely followed by Riley, who quickly overtook him despite his short legs. Riley had purpose in his eyes and a ropelike dog toy in his mouth. In seconds, they reached the other end of the kitchen and disappeared as rapidly as they had appeared. "Bye, Nikki! Bye, Jackie!"

"Uh, bye, Paul." Nikki looked at the doorway, where they had been a moment ago, and turned to Jackie with a grin. "I think the caffeine kicked in. What do you think?"

"Hard to tell who's chasing whom with those two." Jackie replaced the dish towel with a dry one and gathered the used one with the linens from Harvey's luncheon. "Are you off for the day now, or are you doing dinner tonight?"

"I'm done. Laura tells me Harvey's scheduled to spend the evening with Nathan and his family." She checked the clock on the wall. "My sister Hannah will be here soon. We're doing a little shopping. Or, rather, *she's* shopping. I'm just tagging along. I'm in strict savings-mode right now."

"Good for you. You have something you're saving toward?"

Nikki leaned against the counter and sighed with longing. "A house."

Jackie had been walking toward the door but stopped in her tracks. She raised her eyebrows. "A house? How exciting! And aren't you ambitious? You have a place in mind?"

"Yeah. It's one of the reasons I took this job with Harvey. The house is right down the road from here—"

"So Harvey knows? And he's all right with your moving out?"

"Yeah. I mean, I wouldn't be moving anytime soon. Even though I've almost reached the point where I can make my offer on the place, it needs a lot of work. It's been neglected over the last few years. But Harvey knows about my plans. We talked about it before I accepted the job. He said as long as I can still be here for him when he needs me, he's fine with my moving out. He's not really one for surprise requests at midnight and that kind of thing."

Jackie nodded. "True."

"So my room and board here has just been a perk for me, rather than a necessity for him."

Jackie headed for the door again. "Well, I think that's fantastic. I imagine Harvey's that much prouder of you for your determination. I know I am." She pushed the door open and smiled. "Enjoy your shopping, dear. Or, enjoy your tagging along."

* * * * *

Fifteen minutes later Nikki sat on the front steps of Harvey's mansion, waiting for Hannah to pick her up. The front door opened behind her.

"Whatcha doing, Nikki?" Paul walked out and sat on the step beside her. He carried his handheld video game but wasn't yet playing it.

"Hey, Paul. I'm waiting for my sister. She's picking me up so we can go clothes shopping. There are a bunch of weekend sales going on."

"Borrr–ing."

The both laughed.

"Yeah, I guess most boys would rather do just about anything other than shopping, right? What are you and your parents doing this afternoon?"

"We were just going to bring Grandpapa home with us, but he says it's too pretty out to stay inside all day. We're going to pick up a couple of my friends and go hiking."

"Grandpapa is going to hike?" Harvey was sprightly for his eighty-eight years, but she had a hard time picturing him taking on a full-blown hike.

Paul shook his head. "Not very far. The last time we went hiking, he just went a little ways and then he and Riley sat on a park bench and waited for us while we did the rest of the hike."

Nikki nodded. "I'm glad he's getting out with you."

"It's more fun when he's there. He's awesome."

"Yes, he is. My great-grandfather was awesome too. I really miss him. And my great-grandmother."

"They died?"

"Yeah, quite awhile ago. They lived not too far from here—right down the street, actually. Grampa William and his brothers built the house before he even proposed to Granny Lillian. I hung out at their home whenever I could, just like you do with your grandpapa. We spent all the big holidays there too. Christmas was my favorite. My sister and my parents and I would all show up and add our presents to those Grampa and Granny already had around the tree, and our grandparents and aunts and uncles and cousins would do the same. Lots of family and noise and fun. The tree had ornaments I'd practically memorized over the years." She sighed. "I don't know what happened to all those ornaments. I can't wait to get back in that home."

"Get back in it? What do you mean?"

She grinned at him. "Well, neither my grandparents nor my parents were interested in the house after my great-grandparents died, so it hasn't been in our family for years. But whoever owns it right now has had it for sale for some time, and I'm going to try to buy it."

"What do you mean, *try* to buy it? Why don't you just buy it, if it's for sale now?"

Nikki chuckled. Spoken like a true, innocent rich kid. She was surprised she could understand him while he talked around that silver spoon in his mouth.

Hannah drove up, and Nikki stood. "It's not that easy. Houses are expensive. But I've been saving my money and I'm just about ready to make my move." She waggled her eyebrows as she spoke the last three words, pretending to be cool.

Paul laughed at her. "That kind of shopping sounds way cooler than buying clothes."

"I agree." She high-fived Paul before she left. "See you later, buddy. Enjoy your time with Grandpapa."

* * * * *

Nikki's talk with Paul got her excited about the house again, so she put in a call to Estelle, even though it was Saturday. She had to leave a message.

"Just checking to see if I can make my offer on the house this week,

Estelle. Didn't want you to forget about me. Call me as soon as you can on Monday."

Hannah turned the CD player back on once Nikki ended her call. "So you're really going to go through with it, huh?"

"Yep." Nikki bounced in time to the music, her mood getting perkier by the minute.

"I just don't get it. Does Estelle really think this is something you should do with your money?"

"What? Estelle? This is my decision, not hers. Anyway, she's known all along what my investment goals are, and she hasn't discouraged me from buying the place. Investing in real estate is a smart long-term move. *You* bought a place."

"I bought a brand-new town house, Nikki." They pulled into the shopping mall. "Look, I loved Grampa William and Granny Lillian too, but that old home could turn out to be a total money pit for you. Has Estelle seen it?"

"No, she's not my Realtor. That's not her job. She's putting me in touch with a Realtor she recommends. I'll have him take a look at the house before I make an offer, but this just feels right. I've been praying about it for years. Even before the current owners moved out. Everything just keeps falling into place, with the owners putting it on the market, no one making an offer all this time—"

"Yeah, there might be a very good reason for that."

"And then Harvey giving me this amazing job here and paying me well so I could afford to even consider the place. All open doors. You can't deny that."

* * * * *

As low an opinion as young Paul had of shopping, Nikki loved it as much as Hannah did, and she always had to fight the urge to buy when she went. She wasn't easily satisfied with mere window-shopping. But since establishing her goal, she'd been ever-vigilant. Even today she saw a pair of burgundy pumps she would have loved to buy, but she forced herself to walk away from them.

She gave Hannah a wistful gaze and whimpered like a puppy.

Her expression totally deadpan, Hannah said, "You're made of stern stuff, Nicole Tronnier. Stern stuff."

"Tell me about it. Those would look so perfect with that little gray sweater dress of mine. But I need to *Just. Say. No*." They escaped into the juniors' section of the store.

She was in the middle of giving Hannah her honest opinion about a skirt her sister was modeling when her cell phone rang.

"I wouldn't, Hannah. It's more 'granny' than 'hippy chick.' " She turned away and opened her phone. "Hello?"

"Nikki, it's Estelle."

Her heartbeat picked up. "Hey! Thanks so much for calling me back so soon."

"Sure, hon."

Nikki frowned. Something was wrong. Estelle's usual upbeat tone was missing.

"You okay, Estelle?"

A sigh.

Uh-oh.

"I'm fine, sweetie. But I have some pretty bad news."

Nikki turned around and saw Hannah watching her.

Hannah put her palms up, question in her eyes. "What's wrong?" she mouthed.

Nikki shook her head and turned again, trying to concentrate and not panic. She hadn't heard anything about the stock market getting hammered this week or anything like that.

"What is it? Is it my account?"

"No, no, your account is right on track. That's the good news. But I heard your phone message and called Brian—the Realtor I told you about?"

"Yeah?"

"Well, I had mentioned to him, after you and I talked last, that you were interested in your old family home. I asked him to look into it."

"Right." Maybe Estelle thought there was too much work to be done, as Hannah had suggested. Nikki didn't care. She wanted that house.

"Brian talked with the seller and mentioned that he might have a buyer for them if the price was right."

"Well, that's good, right?"

"Yeah, honey, that's fine. And they were asking three hundred thousand, and Brian thought we could probably get as low as two fifty, considering—"

"How long it had been sitting empty. I know. What, they want more? Can I afford more?"

"That's not it, Nikki. Some yahoo came along this past week and apparently fell for the house."

Nikki gasped. She couldn't speak. She clenched her fist against her stomach.

"The seller told him someone else was interested in the house, so he immediately offered them their full asking price."

Nikki tried to keep her voice calm, but sweat broke out all along her forehead. "But I didn't even get a chance to— Can't *I* offer them the asking price?"

"No, you weren't quite there yet, financially. And they've already given him a contract."

Hannah came to Nikki's side, her eyes full of concern. She put her arm lightly around Nikki's shoulders, and the gesture brought tears to Nikki's eyes.

"Estelle, this can't be happening. How could I lose the place in a single move like that?"

"It happens, hon. I'm sorry. But there's always the chance something will fall through on the contract. They won't be able to close for several weeks to a month, at the soonest. Maybe the guy's credit is bad or something. We won't give up completely. Not just yet."

Nikki had to wait a moment after closing her phone before she could tell Hannah what was happening. She knew Hannah would be supportive, even though she wasn't totally on board with Nikki's desire to buy that particular house.

"What's happened?" Hannah kept her arm around Nikki and gave her shoulder a squeeze.

Nikki released a ragged sigh. "I might as well go back and get those stupid burgundy pumps. My bank account is all dressed up with no place to go."

Chapter Eight

....

Now this is more like it. Drew walked into the Sunday service at Cary Community Church the next day, right before the music started up. No one was standing to sing yet, so he was able to see Phillip and Gigi sitting nearer the front than they had before. And as he walked up to join them, he made a falsely casual survey of the crowd.

There she was, near the end of the aisle, fifteen rows or so behind Phillip and Gigi. She wasn't so far away that he was unable to detect a demure smile brightening her expression when her eyes met his. He gave her a quick nod and smiled back. That was all he needed. She definitely recognized him. And if she had been put off by how he'd handled their initial meeting, that no longer seemed to be the case. If she didn't hurry away at the end of the service, he'd approach her and strike up a conversation.

"Well, there you are." Gigi grinned at him when he moved to take the seat they had saved for him. "Right on time."

"Thanks for keeping a place for me." He handed Gigi her Bible and gave Phillip a quick handshake.

The musicians began to play and people automatically stood to sing without being asked. Drew stood too, and the most ridiculous thought popped into his mind. He knew he stood a bit taller than the average congregant. The idea that the pretty woman from the park might notice the little bald spot on the back of his head diverted his attention for a moment.

What was *that* all about? He didn't tend toward vanity. Why now?

Especially when he should be focusing on the words and intent of the worship song rather than his hair follicles—or lack thereof. He shook off the distraction and listened to the song. It was such a small spot, anyway. He fought the urge to reach back and check it.

Two songs later he was completely unaware that his thoughts had strayed again to the young woman until he realized the velvet offering bag had just been extended to him by the person on his left.

"Oh!" He spoke out loud without thinking, and he sensed movement in the row in front of him. Great, now he had distracted others as well. They turned to see who the nuisance was. He took the bag and tried to prop the handle of the bag between his arm and his side. He patted his back pants pocket for his wallet—he had taken the time to write a check this morning before leaving for church. He fumbled his wallet out of his pants and opened it. No check.

"It's all right, Drew," Gigi whispered. "They don't care if you miss a collection."

He sensed she was trying to help not only him but the waiting usher as well. She put out her hand so he could pass off the collection bag.

He pointlessly patted his chest, as if he had stored the check there. He didn't even have pockets there. And at once he was sweating. "No, but I wrote a check and everything." He thought he was speaking quietly, but a woman in front of them turned and shushed him.

"Oh, now, be nice," Gigi said to her. "The poor man's just trying to give to the Lord." She didn't work quite as hard as Drew had to keep her voice down, and the snickers of a couple young girls erupted behind them.

Drew gave up, passed the bag to Gigi, and battled a rapid succession of thoughts so quick that they were mere words. *Disruption. Idiot. Girl from park. Bald spot.*

And *Sweat.*

He pressed the back of his hand against his forehead, blotted the moisture, and tried to refocus.

Help me, Lord. I honestly meant to honor You this morning. I'm acting like a little kid here. I'm so sorry. I love You. Please help me to focus on You and calm down. And cool off.

He breathed deeply, his eyes still closed, and recognized the song being played. He knew this one from his San Diego church. Gigi's pretty singing voice was the perfect encouragement, and he began singing. Within moments he had lost himself in the praise of the song.

Had Cary Community Church used the same song arrangement as San Diego Bible Chapel, he would have blended right in. At a crucial moment, however, the worshippers at Cary Community apparently paused for dramatic emphasis and a chord change, whereas the San Diego worshippers usually belted right along. Which is what Drew did.

And only Drew.

Even Gigi looked at him in surprise. How could she help it? How could anyone? He heard himself bark into the stillness like a trained seal over a bucket of herring. He felt heat rush from his cheeks to the raging bald spot on the back of his head.

He looked at the ground, squeezed his eyes shut, and tried to be as invisible as possible. He felt Gigi's reassuring pat on his arm and ventured a sheepish glance at her and Phil. They were both struggling not to laugh.

Somehow that helped. He had certainly done more embarrassing things in his past. The fact that none of those moments came to mind right now didn't matter. If any people would forgive him for being an oaf, it would be a church full of Christians, wouldn't it?

The pastor saved the day, teaching with such conviction and making enough fascinating points that even Drew forgot about his blunders. As a matter of fact, he forgot about the girl from the park until the service ended. Gigi reminded him as soon as the closing song finished and they stood to leave.

"Did you see your pretty friend here today?"

Phillip chuckled and kissed Gigi on the top of her head. "Don't disappoint her now, Drew. She's been looking forward to this all morning."

Drew smiled and looked behind them. "I did see her when I came in, but it's too crowded now. I was kind of hoping to—"

Then he saw her as she stood to leave. And his hopes fell. A guy was beside her, and he had obviously been sitting with her throughout the service. Even as a guy, Drew could tell the man was good-looking. Now as they were walking out, Drew saw them chatting with such familiarity that there was no way they had just met.

Gigi and Phillip joined him in the aisle.

"Did you find her?" Gigi walked on her tiptoes, trying to see above everyone.

Drew sighed. "I'm afraid so. She's with someone."

"Her sister?"

"A dude, honey." Phillip looked from the girl to Drew and shrugged. "Not necessarily a boyfriend. Maybe he's just a friend."

"Maybe." The guy looked awfully chummy with her, though. Whatever they were discussing, they were laughing about it, and then he briefly rested his hand on her shoulder.

"Okay." Gigi stepped more aggressively into the throng of people walking out of the sanctuary. "I'll see what's up."

Drew managed to stop her before she moved too far from him. "No, really, I'd rather you didn't. I think I've embarrassed myself enough for one Sunday morning."

The disappointment in her expression unmistakable, Gigi acquiesced but crossed her arms and frowned. She looked like a little genie, shuffling down the aisle that way, and Drew couldn't help but laugh.

"You really *have* been looking forward to this, haven't you?"

Phillip draped his arm around her, which loosened her up. "She likes to see people in love; what can I tell you?"

"Well, I'm going to ask around this week, all right?" She gave

Drew a look of warning. "There's no harm in that. No one needs to know I'm asking for you. You can be a mystery man."

He gave her a smile. "I like the sound of that. And who knows? I might even be able to figure out something when we finally get into the fellowship hall." He lowered his voice. "I love this church, but they could use a couple more exits."

"Mmm-hmm. Or faster walkers," Gigi said.

A woman turned and shot Gigi a look of disapproval. Drew recognized her as the one who had shushed him earlier.

"Oh, come on, now," Gigi said to her. "You know you're thinking the same thing."

Drew stifled a laugh. He was going to have to be careful around Gigi. Apparently there was little she was afraid of saying or doing. He glanced at Phillip, who simply nodded as if he knew exactly what Drew was thinking.

By the time they reached the fellowship hall, the girl and her guy—friend or otherwise—were already gone, as far as Drew could tell.

"Hey, Phil, Gigi, I'm going to head out."

Gigi looked around them, obviously seeking the couple in question. "But what about—?"

"No, it looks like they're already gone."

"You don't want to stick around anyway?" Phil asked. "We could introduce you to a few other couples here."

"That's okay. Maybe next week. I should get home and start going through my stuff to figure out what I can get rid of before the new house is ready for me."

"Okay," Gigi said, "but I'm going to have Phil report in with you about this whole extra-man thing." She pointed to the sanctuary as if the girl from the park were still in there with her handsome escort. "I'm sure I know someone who knows someone and all that. I'll get the skinny for you."

He grinned. "I'm sure you will. Thanks, you two. See you at the site, Phil."

Again he was glad to have the house remodeling ahead of him. What with his office-building project and now the virtual certainty that he'd settle on the house in the next few weeks, he was fine with losing out on the girl from the park. Sort of.

As he reached his car, he saw the couple at the entrance to the church parking lot. He risked their spotting him and watched for a moment.

The taller sister was there now. She approached the couple, and they approached her. She definitely hadn't been with them in church, so maybe she was arriving for the late service. He couldn't hear what any of them were saying, but he certainly noticed the guy putting his arm across Park Girl's shoulders.

"Right. That's it, then." He got into his car and took a moment to settle his thoughts. It wasn't as if he'd invested a lot of emotion in the idea of dating her. They hadn't spoken more than twenty words between them. He really didn't need to think about it anymore.

He mumbled to himself while he turned his phone on. "Pizza. That's what I need to soothe my disappointment." While he put in his order, he noticed his offering check sitting on the floor of the passenger side. Should he bother running it back to the church?

He grabbed the check. He didn't want to have to keep track of it until next week. And to be honest, he wanted another peek at whatever was going on at the entrance to the parking lot, assuming they were still there.

What Drew saw made him stop in his tracks. The girl from the park was nowhere to be seen, but her boyfriend was. And her sister was there, flirting with him—he knew flirtation when he saw it. And then she moved in, as if she were going to kiss him.

"Oh, no. Don't—"

After a moment's hesitation, they bridged the distance and were in full-blown lip-lock.

"Drew?"

Phillip's voice made Drew jump. He hadn't realized he was just standing there, staring at the couple.

Phillip smiled. "I thought you were already gone. Did you forget where you parked?"

"Yeah. I mean, no. I got to my car and found my offering check." He held it up. "I'm just running in to drop it off."

"Ah." Phillip started to walk past. "Okay, then. I promised Gigi I'd bring the car around. See you tomorrow."

"Right."

Drew frowned as he went back into the church. This was none of his business, and he had never been one to stick his nose where it didn't belong. Still, even though he didn't know the park girl, he felt protective of her. He was unsure of what was going on, but he sure didn't like how things looked. Why did that guy have his arm around the girl from the park if they weren't together? Why would he attend church with one and get amorous with the other? If his girl was getting two-timed—by her sister, no less—he wanted to make sure she found out. Maybe he'd enlist Gigi's help for that.

And she had looked so comfortable with that guy.

Chapter Nine

....

"Ugh, Hannah, I was so *uncomfortable* with that guy! I couldn't relax until I drove away from church."

Hannah had called Nikki several hours after church. She laughed before she responded. "Yeah, David couldn't tell, but I sure could. You were as stiff as a corpse. He's not that bad, though, Nikki. You have to admit, he's good-looking."

Nikki removed the bok choy and a red pepper from the refrigerator. She was going to whip up a Chinese stir-fry for Harvey tonight.

"I'll give you that, for what it's worth. But I don't know. These online dates of yours... He seemed harmless, but, ew, sorry. He was kind of, I don't know, *cheesy.* He had that fake salesman-type cheeriness, like he thought he was constantly on camera. I half expected him to try selling me a panini grill or a ShamWow or something."

Hannah laughed again. "He is a little over the top. But I think he'll relax that behavior eventually."

"I tried to be gracious with him. I mean, I laughed when he tried to be funny."

"He's managed to make *me* laugh before. I think."

"And what's with all the touchy-feely stuff? *I'm* not dating him. I don't even enjoy *women* getting that physically demonstrative with me, unless they're my close friends. I don't ever want to be stuck with a stranger like that again."

"Honestly, it wasn't my fault. I never expected my boss to call me on a Sunday morning. I don't think she would, normally. This was an emergency. And I got on the road as soon as I could. It wasn't my choice to show up when the service was already over."

"Right, okay. But now that we know it could happen, that's the last time I'm picking up one of your boyfriends on the way to church, okay? No matter how close he lives to me. No more boyfriend-carpooling for me."

"Sheesh. All right."

Nikki sighed. She knew Hannah hadn't had much control over how things worked out this morning.

"The main reason I'm ticked off is because of the cute guy with the dog. From the park earlier this month?"

"Yeah, I know who you mean. What happened?"

"I could have sworn he was looking for me when he walked into church this morning. And he came in at the perfect time, because David was in the men's room and the guy saw me sitting alone."

"Well, that's good."

"Yeah. We had a nice little moment there, when I got over myself and managed what I thought was a confident, inviting smile."

"That's my girl."

"He has a great smile. It was all I could do to pull my focus away from him and place it where it belonged during the service."

"I'm sure the good Lord appreciates your sense of priority."

"Especially after he sang out all by himself on this one song."

"What do you mean?"

"He kept singing when everyone else wasn't."

Hannah's laugh rippled through the phone. "Oh, that's awesome."

"It was just about the cutest thing I've ever seen. And he sounded like he had a horrible singing voice." She smiled just thinking about it. "Even from behind, I could tell how embarrassed he was. And after he seemed so cocky that first time, in the park—" She stopped to remember the way he had teased her.

"Yeah?"

"Well, his humility was kind of endearing."

"Hmm."

"What, hmm?"

"You're always giving me a hard time about falling for guys I barely know, and it sounds like this guy is landing you without even striking up a conversation."

"He's not *landing* me. I just saw something that made me like him a little more."

"Uh-huh."

"And then *you* fail to show."

"Sorry, ma'am. I really do appreciate your keeping David company."

"You're welcome. Who knows. Maybe he was just as uncomfortable with me."

"There, see, I knew there was an understanding woman underneath that sour exterior."

Nikki removed the soy sauce and a bottle of sesame seeds from the pantry. "But I really had to fight the urge to shrug off his hand or arm on my shoulder."

"I'm sure he didn't mean anything but chumminess by it."

"What if the guy with the dog was watching? Making assumptions. Writing me off."

"Don't put so much store into one little misunderstanding," Hannah said. "*If* he even saw. Anyway, if your guy has any sense at all, he'll pay attention in the future and see that David's with me. And you're glaringly alone. Just waiting for him to swoop in and save the day."

"Just make sure you don't dump David before next Sunday so my guy can see you two together."

Hannah spoke in a deliberately flighty voice. "You expect me to date the same man an entire week? After you've pointed out his many egregious flaws? Well, I just don't *know*. However *shall* I commit to one man for seven entire days?"

"Hey, you said it."

"No, you kind of said it too, actually, and you should give me a break. It's not as if I run through them like jelly beans. I'll definitely go out with David some more. But I don't see the point in dating someone once I can tell he isn't the one. You know that."

"Is David the one?" There was *no* way. Nikki was sure.

"How do *I* know? *You've* dated him longer than I have."

"Very funny. I have to cook now. And I'm in a bad mood, in case you hadn't noticed."

"Oh, honey, I noticed. Really, Nikki, church was hours ago."

"No, it's not just church." Nikki sighed. "It's Grampa and Granny's house."

"Oh. Yeah, I'm so sorry that fell through."

Hannah's change in tone made Nikki feel sorry for herself all over again, a reaction she couldn't stand. She tried to shake off the feeling. "I'm still hopeful it hasn't fallen through. Estelle says the financing or something else might end up wonky."

"Then we'll pray for wonky."

Nikki nodded and grabbed an onion from the pantry. "Yeah. Dear Lord, nothing against the other buyer, but please bring on the wonky."

"Love you, Nik."

* * * * *

Two hours later Nikki snuggled up on her bed with her comforter and pulled out a novel to read. She had made an excellent dinner for Harvey, if she did say so herself. And they had a brief but characteristically comfortable chat before he needed to take an overseas call. But now she just wanted to escape into someone else's life for a while. She opened the romance novel she had set aside days ago.

When her cell phone rang, she was momentarily annoyed until

she saw that it was her mother calling. Yes. Mom was exactly who she wanted right now.

"Hi, sweetheart. I just thought I'd check and see how you're doing. Everything going all right? Are you happy? Any problems?"

Nikki laughed. "Hannah called you, didn't she?"

"Maybe."

"I'm fine, Mom. I guess I came down kind of hard on Hannah today."

"Oh, I don't know. You know your sister. I love her to death, but she *will* take that mile if you don't make a big deal about giving her an inch. She seemed to think you might like a little motherly comfort tonight."

Nikki smiled. "My sister knows me too well."

"So what's the problem? Hannah wouldn't fill me in on anything other than the fact that she put you in an uncomfortable spot this morning with this new boy she's seeing."

"Yeah, we're okay on that, though. She really couldn't help it."

"But?"

"I kind of have my eye on someone who might have his eye on me, but that's as far as we seem to be able to get."

"You haven't gone out?"

"We haven't even gone out the same door! At church, I mean."

"Ah. Ships passing in the night, huh?"

"I guess." She shrugged. "He could be a complete jerk, for all I know."

"But you don't think so."

"No. There's something that draws me to him."

"Handsome?"

"Well, yeah. But there's something else. I think he might have a good sense of humor."

"Oh! Always number one on my list."

"Yeah, me too. I think that's because of how you and Dad are with each other."

"You've got to be able to laugh with each other. About each other.

And yourselves. Our family has always enjoyed a good laugh. I have to say that comes more from your dad's family than mine. Not that my parents are stiffs, but you know how funny your grandpa is. Even *his* parents—William and Lillian… The Tronniers have always been able to find the humor in life."

Nikki hesitated just long enough for her mother to react.

"What else is going on, Nikki?"

She lay back on her bed. "Mom, how come Dad's parents sold Grampa William and Granny Lillian's home? And why didn't you and Dad ever try to buy it back?"

"Mmm. Are you having a hard time getting the money together for the down payment?"

"I was doing fine with that. But somebody sneaked in behind my back and put in a contract this past week."

Her mother gasped. "Sweetheart! I'm so sorry!" She sighed. "After all this time with it on the market, I just settled into the idea that you were going to get the place."

"You and me both. But why am I the only one who seems to think the place is worth owning? Aside from whoever just got the contract, anyway. Don't you have the same kind of memories I do? Didn't Grandma and Grandpa?"

"Well, yes, but fond memories don't always equal financial ability or necessary circumstances, honey. Grampa William didn't need to sell the house when Dad's parents were in the market for one, so they bought one of their own that became even more special to them than Grampa and Granny's house. And we would have loved to have bought the house when your father and I moved back to Cary. But not only did we not have the kind of money needed to buy the family home, it wasn't available for sale. And by the time it was, we were comfortable in our own home. This has just been a blessing, that the house became available at a time when you could afford it."

"But the blessing's been yanked out from under me."

"Yes, I see that. And I know that breaks your heart, honey. At the risk of sounding glib, I'm going to tell you that some things are hard for us to understand, but they fit into God's plan for us. Maybe the remodeling would have been a nightmare for you. Or maybe the mortgage would have made you too dependent on your position with Mr. Fennicle, and…well, he's getting up there in age, isn't he?"

"Mom!" She lowered her voice. "Let's not kill off the poor dear before his time, okay?"

"I'm just trying to be practical. I know whatever is going on is part of God's plan for you. He's always looked out for you, Nikki. Take comfort in that."

Nikki nodded. "I'll try." She sighed. "I know you're right."

By the time she and her mother hung up, she had changed her mind about reading her novel. She was sleepier than she realized. Besides, after her mother's assurance, her need for escape had diminished.

As sleep slowly enveloped her, she prayed. For Hannah and her mother, who clearly loved her. For Harvey's longevity and her continued employment with him. She even steeled herself to pray for whoever had bought her dream house out from under her.

She didn't know who the person was, but, as her mother intimated, in some fashion he or she was all part of God's plan for her.

Chapter Ten

....

"I appreciate your taking the time to meet us so I can start making plans, Jolene. Especially on a Saturday. I know this is a busy day for Realtors."

"Us. That's cute." Drew's Realtor glanced at Freddie before she turned the key in the house's lockbox. "You and your best friend, here."

"Did I say 'us'?" Drew rewound. He sure had. He really did need to get out more. He reached down and scratched behind Freddie's floppy ears. "He's my boy, I guess."

"I'm happy to help out, believe me. Of course, I don't want to disappoint either one of you, but Freddie's not going to be able to attend the closing." She smiled and let the golden retriever walk into the house ahead of her.

"I'll have a chat with him. I think he'll deal with it." Drew followed in Jolene's perfumed wake and stepped into his future home. He wondered if he would experience that lingering concern others describe—buyer's remorse—after they closed on the sale. He didn't think so. His only other home purchase had been his place back in San Diego. He had loved every minute of ownership there, even though he never got around to the painting and furnishing he'd planned before he moved out here to North Carolina. And this house felt even more like the one God had in mind for him. How else could he interpret the fact that the house had sat unattended for so long and drew his attention so swiftly? Yep. This was the home he was meant to buy.

Jolene's heels echoed against the hardwood in the empty rooms. "Your paperwork is the kind my mortgage people love. Uncomplicated.

Terrific credit. The seller is thrilled, and they'd probably be willing to let you come to the house without me, even. I just want to play it safe in case anything should happen—like another squirrel invasion. I don't want you getting blamed for something you didn't do."

"So you think the closing date looks solid?"

"Definitely. In less than two weeks, this little baby will be all yours."

He grinned. "It's happening quickly. A month ago, I wasn't even thinking about buying a place. But this place just feels right."

Jolene gestured at Drew's notebook and measuring tape. "You go on ahead and get started with whatever you wanted to do. I'm going to make some phone calls and do a little business if I can. Also, make sure they replaced that broken pane of glass back there like they promised—and if not, I want to put in a call about that right away."

"Sure. But a little pane of glass isn't going to make or break this deal for me. I'd love it if that were the only thing I needed to fix."

Jolene smirked at him. "I'm sure. But I can see those creative wheels of yours turning every time you're here. I think you're looking forward to putting your own mark on this home."

They spent an hour there, while Drew measured and inspected and gauged what might need remodeling and what could be saved. He decided he'd have the kitchen redone first so he could move in sooner. He could always sleep and work in rooms other than those being remodeled, but he'd need a kitchen daily, right from the point he moved in. Even going that route, he knew from his experience at building sites that he was looking at several months after closing before he'd be able to get out of the apartment.

Freddie casually explored the house, stopping to smell a corner here and a closet there. Drew could hear Jolene on the phone in the front room, proposing meetings and deals and making demands. Her busyness helped him relax about her having taken time to serve as a supervisor during his visit here.

She closed her phone as he walked back to the front of the house. "You all done?"

He nodded. "For now, yeah. But I'm not sure if I didn't just raise more questions than I solved."

"Why is that?"

Drew turned and gave the house an overall survey. "I think I'm going to be able to figure out the structural needs of the house easily enough, especially if the town has any blueprints on the place."

"But?" Jolene walked through the front door, apparently now wanting to move him along.

"Freddie! Come on, boy." Drew stepped onto the front porch and unhooked Freddie's leash from his belt loop. "Well, structure I can do. Layout I can do. And I know plenty about architecture. What I'm not very confident about is decor. *You* might see my creative wheels turning when I'm here, but as far as I'm concerned, they're spinning haphazardly. I can't seem to visualize the specific *cosmetic* picture of the place. And it might sound weird, but if I don't have a clue about decor, it will make structure and layout a little more difficult for me. I'd like to be able to put together a complete vision for the interior before I take a sledgehammer to a single slab of drywall, you know?"

Jolene tucked her phone in her purse. "I know exactly what you mean, *and* I know what you need. I'm in touch with a number of interior decorators who would love to work with you on this place."

He couldn't help but envision some of the garish monstrosities he had seen when friends had hired the wrong decorators for the job. And they were never inexpensive. Still, he did need counsel in this department.

"Yeah, okay. Why don't you get me some names and numbers? I'd appreciate that, especially if any of them can show me some of their handiwork."

Jolene nodded. "I'll email you their website links."

They walked toward their cars, but then Jolene set her manicured fingertips on his arm to stop him. "You know what else you could do is visit some of the newer homes on sale. Especially any developments that have model homes open. You might not be looking for cutting-edge decor since your house has that older-home charm, but at least you could get a feel for what styles you like and don't like."

* * * * *

The office complex demanded the bulk of Drew's attention during the following week and into the next. He was just days away from clos-ing on the house before he was able to dash out of the apartment with Freddie and take Jolene's advice about touring the area in search of model homes. He had a pickup basketball game scheduled with some of the men from work, but that wasn't for a few hours.

Even if he didn't see many model homes to explore, he could at least check out some of the landscaping in the area while there was still daylight. That was another hurdle he'd have to face as a new home-owner. There were some dramatic old magnolias and white oak trees on his new property—he paused and savored those words: *his new property*—but the shrubs were overgrown and untidy looking. Back in San Diego a landscaper had advised him that old, overly woody shrubs made a house look shabby. He'd probably need to have some of them replaced. Eventually. But one thing at a time.

He reached over and stroked Freddie's head. "Let's do a little sightseeing, partner. Whaddya say?"

Freddie turned at the sound of Drew's voice and looked happy and eager as he sat up in the passenger seat. Drew chuckled.

They traveled to the part of town where the house was, but there weren't any new developments around there. Jolene had said the developments were likely to have model homes for him to see, so he decided to look for a newer area of town.

He had only driven a few blocks down the road when they approached a beautiful mansion. The first words Drew thought when he saw it were "Southern elegance." He recognized the style as Greek revival, with Italianate touches around the windows. White two-story pillars and trim, a huge wraparound porch, and black shutters against pale yellow brick. The circular driveway set off a small, tasteful fountain and pristine lawn. The landscaping was already gorgeous and lush, even in early April. And he'd bet the interior was exactly what he'd like in his own home. Drew pulled over and let the car idle.

"Man, that's the life, eh, boy?"

Freddie—who actually looked as if he were studying the elegant manor—made no response. At first.

But when a certain feisty little terrier scurried out the front door, followed by a certain young woman holding him with a leash, both Freddie and Drew sat up, alert.

"It's her!"

Freddie seemed to pick up on Drew's heightened awareness. He struggled to stand up on the passenger seat, something that had never been easy considering the golden retriever's size and bucket shape of the car's seat. He pressed his wet nose against the window and let out an eager whimper.

Drew turned off the ignition and fished Freddie's leash from the floor of the car. He wrestled with Freddie in order to clip it to his collar.

"Let's go for a walk, pal."

By the time they exited the car, however, she had turned the corner, and Drew realized he'd have to run up behind her in order to casually run *into* her. He didn't like how desperate and maybe even creepy that could look to her.

He pushed Freddie back into the car, but not without a struggle.

"Come on, boy. Trust me on this."

Freddie's agitation didn't subside until Drew got back into

the car and peeled away from the curb. The dog was thrown off-balance, and he plopped down on the seat and let out a depressed sigh.

"It's okay, boy." Drew drove to the opposite side of the block the girl was walking, and he sought a parking place. "We're still going for a walk, Freddie. We just need—" And there it was, the parking spot he needed. Drew swerved up to the curb, shut off the car, jumped out, and let Freddie join him. Judging by the pace she had been walking, they would meet right up there at the corner, if he played his cards right.

He ran his hand through his hair and glanced down at himself, at his gray UCLA hoodie and faded jeans. Not his best look, but that would only enhance the pretense of this meeting happening by chance.

They reached the corner and…nothing. She and the terrier were nowhere in sight.

"What in the world?" Drew scratched his head. She must have gone straight, rather than just walking around the block. He'd have to try to cross paths with her up at the next corner.

"Come on, boy." He didn't need to tug at Freddie. Freddie was eager to go. So they soldiered on to the next corner and arrived just at the time she would have reached it, by Drew's calculations.

Again, nothing. Now Drew didn't know what to do. She could have gone in a completely different direction once he lost sight of her on these neighborhood streets. He should have just run after her as he originally started to do. He tried one more block ahead and discovered a little park on his right. Could she have crossed over there without his seeing her? He and Freddie ventured that way, and then Drew stopped at the park's edge and blatantly looked for her.

Freddie started to fuss at something behind them. Drew turned, and there she was. She and the terrier approached, and Drew saw amusement in her eyes. He wondered how savvy she was about what he had been doing.

"Did you lose someone?" Her cheek dimpled when she smiled. "Or are *you* lost?"

Hmm. Maybe she *did* know he was looking for her. "What makes you think— Maybe I'm exactly where I want to be and with exactly who I want to be with."

As soon as he said the awkward sentence, he realized it could be construed in a number of ways. He'd *thought* he was being clever, saying he was with Freddie by choice and at the outer edge of this park by choice. But she could very easily assume he meant he wanted to be there—with her.

Which he did.

If anything, she looked confused by what he said. "Ohhhh–kay."

Drew put out his hand. "Considering how often we've crossed paths, I think it's time I introduced myself. Drew Cornell."

She put her dainty hand in his and gave him a strong handshake. "Nicole Tronnier. My friends call me Nikki."

"Then I'll presume to call you Nikki."

"And I'll presume to call you Drew." She glanced at the two dogs, who were busy sniffing at each other. "I remember this troublemaker, but I don't remember what you called him."

"That's Freddie. But to be fair—"

Her dog tried to take off after something at that moment, and Freddie tensed, ready to dash after him. But she had a firm hold on the leash this time, so no antics similar to their initial meeting ensued.

"Riley! Chill!"

Still, she looked as embarrassed as if her dog had started another race into the park. Drew should let it pass.

But he couldn't resist. "As I was about to say, to be fair, I believe it was Riley here who started the trouble six and a half weeks ago." He raised an eyebrow and smiled. "Go ahead and deny it, while you hold fast to that taut leash there."

She looked down and smiled. "Okay. Busted." Then she gave him a sly look. "Six and a half weeks ago, huh? What did you do, write about it in your diary?"

He laughed right out loud at that. "And here I thought maybe you were demure, because of how you always seem to rush away when I see you."

"Hey, I can be as demure as the best of them. My sister's always harassing me for not being bolder than I am."

Oh, yeah. The sister.

"Uh, speaking of bold, do you mind my asking...?" How to tactfully broach this subject? "I've missed the last few Sundays at church. But a few weeks ago I couldn't help noticing the guy you were with—"

"My sister's boyfriend."

"Ah." The *sister's* boyfriend. Very good. And she supplied that information pretty quickly. He liked *that*.

"Hannah—that's my sister," Nikki said. "She was supposed to be there, but she got caught up on a phone conference. She had asked me to pick him up on the way to church, since he lives right down the road from here."

"And you live around here?"

He wondered if he was sinning by omission. He had clearly seen her walk out of that mansion, and now he was pretending he'd just run into her here at the park.

"I live in that big house you saw Riley and me walk out of." She pointed in the direction of the mansion. "Just those few blocks down."

He didn't realize his mouth hung open until she chuckled.

"What? Did you think I didn't see you? It's broad daylight, and you were parked right in front of the place. Single women have to be aware of their surroundings at all times; don't you know that?"

He knew his face was red. Talk about busted. Still, he liked her spunk. She must have seen that in his expression.

"What?" she asked, a twinkle in her eyes as well.

"I'm just wondering when the 'demure' is going to kick in."

Now *she* laughed out loud. She had one of those laughs that drew a man in. Natural, musical, and downright fetching.

She checked her watch.

"I should get back. I need to make Harvey's dinner."

"Harvey?" They started walking together.

"My boss. That's his home I live in."

"Ah. That's not *your* home?" He felt a bit of relief that she wasn't from an economic class so far above his own.

"Hardly!" She pointed at Riley. "This isn't even my *dog*. I'm Harvey's—Mr. Fennicle's—personal chef. I'm part of his live-in staff."

"Fascinating. I've never known anyone who lived with their boss. Well, my old girlfriend lived with her boss briefly after I moved out here, but that was a different situation altogether."

He saw her eyes widen, and he nearly stumbled. "I'm sorry. I shouldn't have said that. I didn't mean to insinuate anything about you and your boss. And that was her private business too. And completely unlike her, I should add. It was, well, she went a little wild after I... Oh, never mind. Way too much information. Ignore what I said."

She nodded once. "All right, done. I've been known to spill stuff I regret spilling too."

The mansion was in sight by the time either of them spoke again. They had already passed his car, and he liked that she didn't stop there to part from him.

She said, "And what brought you to Cary?"

"I'm an engineer. I moved out here to oversee the building of an office complex."

"So you're temporary here?"

"No, I'm here for good. At least that's my plan."

He was about to mention the new house, but he thought better of it. Not only was it not a done deal yet, but after the way he had nearly hunted her down today, he was a little uncomfortable telling her he was buying a house right down the street from her. Besides, even though they seemed to mesh well, if they didn't hit it off long-term, it was probably best not to point out how close they would be living near each other. Better to wait until they knew each other better.

They reached the sprawling yard in front of the mansion, and she put out her hand.

"It was nice meeting you, Drew."

He took her hand but just held it for a moment. "Yes. Do you think you'd like to get together for coffee or something tomorrow? Maybe after work? That is, do you have specific working hours, or—"

"Oh. I can't tomorrow. I actually have a pretty full schedule right now. Harvey has some business meetings going on here, and I need to feed everyone. Maybe in a few days? The weekend?"

"Saturday? Sure. You want to give me your number?"

They pulled out their phones and exchanged numbers.

He made a point of walking away when she did, rather than standing there and watching her leave. He was in too good of a mood now and didn't want her to see just how happy she had made him. Too obvious, and too soon.

He wanted to at least save *some* surprises for the next time they met.

Chapter Eleven

....

Nikki wrestled with opposing emotions on Saturday morning. She busied herself by making raspberry blintzes for Harvey, but her thoughts kept bouncing between her plans to meet Drew for coffee later today and her disappointing loss of the house. She couldn't seem to shake the latter.

"What can I help you with, Nikki?" Harvey broke into her concentration when she brought his breakfast to the dining room.

"Hmm? Oh, Harvey, I'm sorry. Am I that obvious? I thought I was more poker-faced than that."

"I've never been a fan of poker." Harvey sipped his coffee. "And I hope you feel comfortable enough here that you don't feel the need for pretense around me. You've been a bit off your game the last couple of weeks."

She gasped before she caught herself. "Have I? You should have said something earlier! Have the meals—"

He put up his hand to stop her. "I don't mean your work, dear." He leaned back where he sat at the head of the table and gently patted his stomach. "Do I look as if I haven't been eating well?"

Nikki laughed. If there was one thing Harvey was *not*, it was portly. He was actually very slim and seemed in fine health, especially for an eighty-eight-year-old man.

"No," he said, "I mean your—your..." He put up his palms,

waiting for the right words to fall. "You usually give me a harder time than you've been doing lately. You're being far too nice. Almost polite. And that tells me there's something wrong."

Nikki rested her hand on her hip and smiled. "Harvey, you're the most unusual boss."

"Thank you. I aim to be. Now come and tell me what's wrong." He patted the table, and she sat down adjacent to him.

"Well, there are two things, really."

"Two men?"

"No, not two men! There's more going on in my life than romance, you know."

"I'd say everything *but*."

She straightened, her eyes wide. "What do you mean?"

"You don't get out enough. Even Laura seems to go out on dates occasionally, and she has far less *joie de vivre* than you do."

Laura. Harvey's all-business personal assistant. Wow. She had less joie de vivre than a post. Harvey's comparison rankled Nikki.

"It just so happens that *one* of my issues *does* involve a man."

"Ah!"

"And it's *good*."

"What is, dear?"

"Uh, the issue. I mean, I have a date with him later this afternoon, actually. After you leave for your…whatever. And I'm looking forward to it."

"So what's the issue?"

"No issue, really. I'm happy about that. So happy that I've been preoccupied lately. In a good way."

"Wonderful!"

"But that might be part of what you've noticed. Maybe I've been off my game because I'm thinking about him. Drew."

"Well, that's fine. And if things work out with this Drew fellow,

I'd like you to feel free to have him come around so I can meet him. I already know he has excellent taste."

Sometimes Harvey reminded her of her grandfather. She smiled. "Thanks. I'll do that."

"And now the second thing? I gather it's the one that's put that frown on your face the last few weeks."

Nikki sighed. "You remember when you hired me and I told you I wanted to eventually put an offer on the house my great-grandparents built?"

"Yes. Lots of good family memories, you said. Such an admirable goal for a young person. While others are out buying fancy sports cars and throwing money away on technological fads, you're trying to preserve the best from your past. I like that."

She laughed. "Thanks. But I *do* have an iPhone, you know. And my BMW isn't exactly an economy car."

"Yes, but I'm sure that's only because I pay you so exorbitantly. If I didn't, you'd still be focusing on that house at the cost of those amenities. Am I right?"

"I *would* have been. But that's all over now. Someone got in there and made an offer on the house before I was able to."

Harvey had a forkful of raspberry blintz at the ready, but he set the fork back down. "I thought you told me the market was dead on the place. Am I remembering wrong?"

"No, you're right. No offers at all, as far as I know. And the house has been on the market for more than a year. But someone showed up out of the blue, with the full asking price. Just like that." She snapped her fingers. "Gone."

He studied her for a moment before he picked up his napkin and wiped his hands, as if he were ready to leave his breakfast and take action. "Let me make some phone calls—"

"Oh, Harvey, I don't think so. I really appreciate it, but the contract was put on the house weeks ago. My Realtor would have called me in a flash if the house became available again. For all I know, they've already closed the sale."

"Well, maybe not. I'm not saying I would do anything unethical, but if there were the slightest chance of having the contract fall through, maybe I could influence—"

"No. Thanks. Just thinking about doing something like that gives me an upset stomach. I don't think God would want me to get the house that way. I need to trust that there's a reason I didn't get the house. Maybe I'm putting too much store in an earthly thing."

"But that's just it, dear. You were putting store in those memories, not the house, per se. Right?"

She didn't even have to think hard about the answer, so she had a pretty good idea where it came from. "I can still have the memories, Harvey. I think I have to let my desire for the house go."

Now Harvey sighed. "All right. If you say so." He picked his fork up again. "But you let me know if there's any way I can help out. I want you to get back to harassing me again."

She mustered a smile for him. "Fine. Eat those blintzes, for goodness' sakes. I slaved for hours, and you've let them get cold. How's that?"

He considered her remark before giving a brief shrug. "It's a start."

* * * * *

Harvey's concern and offer of help hadn't come as a surprise to Nikki. That all fit his personality perfectly. Still, he had perked up her attitude considerably. That—coupled with the anticipation of her coffee date with Drew—had her in good spirits that afternoon when she headed out of work. She was a little early, but that just helped her to feel relaxed about the date. She tended to stress when she ran behind schedule.

She took one last check of herself in her car's rearview mirror before she headed toward Ashworth's Drug Store. She had suggested to Drew that they meet at the old-fashioned soda fountain in the shop rather than at one of the trendy coffee bars in town.

"The place has been here all my life," she'd told him on the phone earlier that week. "I think you'll get a bigger kick out of Ashworth's than one of the modern coffee bars. It's a little like a scene from *It's a Wonderful Life*."

That had been a test, of course, whether Drew knew it or not.

"Oh, yeah! Where Jimmy Stewart worked as a kid."

Ah, well done. Sounded as if he liked old movies, as she did. "Exactly. You'll see what I mean. And if you're nice, I might even treat you to a hot dog."

"*Please*. Don't insult my sense of chivalry." He spoke with mock indignation and bluster. "If any hot-dog buying goes on today, I'll be doing it, young lady. And I'll hear no more about it."

So Nikki drove away from Harvey's thinking of nothing but seeing Drew and getting to know him better. Still, she never drove past Grampa and Granny's house—as she would always think of it—without giving it a wistful glance.

And this time she saw several men walking into the house. Without a second thought, she pulled over onto the other side of the road. They had left the front door open, as if they planned to walk right back out again, but no one exited while she watched. They had been dressed casually, in jeans and T-shirts. Could someone actually be moving in already? It had only been…what, four weeks? Five? She couldn't remember when Estelle had dropped the bomb about her losing her house to that…that house swiper.

Her house. Ugh. She simply couldn't shake that proprietary feeling. She clearly needed to pray about that.

And she would. But not just now. Right now she was dying to see who the usurper was. She shut off her car and stepped out before she could change her mind. In fact, the closer she got to the front door, the more steam she seemed to build up and the more aggressive she felt toward whoever had ruined her well-laid plans.

An older, wiry, leather-skinned man wearing a ball cap stepped out of the house just as she walked up the porch steps. She hesitated, midstep.

The man tipped the brim of his cap at her and gave her a friendly smile. "Afternoon."

"Oh. Yes. Good afternoon. Are you the, uh, person buying this house?"

He cocked his thumb over his shoulder. "Nope. You'll find him inside." He pulled a pack of cigarettes from the rolled-up sleeve of his T-shirt.

"Thanks." She stepped to the front door and experienced such an emotional rush of memories that she literally had to stop moving. It used to be so natural, entering this home without knocking. Knowing her great-grandparents would welcome her anytime. Now she was about to barge in on someone else's property. Or what would soon be someone else's property. She couldn't stand it. Maybe she should just leave. The last thing she wanted to do was become a crying, slobbering mess in front of some stranger who was clueless about her connection with the house.

She heard voices, although she couldn't hear what they were saying. It sounded as if they were back in the kitchen. Her kitchen.

Ugh. She had to do it. She tapped on the frame of the front door, still uneasy about walking in. "Uh, hello?"

No answer. Not even a pause in the discussion back there. She knocked more loudly and spoke up.

"Hello? May I—?"

"Just go on back there, miss."

Nikki turned and looked at the fellow on the porch. She wanted to tell him to stop flicking his ashes on the porch. But it wasn't her porch.

He lifted his chin to point at the inside of the house. "They can't hear you. But go on back. They won't bite."

Huh. It wasn't *their* bites she was worried about.

She stepped in and headed toward the kitchen. Just being in here now, under these circumstances, made the loss feel so acute. She clenched her jaw to keep from getting too emotional. She reminded herself that she would still have her memories even if she didn't have the house.

As she reached the kitchen, she heard one of the men say, "Hey, listen, I have an appointment. You go ahead and lock up when you go. Maybe give me a call tonight and let me know how long you think it will take to gut the kitchen."

Gut the kitchen! Granny's kitchen?

She heard his steps as he spoke, and he walked out of the kitchen and nearly collided with her.

She didn't know who looked more shocked, but Drew's expression was definitely full of surprise and utter confusion.

"Nikki!"

"You?" She struggled with the disorientation of seeing him here, when she'd pictured him at the soda fountain, possibly waiting for her.

He broke into a grin. "How did you know to find me here? I was just about to head for the soda shop."

And finally it settled in on her. "You!" She tried to tame the anger in her voice. "You're the one who's buying this house?"

She watched confusion cloud his expression.

"Uh, yes. I actually closed on it yesterday. It's a great house, don't you think? I was going to invite you to come see it after coffee. Is—is something wrong, Nikki? You okay?"

He was so clearly proud of the place. And he wanted to share his new homeowner's joy with her. With a jolt, she got a heaven's-view picture of her outraged heart, and the heat in her face was suddenly more about shame than anger.

"I, um, yes, I'm fine. I knew the house had been sold, and I—I was curious about who the new owner was. You're right. It's a terrific house."

He looked away from her and took in the big, empty place. "I know there's a lot of work to be done. You know, repairs and remodeling. But there was something about the place that caught my attention right away. I'd love to restore it to its original charm."

She released a resolute sigh. How could she fault the guy? Yes, he had stolen her dream, but only because it was the same dream he had. Kind of.

A quick prayer passed through her thoughts.

Lord, please help me to be gracious here. It's not Drew's fault that I lost the house. Well, it is, but he didn't mean to rip my heart out. I'm sure he'd feel awful if he knew. No point in both of us feeling awful. But I definitely need You to step in here and keep my mouth shut for me. Truth be told? I'm fighting the temptation to spoil his joy just a little bit.

Chapter Twelve

....

Nikki was right. Ashworth's did remind Drew of those soda-fountain scenes from *It's a Wonderful Life*. He was glad to sit across from her in the booth so he could look directly into her deep brown eyes—except for the fact that she immediately focused her attention on what was happening outside the window.

"Sometimes I come in here on my own just to relax. I like to sit and watch the people go by." She tucked her long dark hair behind her ear, and he noticed a small scar at the edge of her eyebrow. He felt an odd relief at that small imperfection.

She sipped her coffee and gave him a comfortable smile before she glanced back out the window. "I always see the same small group of people at work. This is a nice change."

The day was working its way toward sunset, and a peach-colored light filtered through the window and warmed the color of her face. He liked how delicate her features were. And her short, frilly dress made her look like a dancer. She had a classic beauty about her, but he loved her artistic bohemian flair too.

She turned and caught him staring at her. He started speaking right away to try to cover that. "People-watching. Yeah, I can imagine you'd get stir-crazy working in someone's house like that."

"Well, I wouldn't say that."

"No, not stir-crazy, that's not what I meant—"

"It's a huge house, after all," she said. "So no, not stir-crazy."

"Bored. You get bored."

She frowned, and he did too. They both chuckled uncomfortably.

He shook his head. "Ignore me. I blurted the first thing in my mind because you caught me staring at you. I didn't want you to think I was some, uh…"

"Weirdo?"

He laughed. "All right. Let's go with that."

"I guess if you're concerned about seeming like a weirdo, you're probably *not* a weirdo."

He waggled his eyebrows at her. "Ah, so my plan is working!"

Yes, delicate features enhanced by that smart, sardonic smile.

"So what prompted you to walk into my house today?" he asked. "That was such a pleasant surprise."

The smile wilted. It was followed swiftly by a frown and finally replaced by a wide-eyed innocence that didn't look altogether genuine.

"I was…curious. I knew the house had been on the market for quite a while, and when I saw people there, I just wanted to see if the new, um, owner was there."

"Small world, huh?"

She gave a little cock of her head. "You have no idea."

He wondered if she was referring to the fact that he kept showing up where she was—at church, in the various parks around town, in front of her house…. He really could be giving her the wrong impression, he supposed. Except in the case of his house, he was there first, so she couldn't blame him for that one.

"So, you've noticed the house before, huh? Have you lived in Cary for long?"

She nodded and still looked a bit on guard. Maybe she had her awkward moments on first dates too. "Yeah, I've lived here my whole life. Well, except for when I left for college—"

"At?"

"Johnson and Wales. In Charlotte. A small private university. So I still wasn't terribly far from home, really. And then I worked for Armand in Charlotte for several years—trained under him, actually. Armand Gaudet. Ever heard of him?"

"Sorry, no."

She shrugged. "It's an industry thing. I've probably never heard of the titans in the engineering field either. Or even the small fry."

"Ah, the small fry." He gave her a casual salute. "That's where you're wrong."

She laughed. "So you're the small fry?"

"Mr. Fry at your service." He put out his hand as if to shake hers.

She played along and took his hand. He wasn't sure, exactly, who was in charge at that particular moment, but neither one of them released the other all that quickly. At once, the friendly gesture felt intimate enough that they both reacted. Judging by the heat rising up his neck, he figured he reddened as much as she did. But he was as pleased as he was embarrassed.

"You all need a warm-up over there?"

They dropped each other's hands and turned to face the woman behind the soda counter. She held up a coffeepot, the picture of innocence.

Drew slid from the booth, his mug in his hand. "Thanks. Hang on, I'll bring them to you." He looked to Nikki. "You need warming up?" He took great care to keep his expression almost neutral.

And there was that playful scorn in her smile again. She had obviously recovered from any shyness their hand-holding had brought on. "You're too kind." She handed him her mug.

He was certain, by the time he returned to the table, that she was having fun so far.

"So who else is on the live-in staff there in that big old mansion?"

She counted off on her fingers. "Jackie is the housekeeper, and she helps me sometimes when Harvey has big groups over for luncheon meetings and things like that. And Edward is Harvey's valet slash chauffer. Laura is his personal assistant. That's it!"

"No butler?"

She smiled. "It's a big place, but Harvey's not a terribly formal man. Jackie's usually the one who answers the door unless another of us is nearby. And there are other employees there during regular office hours—employees of Harvey's companies, I mean. They're just not part of the live-in staff. Harvey has outside services that come in for a lot of the other work around the home too. A big housecleaning crew, a landscaping company, that kind of thing. We live-in employees are really there just because the house is too big for Harvey to navigate on his own. And I think he likes the company."

Drew nodded. "That last part sounds a little sad."

"Yeah." She tilted her head. "I think so too, sometimes. I can tell he really misses his wife. She passed away the year before I started working for him. But he tries to keep upbeat and lively. His grandson and his family dote on him. He doesn't seem to lack for visitors. He's well-liked. And respected."

"You really like him, don't you?" Drew studied her. "I can see it when you talk about him."

She sighed. "I have fond memories of my great-grandparents, William and Lillian. Sometimes Harvey reminds me of Grampa William."

"Did they live around here, then?"

Her wistful expression dropped away as if she had just remembered something bothersome. She straightened and got that same wide-eyed expression he saw before.

"Yes, but enough about me. Time to switch places. What's the story about your family?"

He chuckled. "You haven't actually told me about *your* family, you know. Just your work family."

"Right, right." She waved the comment away. "We've talked enough about me for now. We'll switch again later."

Well, there was some promise of more time together in that, so he relaxed and sat back in the seat.

"No siblings. My parents are back in San Diego, where I grew up. Dad—also an engineer—had a heart attack last month. Not that that's his defining feature, but it's what I remember first when I think of him these days."

"I'll bet! That's awful. And you were out here when it happened?"

"Oh, yeah. I've been here for about nine months now. And they told me not to fly back. They did bypass surgery on him so quickly, I couldn't have gotten out there in time anyway, and they were confident of his surviving the attack. Still, it's hard to be all the way on the other side of the country, knowing he's susceptible to another one. So I stay in pretty constant touch."

She smiled. "You have a close family, then."

"Very. I certainly had my own little form of rebellion in my youth, but I never went through that stage kids go through when they're embarrassed to be seen with their parents."

She lit up at that, tapping her chest. "Me neither! I know exactly what you mean! So many of my friends were like you said—they wouldn't be caught dead hanging out in public with their parents. My sister, even. She's just the opposite of me in that. I mean, not that she went through a particularly bad time in her teens, but even now she doesn't seem to cherish family the way I do. I see it as appreciation, but she sees it as a lack of independence. Which is funny, considering she lived at home until she was twenty-four. I'm glad to hear I'm not the only...the only—"

"Weirdo?"

She laughed. "I don't think that was the word I was looking for."

"Yeah, I wasn't looking for it earlier, but you were kind enough to help me find it."

She had a twinkle in her eyes, but he saw her shoot a quick glance down at her watch.

"You don't have to go already, do you?" He leaned forward. They had barely begun to get acquainted.

"No. I was just wondering if my stomach is ahead of the clock."

"You're hungry?"

She shrugged. "I'm definitely considering taking you up on your offer to be chivalrous and buy me a couple of hot dogs."

Ah, that was more like it. He stroked his chin and gave her a suspicious look. "A *couple* of hot dogs, is it now? Hmm. I'm not sure you were clear I would run into that kind of financial outlay here."

"I'm sorry. A promise is a promise. No snaking out of the deal now."

"Hey, I have a better idea. Why don't you let me take you out to dinner for real? Any reason we can't do that? I'd need to swing by my apartment to walk Freddie first, but it feels too soon to call it a day."

He watched her consider, and then they both smiled at her answer.

"Why not? We both need to eat, right? No reason we can't do that together."

All right, maybe she wasn't swept off her feet. But she was still willing to spend more time with him, and he certainly wanted to spend time with her. They hadn't even scratched the surface yet.

He was tempted to ask her what she thought of the house he bought, but he decided to wait on that. Probably better to talk about the things they had in common first. He didn't want to bore her by discussing subjects she probably didn't care much about.

Chapter Thirteen

....

Nikki parked her car at Harvey's and joined Drew, who awaited her in his car. She experienced the strangest emotional juxtaposition around him. He was, after all, the man who had stolen her family home right out from under her. When she first saw him in Grampa and Granny's living room, she'd struggled to keep from showing her anger with him.

But now she realized her anger had abated almost as soon as it arose. That irked her to no end.

Maybe she should have thought through that prayer for graciousness before she prayed it.

Of course, she knew herself well enough to suspect that she was giving him a bit of a break because he had charmed her with his humor, green eyes, and dark good looks before they crossed paths at the house. He definitely had an effect on her, which led to another emotional contradiction for her. One minute she was as comfortable with him as she was with any other man, and she felt confident and funny. And then when she wasn't watching for it, something would happen to make her suddenly aware of him as a, well, as a man whose handsome face she really wanted to take hold of and kiss. In the past two hours with him, her body had undergone so many temperature fluctuations that she had newfound empathy for her poor menopausal mother.

Right now, for instance. His little Audi sports car was a stick shift, and even though he had the engine fully opened up and had stopped changing gears, he still rested his hand on the gearshift. Nikki became ridiculously aware of how close his very masculine hand was to her knee. She thought she could even feel its warmth.

So what? It was just a hand. Just a knee. Still, she had to crack the window to let the cool air flow onto her face.

"This is a nice apartment complex," she said when they approached his place. She would have said that no matter what, just to mask her silly emotions. But they actually were pretty buildings. They were brick-front garden apartments, well-tended outside and fairly new-looking.

"Yeah, they're all right. The location is convenient to my construction site and most stores. But they're small. I mean, I can live in small quarters, but this has been hard on Freddie. I'm eager to let him run free in my new house and that spacious yard."

As had happened every time he called Grampa and Granny's house "his," she cringed just a little. Yes, other people had owned the house over the years, but this was honestly the first point in her life that she didn't envision owning the house herself someday.

Nevertheless, when Drew opened the apartment door and Freddie just about jumped into his arms, she felt again that she couldn't stay mad. And she loved the affection Drew obviously had for his dog. His voice was full of sympathy for Freddie while he hugged him up.

"Aw, was it a bad day, buddy? Were you bored? That's a good boy. Let's go for a walk. You wanna go for a walk?"

He looked at Nikki and chuckled. "I'm one of those chatty dog owners. I discuss matters of the day with him, the latest news—"

"Discuss? You mean he answers you?"

He pulled back and looked at Freddie. "In his way. He sets his head in my lap and makes big, adoring eyes at me when he agrees with me."

"And when he doesn't agree?"

"Oh, he always agrees."

She laughed. "Dogs are awesome. My parents didn't buy another after Barkley, our family dog, died. So Riley has been a bright spot for me there at Harvey's, even if he doesn't always agree with me."

"I'm afraid my chatting at Freddie makes him miss me all that much more when I'm gone."

But Freddie took time to greet her as well. "Hey, Freddie." She rubbed his head but kept her distance. She didn't want to smell like dog when they went out to dinner.

"You want to come with us while I walk him, or would you rather wait here? We won't be gone long."

"Oh no, I'll go with you." She'd feel odd staying behind—she didn't know him well enough to be comfortable, alone with all his private stuff. Anyway, she wanted to get to know him better. Even if nothing came of their relationship, she hoped to feel better, knowing who lived in the Tronnier home.

The weather had been rainy earlier, so there were puddles here and there along their walk.

"Great. Freddie's never seen a puddle he didn't like." Drew attempted to keep him from getting muddy without tugging on the leash too stringently. Still, the retriever's golden fur seemed to pick up plenty of dirt without Freddie's even trying.

"Riley's the same." Nikki took care to walk far enough from Freddie that he didn't splash on her. She probably shouldn't have worn pastels today, but she really loved this new top and skirt and couldn't resist. "But Riley is small and pretty easy to tidy up. It must be a hassle for you, keeping your apartment clean. I'll bet Freddie can cover the whole place in puppy prints pretty quickly."

"You'd win that bet. But there isn't much carpet, and I keep a towel near the door. I'll wipe him clean before I let him into the apartment. I hope you don't mind if I take a two-minute shower and change?" He lifted his chin to point in her direction. "You're all fresh and frilly. But I've been working at the new house and will probably smell like Freddie by the time I wipe him down. Will that make you feel uncomfortable?"

"Your showering, or your smelling like a dog?"

He smiled. "I suppose I should ask which of those choices you're most comfortable with, since they're diametrically opposed to each other."

"I think a shower sounds like a wise way to spend two minutes."

"It's a plan, then."

When they returned to the apartment, Drew juggled both his keys and Freddie, who was still active on the other end of his leash. The keys dropped to the floor, and without a moment's hesitation, Nikki bent down and picked them up.

Drew reacted quickly. "Oh! No, don't—"

But he wasn't quick enough. Nikki jangled the keys, which seemed to serve as a Pavlovian signal to Freddie. He jumped up at her, exactly as he had done when Drew first arrived home. But she was far less prepared than Drew had been, and Freddie was far dirtier than when they stood at the front door before.

"Freddie, no! Down!" Drew pulled at the dog, who obeyed at once.

Drew and Nikki observed a moment of silence for her pretty pastel top. She stared down at her dirty chest and wasn't sure how to react.

"Nikki, I'm so sorry. He gets all wired up at the sound of the keys."

She hadn't looked up yet. "I see that." They were going to have to drive back to Harvey's so she could change. She could only hope no one needed her for anything. She was free for the evening, but if she stopped at the house, it would be difficult to say no to anything others considered pressing. That was just the nature of being on staff.

Drew opened the door and grabbed a towel from the coat closet. "Here, come on in." He held up the towel. "This one's clean. Newly laundered." And he reached toward her as if he were about to wipe her down.

She gasped and grabbed the towel from him. "Uh, how about you wipe *Freddie* down?"

He rattled his head, as if he had just been kicked. "Oh, man. Of course. You must think I'm a complete clod."

She tried to repair the damage to her top, but she only succeeded in spreading the mud around. "I guess we'll have to swing back over to Harvey's so I can change."

"Sure, no problem." Drew worked on Freddie's legs before he looked at Nikki again. "Or *will* that be a problem?"

She shrugged. "I'm not crazy about popping back in. There's usually someone who needs me whenever I get home, even if I'm off for the night."

"No, we can't have that. We don't want to do anything to spoil such a successful first date."

She couldn't tell if he was serious or not. She glanced at her chest again and allowed the slightest frown before she saw his eyes crease at the corners.

"It's not that bad," she said. "I've been on worse dates, believe me."

He laughed. "Take it easy. Such glowing praise might go to my head. But I really am sorry about your top."

"This is washable. I just don't want to stop in at Harvey's."

"Maybe I have something you could wear."

Nikki appreciated having a good excuse to give him a once-over. "I doubt we wear the same size. Are you saying you have some women's clothes here?"

"Oh. No. Sorry. But I have a few lightweight cotton sweatshirts that are pretty small on me." He tilted his head. "We could try."

* * * * *

The smallest top he had was a pale-blue, loose-weave cotton sweater. Nikki took it into the bathroom and changed. It might have been small on Drew, but it nearly covered her skirt. Only the frill at the bottom peeked out. But this was better than interrupting their date. She stepped from the bathroom and went looking for Drew.

He was in the kitchen with his back to her, talking quietly on his cell phone. She heard concern in his voice.

"Now you know I'm not going to tell you what to do. I know you hate that. But could you please take the time to develop a friendship—I know, I know, I've said that before. But, Isabelle, you keep jumping into these so-called romances and getting hurt—"

At that moment he turned and looked at Nikki.

"Wow." He lost his grip on his cell phone, as if her appearance knocked him, physically. He grabbed for the phone as it fell to the floor. From what Nikki saw, he actually smacked the phone in his efforts to catch it, and the battery shot right off the back when it landed. It stopped at Nikki's feet.

He shook his head and laughed. He bent down and picked up the phone. "What a klutz. I'm sorry. I'll have to call her back just to hang up."

"Is it all right if I pick up the battery for you, or will Freddie attack me if I do?"

"No, batteries do nothing for him. You look fantastic, by the way. My sweater never looked so cool."

"Cool?" She handed him the battery.

"Yeah. You have that kind of feminine, bohemian style anyway, and now you look like a model out of one of those trendy clothing catalogs or something."

She looked down at herself. " 'Or something' is right." She saw he was placing the call again. "I'll wait in the living room."

"Oh, no, stay. I'm only going to explain why I hung up and then I'll hang up again."

And that was exactly what he ended up doing with this Isabelle person. Was she the old girlfriend? The one who went a little wild after they broke up? Lived with her boss? Drew sounded as if he were talking to his little sister, but he had said he didn't have siblings. Then she noticed a smile, and he glanced up at her.

"Yes, I have a date." His eyes twinkled with amusement meant for Nikki, obviously, although it sounded as though the woman on the phone was teasing him. "Uh-huh. The one I told you about. Freddie even likes her. Yes, I will. Gotta go."

"Yes, you will *what*?" Now Nikki was especially intrigued.

He scratched at his eyebrow. "Listen to my own advice. That was my old girlfriend. I think I mentioned her to you before. She hasn't been making the best relationship decisions, and I've often told her she rushes into romances without building friendships first."

Nikki wasn't actually sure she liked the idea of this woman cautioning him about his relationship with her. But she couldn't fault the advice.

* * * * *

They went to Biaggi's for Italian food, and halfway through their capellini di mare and rigatoni alla Toscana, Drew finally talked about the house.

"I'm working on plans for remodeling, and I have a good idea of what I want to do. The kitchen needs to be completely redone—it's way out-of-date. The appliances look like they're from the seventies, and I think the layout could be a lot more convenient. But I'm hesitant about some of my other plans because I'm clueless about style."

"What do you mean?"

"Whenever I see a place that I think has terrific decor—you know, the paint colors, the molding, the wainscoting, that kind of thing—I know I like it. But when it comes to envisioning what to do with my own home, I don't trust my taste. My home in San Diego was already done when I bought it. But this is starting from scratch. I don't want to take away from what's so beautiful about this old place."

"Oh, I'm so glad to hear that." She realized too late that she spoke as if she had something at stake with his choice of decor.

He smiled. "Well, I'm glad you're glad. You appreciate old beauty too, then?"

"Absolutely. I like contemporary decor, and I think it's possible to give an old house a modern feel. But not at the expense of such beautiful enhancements like the crown molding that goes up the main staircase and, as you said, touches like the wainscoting in the dining room—"

"Wow, you really *are* familiar with the house, aren't you?"

What was the matter with her? For a moment she wondered if her subconscious was deliberately trying to arouse his curiosity about her history with the house.

She shrugged, with the hope of suggesting nonchalance. "It's an impressive place, I guess. In my business, I've been in my share of expensive restaurants and private homes—Armand catered back in Charlotte—to get a good feel for what I think is classic beauty and what's just over the top. Gram—" She caught herself. "Your home deserves classic beauty in its decor."

And with that final verbal misstep, she shut her mouth about the house. It was obviously best that she not offer any more comments about how the house should look. If he ended up making a mess of Grampa and Granny's home, she'd keep telling herself, *It's just a house.... It's just a house....*

It wasn't her place to tell Drew what to do, but she was so emotionally attached to the place. It would probably be best if she avoided being there while he had the remodeling and decorating done.

Drew's eyes took on the spark of a new idea, and he leaned forward, eagerness in his smile.

"You know, my Realtor gave me the website links for a couple of interior decorators, and I checked them out. There were all kinds of those over-the-top things you're talking about."

"Oh, gosh. Don't use them, Drew." She shook her head and put up her hand to stop her comment. "I mean, use whoever you want. It's none of my business, and I should keep my nose out of it."

"On the contrary. Nikki, how about *you* act as my decorating advisor?"

Chapter Fourteen

....

Drew couldn't quite figure out what caused Nikki's discomfort. It seemed to come and go as they spoke, and right now it was definitely here.

"What? You don't think you could tell me how to decorate? I'll bet you could." He gestured at his sweater, which never looked so good as it did on her. The light-blue made her warm brown eyes look darker and more soulful. And the layers of her long brunette hair waved loosely around her shoulders in a casual yet somehow perfect way. "You have such a cool style about you, Nikki, and you said yourself you've been in plenty of fancy restaurants and homes to have a good idea of what works where."

"Thanks, but I'm too busy working for Harvey." She glanced at her watch. "As a matter of fact, we should probably wrap up the evening so I can get back."

"It wouldn't be a full-time thing, though." Drew signaled to the server for the check. "Just come by and talk to me about what you envision. I'd be willing to pay for your time."

"Oh, no, I couldn't charge you."

"Then you'll do it?"

She frowned and released an exasperated—and exasperating—sigh. "Let me think about it. Okay?"

"Sure. You just let me know. In the meantime, I'll start looking for sales on pink flamingos and velvet Elvis paintings."

After she gave him that smart smile again, she seemed to relax.

When they got outside to his car, he stepped ahead of her to open her door. He didn't mean to cut her off, but she came close to bumping into him before she realized what he was doing. She righted herself, but he helped by taking hold of her. He couldn't have planned it better if he'd tried, and now the two of them were mere inches from each other. He would have to pull away just to see more than her eyes. He found he had no desire to do so.

"Sorry." She spoke softly, and he was unable to answer her. Before he could change his mind, he bridged the short distance and kissed her.

He knew she would have soft lips. They had distracted him all evening.

She pulled back just slightly and seemed to think for a half second before she kissed him back.

Until then, he had been unsure whether this attraction was mutual. He smiled at her when she pulled away again, and she suddenly looked embarrassed.

"That was awfully forward of me," she said. "I don't usually…"

Now it was his turn to speak softly. "I'm going to take that as a wonderful compliment."

* * * * *

They talked of everything *but* romance on the short drive back to Harvey's.

"Are you going to church tomorrow?" She didn't look at him, as far as he could tell when he glanced in her direction.

"No, I'm going to have to lean on a simple at-home Bible study, I'm afraid. I have too many things to do at the house, especially since my week promises to be hectic at work."

"Problems?"

"Nothing out of the ordinary. There are just a number of different crews there right now, and I'm usually needed in ten different places at once at this stage of a building project."

"Who are those people you go to church with? That couple. I've noticed them before. He's kind of hard to miss, and she's so tiny next to him."

He laughed. "Yeah, that's Phillip and Gigi. Phillip and I work together. He's the one who told me about Cary Community Church." He refrained from telling her that Gigi had done reconnaissance on Nikki's relationship status, which proved to be unnecessary, thanks to their meeting again near Harvey's home. "Maybe next time I could sit with you instead."

There was a pause before she finally answered.

"I'd like that."

He looked at her, and in the passing light of the street lamps, he was sure he saw her smile.

But her smile vanished when they drove up Harvey's driveway. There was a police cruiser at the front entrance.

"Oh no." Nikki jumped out of the car the moment Drew stopped.

He pulled on the hand brake and jumped out after her. "Nikki, wait. You don't know what's happened. Let me check that it's safe before you—"

A policeman and a man of about fifty walked out the front door.

"Edward!" Nikki ran up the porch steps, and Drew followed.

The policeman said a word or two more to Edward before tipping his hat at Nikki and Drew and heading to his cruiser.

"What's wrong? What happened?" Nikki looked from the departing officer to Edward. "Is everyone all right?"

"Yes, I think so. Don't worry. Harvey took a fall."

"Oh no."

Drew wanted to put a comforting hand on her shoulder or something, but he didn't want to intrude.

Edward gave him a distracted, polite smile, so he extended his hand. "Drew Cornell."

"Edward. Edward Shannihan. Mr. Fennicle's valet." He looked back at Nikki. "They took him to WakeMed in an ambulance."

Nikki gasped as Drew asked, "WakeMed? That's the local hospital?"

"Yes, sir." Edward did what Drew wanted to do. He rested his hand on Nikki's shoulder. "Don't worry, Nikki. He seemed to be all right. His doctor just didn't want to take any chances. Harvey was conscious and didn't appear to be in much pain."

"Much pain? He was in pain?" Tears sprang to her eyes. "What happened?"

Edward shrugged. "As far as I can tell, he went down to the kitchen for a late-night snack. I think he tripped over Riley, because the poor little rascal looked so concerned and guilty. Anyway, that's what I think Harvey said before Jackie and Laura got involved and started making calls and fussing over him. He was able to get up and sit in a chair with my help. So don't you worry."

But Drew could see more than worry in her eyes. Apparently Riley wasn't the only one struggling with guilt.

"I'll leave you two now. Nice meeting you, Drew." Edward walked back into the house.

Nikki wiped away tears. "I should have been here. He doesn't usually want anything like that at night. I thought… Oh, I should never have gone out. I should have checked back when my top got dirty."

"Nikki, this wasn't your fault. From the sound of it, even if you hadn't gone out, do you think Harvey would have summoned you to—?"

"This is exactly why I'm with the *live-in* staff! I'm supposed to be here whenever he needs me." She frowned at Drew. "And he doesn't *summon* me. He's sweet and gracious and—"

"Hey, I didn't mean anything by that. I just think you need to not take this burden on your own shoulders. You can't control every—"

"Oh, is that what I need to do, Drew? Thanks for that advice."

Uh-oh. He had just done exactly what Isabelle always cautioned him against. "I'm—I'm not trying to tell you what to do. How…" He was clueless. "How do you feel?"

She looked at him as if he were crazy. "What? Why are you asking me how I feel? This isn't about me."

Women. He needed to leave so he could go home, have Freddie jump up on him, push Freddie down, and flop onto the couch, rather than navigate these eggshells.

"Right. Okay, well, I'll leave you to it, then, unless there's something you need."

She barely seemed to hear him. She nodded and turned away.

He was at a loss. She seemed crestfallen and prickly at the same time. It was almost as if she included him in whatever guilt she had embraced with regard to Harvey. As if they were complicit together in leaving him unattended. Good thing he hadn't tried to physically comfort her. And as nicely as their drive home had started, clearly, a good-night kiss was out of the question.

"Shh." Nikki looked around them as the crowd slowly exited the sanctuary. "I don't know who knows him around here."

"So what? You have something negative to say?"

"No, but—" She lowered her voice and leaned in toward Hannah. "This isn't exactly a gossip-free zone."

Hannah gave her an exaggerated wink. "Gotcha, superstar. We'll try to avoid the paparazzi in the fellowship hall too."

"He asked me to help him pick out the decor for Grampa William and Granny Lillian's house."

"Awesome! Did you tell him yet that the house—"

"No, I didn't tell him it's their house. It's become too awkward now to say anything."

"What are you talking about? You're getting closer to him, aren't you?"

Nikki shrugged. "It's kind of like not remembering someone's name and then getting to know them really well—by then it's too late to ask them. At this rate it would be really weird that I hadn't told him about the house by now."

"*Is* really weird, Nikki. It *is* really weird that you haven't told him."

"See? So I can't say anything. Who knows? Maybe we won't work out. Then I won't ever have to tell him and there's no problem."

"That's my girl. You go on with your positive self. So are you going to help him decorate?"

"I might."

"Could be the next best thing to decorating it for yourself, I guess."

Nikki nodded. "At least the chances would be better for the place to be restored to its old coziness." She sighed. "Of course, that's assuming he's still talking to me."

They walked into the fellowship hall. Hannah quickly scoped the crowd before responding. "No David yet. He's as bad as I am." She opened her massive hobo purse and rummaged around inside.

Chapter Fifteen

....

"So I take it Harvey's all right?" Hannah followed Nikki [
aisle when the church service ended the following morning.
arrived late, and Nikki had refused to chitchat until the ex
played. "Because I know you wouldn't have come to church ot
You sounded pretty shaken when you called last night."

"Yeah, he's got a bruise on his knee, but that's all. Laur:
with him this morning—"

"Laura?"

"You know, his personal assistant?"

"Ohh, right. The sourpuss."

"She told me they would have actually sent him back hon
night, but they wanted to observe him overnight to play it safe.
going to stick around this morning to be sure I was there whe
got home, but she encouraged me to go ahead to church since Ha
wouldn't be home until after the lunch hour."

"You sure old tight-lips wasn't setting you up? She's always t
kind of anti-*you*, hasn't she?"

"No, I think I was wrong about that. Her snippiness isn't perso
toward me."

"An equal-opportunity snip."

"Something like that. And she and I just have such different perso
alities. But she's lightened up since she started seeing this accounta
guy who works for one of Harvey's companies. I think she's in love."

"Hey, that reminds me. What's the status with Drew?"

"Okay, Typhoid Mary, what did you do now? Why wouldn't Drew be talking to you?"

"I snapped at him right before he left. He was telling me Harvey's falling wasn't my fault."

"The cad!"

"I know. I was a jerk. I was just upset about Harvey."

"Mmm-hmm." Hannah nodded as she pulled a pair of shorts from her purse. "That is so you."

Nikki planted her hand on her hip. "Well, thank you very much. You're so hard on me sometimes."

"Oh, please. You're just as hard on me. Come on, I want to stop at the ladies' room and change before David gets here. We're picnicking. I'm sorry, sis, but it's the honest truth. You lash out at people who try to help you when you're upset."

Nikki couldn't argue with that. She already knew it was true, and she knew that's what she'd done to Drew the night before.

The restroom was quiet, a nice contrast to the noisy between-services crowd in the fellowship hall.

Hannah went into a stall while Nikki combed her hair.

"Yeah, I need to apologize to him. Especially after he was so sweet all night." Nikki grinned, knowing the reaction her next comment would get. "And *really* especially after he gave me such a fantastic kiss."

A loud, long gasp emitted from behind the stall door. "I can't believe you didn't mention that first! He kissed you?"

"And then I kissed him."

"You scarlet woman, you! And?"

Nikki smiled when she remembered how romantic the moment had been.

"And I'm embarrassed at how *much* I kissed him back."

"You mean, for a long time?"

"No. Just with such...gusto. Arms around the neck and everything.

I have to admit, I surprised myself. I mean, it was like not realizing I had been thirsty for years and then suddenly drinking a long, cool glass of water."

Hannah laughed. "Sure, you're thirsty! You've had your nose in cookbooks and kitchens for so long that you've forgotten there's more to life than the perfect pâté or the fluffiest soufflé."

Hannah emerged from the stall wearing shorts and an expression of rapt curiosity. But before Nikki could answer, they heard a flush of water. They both jerked their heads to see a short, petite woman walk out of a stall at the far side of the room, a sweet smile on her face.

Nikki recognized her. She thought she remembered Drew saying her name was Gigi. They all uttered quiet greetings to each other.

Hannah and Nikki exchanged wide-eyed glances, but Hannah looked ready to laugh. They had briefly discussed Drew's church buddies in the past, so Hannah knew who Gigi was too.

While the three of them silently washed their hands, Nikki reviewed the conversation she and Hannah had been having. Were they still talking about Grampa and Granny's house while they were in the restroom? She thought they might have changed the subject before they walked in.

She ventured a quick peek at Gigi, and it seemed Gigi was just waiting for that look. She smiled at Nikki as if she absolutely loved her to death. Or found her highly amusing.

Ugh. The talk about kissing! A long drink of water after her parched years of spinsterhood. Had it really been necessary to wax poetic like that? She sounded like some cheesy film noir dame or something.

Both Nikki and Gigi reached for the paper towels at the same time.

"Oh, sorry. You go ahead." Nikki smiled and took a towel after Gigi.

"I'm Gigi Nester. You're Nikki, aren't you? Drew's friend?"

They shook damp hands. "Uh, yes. And this is my sister, Hannah."

"Hey." Hannah smiled but still had her soapy hands under the water.

Gigi pointed at Hannah. "Yes, I've seen you with that nice-looking blond guy. He's new here, isn't he?"

"Wow." Hannah flicked water from her hands and grabbed a paper towel. "You're observant."

Nikki would have kicked Hannah if she could do it without Gigi noticing.

Gigi responded with a delightfully honest laugh. "Let's call a spade a spade, honey. I'm nosy."

Both Hannah and Nikki laughed.

"But I'm not like that with everyone, girls." She pointed at Hannah. "I only noticed your business because I was being nosy about your adorable sister here." Then she pointed at Nikki. "And I'm only being nosy about you because I know what a terrific guy Drew is. And I think he likes you."

"You and me both." Hannah tossed her paper towel in the trash. "I'm just happy to see her venturing back into the dating scene. She's been all work and no play for *way* too long."

"Well, you couldn't have chosen a finer man to venture back with. And…I'm going to just go ahead and say it. I heard what you were talking about when you came in. I guess you didn't know anyone was in here."

No, indeed. Nikki panicked and tried to subtly communicate with her sister using only her eyes. She hoped Hannah didn't clarify what they had been talking about when they walked in, especially if she *thought* Gigi meant the house issue.

"Anyway," Gigi continued, when neither sister responded, "Drew has pretty thick skin. A real man's man, if you know what I mean. If you snapped at him when you were worried about someone, I seriously doubt he took it too much to heart. That's not like him."

Ah. At last, a comment that carried some comfort. "That's good to hear," Nikki said. "And that *does* sound like Drew."

"But I'm sure he'll appreciate your apologizing anyway." This last comment was punctuated with a quick smile that seemed to insinuate that Nikki would fall short as a decent person if she ran roughshod over Drew's good graces.

Even though she bristled at the smile, Nikki agreed.

Gigi said, "It shows what a nice girl you are to even notice that you snapped at him. Sometimes I'm like that with my husband, Phil, and I don't think about it at all. It's a wonder he stays with me. *He's* a wonder."

Now she had both Nikki and Hannah smiling. Nikki couldn't help it. Happy marriages had that effect on the Tronnier women.

"And Drew is a wonder too," Gigi said.

The door opened and a pretty, teenaged version of Gigi peeked in and chuckled. "Mom! I thought Daddy lost you. He said we need to go as soon as possible."

" 'Kay, baby." Gigi walked to the door and tossed another comment over her shoulder to Nikki. "Anyway, you don't want to let that one get away. Nice meeting you girls."

Hannah and Nikki called out their good-byes. Nikki waited for the door to close before she spoke again.

"I wonder how much of this is going to get reported to Drew."

"Ten bucks says she's pulling her cell phone out as we speak. And she'll tell him everything but your shoe size, and only because she can't figure that out on her own."

"I don't think we were talking about the house at all in here, right? So she won't say anything about that."

"No, I don't think so either. She'll only be able to tell him you were floored by his kiss."

Nikki groaned. "How desperate do *I* sound?"

"Judging by what you've told me so far, the guy is due a little encouragement. You haven't been the easiest catch, that's for sure."

"Hey, I'm not caught yet."

Hannah turned her palm up at Nikki. "Case in point."

"There's nothing wrong with moving slowly."

"Whatever. I don't get the impression Gigi shares that attitude. Not about romance, and probably not about spreading the word to Drew."

"She can't be calling him already. Not if her hubby is hurrying her to leave."

"Hey, I have to get out there too," Hannah said. "David's supposed to meet me here."

They walked out of the ladies' room together.

Nikki pulled her keys from her purse. "I'm just going to have to call Drew before Gigi gets to him. I don't want him to think I'm only apologizing because she told me to."

"There's David." Hannah waved at him, and the sisters walked in his direction. "Then you'd better call him on the way home. I don't get the impression news sits idle at Chez Gigi for long.

Chapter Sixteen

....

No matter how hard he tried, Drew couldn't quite wipe the smile off his face.

"What are you so happy about?" Nikki gave him that smile of hers, the one that went along with an amused but suspicious sideways glance. "Haven't you ever been apologized to before? It's not very valiant of you to gloat, you know."

They were driving to the home design center together. Several days had passed since Nikki called and apologized for being so rude to him. But this was the first time they'd gotten together since then, and one of the first things he had done was tease her about how obviously difficult the apology had been.

"I don't mean to gloat. This is happiness you see, not gloating. It says a lot that you apologized, and I'm glad you're not still angry with me."

"I told you, I wasn't actually angry with you. I was angry with myself."

He nodded. "Then I hope you apologized to yourself too. Everything worked out all right, didn't it? And Harvey's home, safe and sound? And best of all, you haven't let his fall keep you from leaving his side once in a while and seeing me. And saving me from making my beautiful house a nightmare inside."

And there it was yet again, that subtle cloud across her features. Something just didn't sit right with her about him. But he wasn't about to rock the boat, not now that things were going well between them. She'd open up with him eventually. He was sure of it.

Several hours rushed by while they strolled through the design center and discussed decorating options. Drew happened to glance at a clock on the wall.

"Is that a display clock?" He looked at his watch. "No, it really is four! Man, I usually hate window-shopping, but this has been fun. For a number of reasons."

She returned his smile. "The company you're keeping has a lot to do with it, I assume?"

"That's the main reason, yes." Nikki's hand brushed against his. He took hold of it as casually as he could, and she didn't pull away. "And you have great ideas. I knew you would."

She pointed to a display wall. "Drew! *That's* the color I was talking about for the living room. What do you think of that?"

It was yellow, as far as he could tell. "Um…it's…nice?"

She laughed. "You see how it has creamy undertones, like custard, rather than a sharp, lemony feel?"

"Hmm. Why is that wall suddenly making me hungry?"

"And if you incorporated some molding along here"—she pointed to the edges of the display-room walls—"it would give the room such character. And even use a bit of sheen, just the slightest bit, like eggshell. Then you'll get a bit of warmth reflecting off other items and fabrics in the room."

"Oh, yeah. I like that idea."

"I know you're thinking about taking down that wall between the dining room and living room, and I agree with that. It should never have been added. But if you just put in a half wall, with…with maybe a half post from the wall up to the ceiling? You know—so you'd still see from one room into the next? You'd hint at separate rooms without losing the openness you want."

He watched her as she spoke. She clearly had a vivid image in her mind now, almost as if it were a memory rather than something she imagined for his future home.

She said, "You'd be able to prepare the table for your family while they gathered in the living room. And you'd still be able to be part of the conversation. No one likes when the cook has to be apart from everyone else while she's preparing the meal."

"Are you remembering a room from one of the homes where you and Armand catered?"

She looked up quickly. "Uh, no." She looked away, referring to the little notebook she'd brought with her. "Let's go find that salesperson again and ask what this paint is called—what do you say?"

Hmm. Maybe an old boyfriend's home inspired her vision and she didn't want to talk about it. Whatever. It wasn't a problem for him. He loved her ideas.

"Sure. Find the salesperson. Sounds like a plan."

They walked away from the display.

"And then how about we check out that model home you mentioned?" he said. "And after that maybe we could get a bite of dinner. Do you have to get back to Harvey?"

"Not tonight. His son and daughter-in-law are back in town from their trip to Europe. They've talked him into spending some time with them, since he's supposed to relax for a few days."

"So you're free for those few days?"

She smiled. "Not completely. I'm sort of on call. Harvey took me aside and confided that he wasn't sure how long he'd last at Morgan's place. They clash sometimes."

"I thought you said they were really close."

"That's Harvey and his grandson, Nathan. The two of them are tight. Very similar personalities and priorities. Apparently Morgan, his son, has never had much interest in Harvey's business. Or in Harvey, really. He and his wife travel all the time. He writes articles and books about travel. But Nathan has always found his grandfather and his work fascinating. He'll be the one to take over someday, I'm sure."

"Interesting to have the camaraderie skip a generation like that."

"Mmm-hmm. Personally, I was always really close with my *great*-grandparents, Grampa William and Granny Lillian. I mean, I was still fairly young when they passed away, but I absolutely loved spending time with them. I really miss them."

"Were they from around here?"

She nodded, and an expression crossed her face as if he had just caught her in a lie. What was it with her? His little mystery woman.

"Yeah," she said. "Oh, there's our salesman." And she rushed ahead, nearly leaving him behind.

As they finished up, the salesman gave his business card to Nikki.

While they walked to the car, Drew's curiosity got the better of him, and he decided to plunge in. "Nikki, is there something you need to tell me?"

She paused in her step for the briefest moment before walking on. She smiled at him, but a little frown marred her expression. "No. I think we're off to a really good start with these ideas. Don't you like what I've suggested so far?"

"Oh, I love the ideas. It's just that sometimes you get this…look." He smiled in an effort to keep the conversation light. "It's as if you're an amnesia patient in one of those soap operas and little bits of trouble keep dropping back into your memory."

They both laughed at that.

She looked ahead, at his car, as she spoke. "No, no amnesia here."

"And sometimes the look is more like…" He wasn't sure he wanted to say this. It made him sound a little needy. He opened the passenger-side door of his Audi for her.

She tossed her purse onto the floor of the car, got in, and opened those beautiful brown eyes at him without the slightest hint of discontent showing. "Thanks. Like what?"

"Like I'm getting on your nerves." He gently closed her door and walked around to his side of the car. When he looked at her again, he could tell she was trying to either figure out what he was referring to or decide whether to lower the boom on him. Now he wished he had kept his mouth shut. They obviously had chemistry. Whatever it was about him that bothered her was sure to work itself out. This pressure could annoy her right out of his life before they really got a chance to—

"Drew, you haven't gotten on my nerves at all. I think you're— Well, I really love being with you. I can't remember the last time I looked forward to seeing someone like I do you. Why are you looking at me like that?"

"Like what?" He knew exactly how he was looking at her. He just wanted to hear her describe it.

Her smile turned up on one side, as if she could only keep half of it from happening. "All romanticky."

He burst out laughing and saw the other half of her smile turn up. "I guess you make me feel all romanticky." He leaned toward her and gave her a kiss. Right there in the home design center parking lot. And she kissed him back, almost as enthusiastically as she had outside the restaurant. They were starting to develop a pattern: conduct some form of business in a building, leave the building, and kiss. He quickly formed a mental list of all of the buildings they might visit over the coming days.

He realized she hadn't answered his initial question, but at the moment he struggled to remember what the question had been.

Still, he slowly pulled away and saw she had more to say.

"I think I've been giving you the wrong impression without realizing it," she said. She sighed. "It's about the house."

Oh no. He had been certain she liked the house. Yes, the two of them were a new couple—hardly even a couple yet, really. But he loved involving her in the remodeling, having her be a part of making it beautiful.

"You don't like the house?"

"Oh, I love the house. That's just it."

He drew the back of his hand across his forehead and grinned. "Phew! You had me worried for a second. I swear I felt something almost divine when I first saw the place. I was sure God saved it for me, especially when I learned it had been on the market for so long before I found it. I can't wait to finish restoring and remodeling it."

That little frown returned to her features, even while she nodded. "I can imagine exactly how you feel."

"So what's wrong with the house?"

His cell phone interrupted them.

"It's my mom. Excuse me just a second." He took the call. "Hi, Mom."

She started crying the moment he spoke. "Drew?"

"Mom? What is it? What's wrong? Is it Dad?"

"Oh, honey. It's another heart attack. I'm at the emergency room."

Drew shot a look at Nikki and saw she already looked concerned. He shook his head to signal his dismay.

"I'll come out there. Should I? You want me to come out there?"

His mother hesitated a moment. "I–I'm not sure. I don't know how bad it is this time. The doctor—"

"You know what, Mom? I'm just going to come out. I don't want to take a chance that—" He looked at Nikki again. "Well, I'll just get there as quickly as I can. I'll let you know when to expect me as soon as I know, but I'll take a cab from the airport. You call me after you hear from the doctor, okay?"

The moment he hung up, he started the car. "He's had another heart attack."

"Oh, Drew, I'm so sorry."

"I've got to get out there."

"Of course. Just drop me off at Harvey's. You want me to see if I can get your flight booked while we drive?"

They spent the rest of the drive tending to details, and he called her on the way to the airport. "I just talked with Mom again. They're going to do another bypass. But they're pretty confident he's going to pull through."

"I'll pray for him."

"Thanks, babe."

Neither of them spoke for a moment. Had he just called her "babe"? He grimaced. He had indeed. His feelings for her had definitely been growing, but that was pretty forward. And some women hated that endearment.

"I'll pray for you too," she said.

He wasn't certain, but he was fairly sure he heard a smile in her soft voice.

"Nikki, when Mom called, you were about to tell me something. About my house."

"Oh. Yeah, let's just leave that alone, okay? It's not important, and it's not about the house. It's about me. I have an issue I need to pray about. Everything's fine between you and me, and everything's fine about the house. You just focus on your dad and give me a little time to work this out. Will you do that?"

He didn't really have a choice. He preferred open communication—it was one reason he tended to work well with people. It was why he and most of his old girlfriends remained friends. But Nikki obviously needed time before she was comfortable telling him whatever bothered her.

"Okay, let's drop it for now," he said. "Maybe when I come home we can talk more. But I can take a hit pretty well, so don't keep quiet on my account."

"Wouldn't think of it."

Chapter Seventeen

....

Of course she had kept quiet on Drew's account. The last thing he needed now was her petty problem on top of his important concerns about his father. He had just as much right to the Tronnier house as she did.

She laughed at herself. Legally, he had *more* right to the house than she did. As in, he had all the rights and she had none.

She would make peace with that and depend on God to help her deal with her disappointment. She said as much to Hannah the next time they spoke.

"His father's heart attack really put it all into perspective. I'm frankly embarrassed that I was pouting so much—or whatever I was doing—that he felt compelled to ask me if he was getting on my nerves."

"But why haven't you told him about the Tronnier connection to his house?"

"Because it was beyond awkward. And doesn't matter. There isn't a Tronnier connection to his house anymore, and I don't want him to think there is."

Drew called her from San Diego two days after he left Cary.

"Dad's pulling through beautifully," he said. "He's a tough old guy. They think he's going to be fine. He's already complaining about not being able to have his nightly bowl of ice cream anymore."

Nikki laughed. "You'd think they would have made him give that up after the first heart attack."

"Uh, yeah. They absolutely did."

They both laughed.

"When I say he's tough, I mean he's stubborn too." Drew sighed. "I miss you, Nikki."

She grinned. Speaking of hearts, hers did a little flip. She answered softly, "I miss you too. *Babe.*"

She loved his soft chuckle, and she swallowed before speaking again. "Hurry home, Drew."

"Can't wait to see you."

She sighed after ending the call. Somehow the crisis with Drew's father had drawn them closer. She supposed real, honest, messy life had a way of doing that.

Still, she made a point of tucking away her feelings of nostalgia about Grampa and Granny's home when Drew returned. She was certain that was the proper, Christian thing to do.

She focused on the fun she and Drew had when they got together. She loved watching Grampa and Granny's house be restored to a modern version of the classic beauty it once was. It no longer mattered that the home of her childhood belonged to someone else.

Nope. It didn't matter.

Not one bit.

Truly.

They worked together and played together over the summer and well into the fall, whenever both of them were able to get free from their professional obligations. And every time she passed the house or stopped by, Drew had remodeling crews working there. They had almost finished the remodeling and were close to implementing the decorating ideas Nikki had given him. But she was already pleased to see he'd taken her suggestion about the half wall between the dining room and living room. She remembered that half wall from when Granny, Grandma, and Mom would lay out a big family meal on the dining room table, adding their collective six cents to whatever lively conversation was going on in the living room.

Whenever the familiar disappointment crept up, she pulled a Second Corinthians and took captive those thoughts. She handed them over to God. Over and over.

The fact that she sometimes struggled even a tiny bit with the circumstances irritated her to death. She just wanted to get *over* it already.

On the crisp fall day that Drew went with Nikki to meet her parents, she walked out of Harvey's home and embraced the excitement of merely seeing Drew's handsome face. Just taking in that tall, gorgeous, kind man who had been nothing short of considerate, accommodating, and a mighty fine kisser over the past months.

And he blended in with the family as if he had been a part of it all along. He accompanied Nikki's dad out to the garage to let him show off the 1952 Buick he was restoring.

Nikki's mother watched the two men from the kitchen window while Nikki and Hannah set the dinner table.

"Nikki, if he's as sweet as he is good-looking, you be sure to hold onto him."

Hannah laughed as she folded the cloth napkins. "I get the picture that the holding is mutual. And often."

Nikki smacked at her playfully. "He's lasted longer than poor Bradley did, anyway. You're so mean."

Bradley had come along after Hannah split from David.

Hannah sighed without a hint of true remorse. "Poor Bradley. I just couldn't take his...blankness any longer."

Nikki would have asked for clarification, but she had seen Bradley's empty stares. Nikki knew exactly what Hannah meant.

But their mother turned from the window and carried dinner plates into the dining room. "Blankness?"

Hannah shrugged and took the plates from her mother. "I just don't think he has many original thoughts, you know? I mean not clever ones. He had thoughts like 'I should cut down on how much corn I eat.' But that's about how stimulating conversation got with him."

"You see how mean she is, Mom?" Nikki went back to the kitchen and opened the refrigerator to get the iced tea. "Good grief. What's with all this milk in here?"

"Oh." Her mother stood in the kitchen doorway and rested against the frame, her arms folded across her chest. "The weatherman's calling for possible snow. Early for snow, but that's what they're saying. And the two percent was on sale this week. And I had a coupon."

"But you have three gallons in here, and it's just you and Dad. You guys hardly even drink milk as it is."

Hannah walked in and stood next to Nikki at the open refrigerator door. "Wow. That there is what you call a boatload of milk."

Their mother laughed, clearly realizing she had overbought. "They said it could be a *lot* of snow. How do I know when my next chance to buy milk will come along?"

Nikki looked at her, and they both laughed at the absurdity of her comment. The closest grocery store was actually within walking distance.

Hannah reached in and pulled out one of the gallon jugs. "Well, I'll do my part and have some with dinner. Does a body good. But they're calling for a possible snowstorm, Mom, not a nuclear holocaust. I think there might still be a few dairy cows around after the great thaw."

Drew and Nikki's father walked in from the garage to find all three Tronnier women laughing together.

"Ben, honey, tell your girls to stop picking on me."

Nikki's father scowled at his girls. "You leave your dear old mother alone."

"Old?" She planted her hands on both hips and feigned indignation. "Never mind helping me, mister."

Nikki watched Drew through this exchange and felt a flush all over. He wore a genuine smile as he watched the teasing. He fit this family perfectly.

He suddenly turned his smiling eyes on her, and they had their own private moment of appreciation. Talk about a great thaw. She could have just melted.

Dinner went smoothly, and Nikki thought she couldn't have asked for a better time to have introduced her family to Drew.

Afterward, as he helped her into her coat, her father said, "Now where do you live, Drew?"

Hannah and her mother were talking to Nikki about the coming week, but from a distant point in her mind, she sensed a reason for tension.

Drew said, "I'm at the Cambridge Garden Apartments right now, just renting while I have my house remodeled. We're almost done, so it shouldn't be much—"

"Oh, that's right," Nikki's father said. "You're the one who bought my grandparents' place. I almost forgot about—"

Apparently her father had just noticed the sudden silence in the foyer.

Drew was wrapping his scarf around his neck, but he stopped mid-wrap, tilted his head as if he doubted his own hearing, and said, "Did you say your grandparents' place?"

"Uhh…" Her father simply looked from Nikki to his wife and back to Nikki again.

Drew's confused expression slowly scanned across the mute Tronnier family members, one by one, and Nikki saw something more than confusion there by the time he finally stopped at her.

"Drew, we need to talk."

He said nothing, so she took him by the arm and practically shoved him out the door. She followed right behind and glanced back at her family. They all looked concerned. Well, her mother looked concerned. Her father looked guilty, and Hannah's thoughts couldn't have been more clear had she held up a giant placard that read: "I Told You So."

Chapter Eighteen

....

Drew felt a rush of conflicting emotions, and he wasn't sure which to express first. Nikki had been talking at an auctioneer's pace, explaining herself, the entire time they had been driving. Now they were near Harvey's mansion, and Drew breathed deeply to keep from sounding too angry when he talked.

"Why in the world would you deliberately keep something like that from me, Nikki? Were you only dating me because I was the one who bought your grandparents' home out from under you? And to what end? What did you think—?"

"No!" She sat facing him as he drove. "I was dating you because I—I liked you. And I never planned to not tell you. I just *didn't,* and then too much time went by and we kept dating and it would have been weird to tell you after we got so…involved."

His laugh was short on humor. "Oh, that was a good plan. *This* isn't weird at all. I mean, I feel as if I've been the brunt of some bizarre joke the entire time we've been seeing each other." He pulled up Harvey's driveway and parked. "Your family—what did you do, tell them to wait until I left before openly discussing what a jerk I am for interfering with your plans for your family home?"

"Obviously not! Couldn't you tell my father completely forgot about it until you two were talking on our way out? I stopped fussing about losing the house quite awhile ago."

"I guess so, since *I* never heard about it." And then it dawned on him. He pointed at her. "*That's* what the funny looks were about. Oh,

Nikki, there were *so* many times you thought about it, weren't there? I even asked you about that, about the annoyed faces you kept making, back ages ago. I asked if there was something I had done that bothered you. You had plenty of chances to be honest with me." He held the steering wheel and stared outside. "And I kept going on and on about 'my house this' and 'my house that.' I feel like such a selfish jerk."

"That's not how I see you."

Now the past several months streamed through his mind. He groaned and gripped his forehead. "What you must have thought when I asked you to decorate for me." He looked at her again, still baffled. "What *did* you think? How could you do all of that without coming clean? You just let me be an idiot with my stupid little project."

"But you weren't an idiot. And it wasn't a stupid project. It was the same project I would have had if…"

"If I hadn't swooped in and trashed your big dream."

"Drew, look. I was upset at first, I'll admit it. Maybe longer than just at first. You bought the house just as I had saved enough to make an offer. My Realtor had expressed an interest to the seller—"

"That was you! You were the other person interested in the house! That's why I offered them the full asking price."

"But we didn't know each other yet, Drew. I'm sorry I ended up costing you money."

He heard a hint of anger—or maybe hurt—in that comment. He tried to soften his tone.

"That's not even an issue, Nikki. If you honestly didn't know I was the buyer, you couldn't have deliberately affected what I paid. And I had already made the offer by the time we met. That's right, isn't it?"

She nodded. "I think so. It was all happening about the same time, I think. I didn't realize you were the buyer until the first day we went out. Right before we went to Ashworth's soda fountain—when I stopped at the house and you were in the kitchen with your general contractor. I guess I thought I'd tell you about my great-grandparents if we ended up liking each other enough to keep seeing each other. And then I just couldn't find a comfortable time to tell you. But what I was going to say is that I no longer look at you and see the man who—how did you put it? Trashed my dreams?"

"You no *longer* see me that way? Nikki, how could you? I mean, we've been—" How could he delicately ask how she could have let him kiss her and stroke her face and gaze into her eyes all these months when she resented him even a little? The thought embarrassed him all over again. "I mean, what's *wrong* with you?"

He saw her flinch, and then she looked down at her lap.

The meanness of his question lingered there in the air after he said it. But he couldn't bring himself to take it back.

"I don't know," she said, her head still down. "I honestly don't know what I was afraid of." She looked up at him, and he saw that she was fighting tears. "I guess I was afraid of something like this." She gestured back and forth between them. She opened the car door and stepped out.

"Nikki."

"Mmm-hmm?" Her voice was falsely light, and she didn't bend down to look at him through the window. He doubted she'd be able to say anything else without crying.

He leaned toward the passenger seat so he could look up at her. "I'm sorry I've been so angry. I was just caught by surprise. I think I need to do some thinking. Can I call you later?"

She gave him a polite smile and nodded. She lifted her hand in a negligible wave before turning and walking swiftly toward the mansion.

He drove down the driveway and passed the spot where he and Freddie had first seen Nikki walking out of Harvey's house with Riley. That had been the day he'd thrown the leash on Freddie and sought her out. He had tracked her down as if she were the sweetest prize.

That seemed so long ago. A lot of time had gone by. Now he knew her so well. Or did he?

This new facet of their relationship—new to *him,* anyway—was important enough for him to weigh seriously. How had it changed the way they would relate to each other? Did they need to *fix* something between them? Could they?

He headed home. If he had any hope of making clear-headed decisions here, he was going to have to spend a little time in prayer.

Chapter Nineteen

....

Harvey happened to be walking through the front foyer of the mansion, accompanied by his valet, when Nikki walked in. She tried quickly to wipe her eyes dry before they could tell she had been crying. She noticed Harvey wince as he walked, and that was enough to distract her from her own problems.

"Are you in pain, Harvey?"

"Pardon?" He turned, placed his hand on Edward's arm for support, and managed a smile for her. "Ah, welcome home, Nikki. No. I'm just stiff from sitting too long. Had an early-morning conference call with the Hong Kong office—"

Without thinking, Nikki checked her watch as she fell into the slow stride next to them. It was well past dinnertime.

"—Early morning for *them*, I mean," Harvey said. "And they were all full of vim and vigor after a good night's sleep." He patted his chest. "This old fella has been working all day. Two hours of sitting still tends to make my body feel as if concrete has been poured into my veins."

Edward said, "We were just going to spend a little time in the gym. A little walk on the treadmill to loosen things up."

When she looked back at Harvey, he was studying her eyes.

"Why don't you come with us? I have a few things to run past you."

She nodded. It would be good to think about work right now, rather than going to her room and wondering if it was time to pack away the photo of Drew that adorned her nightstand. "Sure. Let me just hang up my jacket and put my purse away. I'll catch up."

Harvey chuckled. "At the pace I'm moving, I imagine you will."

She ran up to her room, dropped her things on the bed, and checked her eyes in the mirror. If she truly let herself experience what was coursing through her heart, she could very easily break down in full-on sobbing. Instead, she took several deep breaths and ignored the picture frame on the stand near her pillow. She tugged her sweater straight as if she were wearing a suit and donned her pert, professional manner.

Edward and Harvey had picked up the pace, apparently, the longer they walked. Harvey must have been telling the truth. He was just stiff from sitting too long.

That's right. Harvey tended to be frank about what was going on. Unlike her.

He was already on the treadmill, and he and Edward were pushing buttons to get it running. Usually Harvey had a trainer come work with him several days a week, so neither Harvey nor Edward ever paid much attention to how to program the treadmill. "Ah, Nikki. Come walk with me. Maybe you can figure out this contraption for us. It's like programming a space launch. Oh! There, that got it, Edward." The belt began moving before Nikki reached him.

Harvey had several treadmills side by side in his gym, since he often conducted business while doing his simple exercises and wasn't averse to having his employees walk beside him. Sometimes his grandson, Nathan, and great-grandson, Paul, joined him for a generational walkathon, which Nikki found especially endearing.

For now it would be just Harvey and her.

"Edward, would you mind coming back in a few minutes so Nikki and I can have a little privacy?"

"Sure, Harvey. You two will be all right, then?" He tapped the face of Harvey's treadmill. "Do me a favor and clip the emergency stop to your sleeve or something, will you?"

Rather than giving Edward a hard time for his mother-hen attitude, Harvey simply winked at Nikki and clipped the cord to the hem of his shirt.

"There you go, Edward. Give us fifteen minutes, and then I'll be ready to head on to bed."

Once Edward closed the gym door behind himself, Harvey gave Nikki a grandfatherly smile.

She smiled back. "Am I going to need to write anything down? Is this about the menus for this week? Are you craving something in particular?"

He held the treadmill handles, looked off into the distance, and pushed his lips out, as if he were giving great consideration to her questions. Then he looked at her and said, "No, I thought we might talk about you."

She tripped over her own feet and had to grab the handles herself.

Harvey said, "Do we need to attach the emergency cord to you too?"

She laughed softly. "No. You just caught me off guard. What do you mean, you want to talk about me? Did I mess up somewhere?"

"You tell me. You came home looking pretty unhappy. I know it's none of my business, but I'm sorry to say that seems to be the trend between us these days."

She gasped. "Harvey, what do you mean? What's the trend?"

"The widening gap. When you first started working here, it didn't take long before you seemed very comfortable around me."

"That's true. That's because of you. You're easy to be around."

"Thank you, dear. But over the past several months, I've noticed that you seem to keep more to yourself. Oh, I'm happy to see you going out with your young man. That's a definite improvement. At least I think it is."

She looked away from him. She really didn't want to be the crybaby on the treadmill.

"Nikki, is there something about your relationship with…Drew, is it?"

"Yes."

"Yes, well, I notice you've never had him over to meet anyone here. Edward tells me he's chatted briefly with him out front a few times and he seems like a pleasant fellow. Is there something about Drew that you're ashamed of?"

She was perspiring now, even though they were walking as slowly as a New Orleans funeral procession. She wasn't sure why she had kept Drew at a distance with regard to Harvey and her parents. And Drew had never complained, even though he had included her several times in social events with his local friends. He seemed to assume that she preferred to take everything very slowly.

"No, not Drew. I'm ashamed of myself."

"It takes *two* to make some bad decisions, Nikki. And I want to be sure no one is treating you in an ungentlemanly way."

She had to walk for a while before she realized what he was saying. She gasped and felt a rush of heat in her face.

"Harvey! Oh, no. Drew is a perfect gentleman with me. I've been the one to treat him unfairly. But that wasn't my intention. Ever."

And she spilled out her circumstances. She told him about her discovery that Drew was the person who bought "her" house. She explained that she had tried all along to keep separate her feelings of loss and her growing affection for Drew.

"But by putting off telling him about the house's history, I put a strange tweak on our relationship. I kept a distance between us. I made too big a deal out of what might happen if I told him I had always planned to buy the house he bought. And by keeping him in the dark, I actually did make it a big deal. When he found out today, he was really angry that I hadn't told him all this time. Or hurt, I guess."

Harvey nodded. "Sometimes it's hard to tell one from the other with us men. At least that's what Louise used to tell me."

"I think one reason I kept Drew separate from my work family and my own family was because I knew sooner or later someone would slip up and he would hear how he took away my dream for Grampa and Granny's house. I always thought I'd tell him myself first. But I never did."

There was a tap on the door before Laura peeked in. "Sorry to interrupt. May I come in?"

"Certainly, Laura." Harvey waved her in. "What can we do for you?"

"I just needed to make sure we were definite on the meeting with the Canadians tomorrow. Earlier you sounded as if you preferred to put that off. But I'll need to call them first thing if we want to reschedule."

Harvey shook his head and searched the array of buttons on his machine before he finally turned it off. "I was just being crotchety. I'm fine with the meeting. Thank you, though, Laura, for double-checking with me." He looked from Laura to Nikki, who turned her treadmill off as well. "You ladies are absolute gems, you know."

Nikki smiled at Harvey before she looked at Laura. She was surprised to see that Laura had done the same thing. And then Laura gave Nikki a genuine smile of camaraderie.

"The chicken Parmesan was delightful tonight, Nikki," Laura said.

The compliment was not only out of the blue, but it was probably the nicest thing Laura had ever said to Nikki.

"Oh. Well, thanks. I made that last night, though. You didn't have it until tonight?"

Laura looked positively friendly. "I wasn't home for dinner last night. It heated up beautifully tonight. A real treat."

"Thanks."

When Laura left, Nikki gave Harvey a look of incredulity.

He lowered his head and looked up at Nikki with a sage lift of one eyebrow. "I believe love has done wonders for Laura's demeanor."

Nikki smiled. "Good for her. I'm happy to see it."

"And I would be happy to see that for you too."

They stepped down from the treadmills.

Harvey said, "How do you feel about this young man, this Drew fellow?"

She inhaled deeply and sighed her breath out. "We haven't *said* the *L* word, Harvey. But I have to admit I feel it."

"You feel it, but you can't say it?" His smile went crooked.

She pressed her fingers against her forehead. "At this point I don't know if he wants to hear it."

Edward walked in as Harvey responded, but Harvey held up his hand to signal that he should wait a moment. Edward gave a nod and stepped out.

"My dear," Harvey said, "if I have a proper read on what you've just told me, I'd say that's exactly what the young man *needs* to hear."

"He's pretty upset, Harvey. What if he shoots me down?"

He rested his hand, wrinkled and spattered with age spots, on her arm. "Nikki, in my many years, I've learned it's always best to be as forthright as you possibly can without inflicting harm or unnecessary hurt on a person. Even when your comments might cause you or the other person some discomfort…there's a funny thing about that kind of discomfort. If you grip what you need to say closely to your chest and try to hide it, it tends to gain power. But if you release it—put it right out there in the open—eventually its power weakens. Eventually it won't seem uncomfortable at all. Your secret about Drew's house is out there now, and the main reason it was a big deal is because you held it too close for too long."

She nodded. "Mmm-hmm."

"Now, if you honestly do believe you're in love with Drew, I would suggest you tell him and take your chances about his shooting you down. You owe him that much honesty, don't you think?"

Chapter Twenty

....

"I'm telling you, Phillip, I feel like I don't know who she really is." Drew ran his hand through his hair and looked up to see Gigi watching him from the kitchen. Judging by the look on her face, he wasn't sure he wanted to hear what she had to say.

Phillip, on the other hand, was a guy. He could identify with how poorly Nikki had treated him. "I hear you, man. Women are supposed to be all about talking." Phillip followed Drew's gaze and laughed at Gigi's cutting expression. "I'm sorry, honey, but you know it's true. You know you blow out ten words for my every one."

"Blow out," Gigi said. She put a bowl of corn chips and guacamole on the coffee table in front of the men. "I feel *so* appreciated."

"Thanks, Gigi." Drew took a chip and was unable to break eye contact with her. "All right, I know you want to *blow out* a few words about this topic. I can see it all over your face. Am I *wrong* to be mad at her?"

"Honey, here's what I see. You can be wrong. Or you can be right. Or you can be happy."

Drew stopped chewing and swallowed.

"Be careful here, Drew," Phillip said. He reached forward with a chip and scooped a big dollop of guacamole from the bowl. "She's going all Yoda on you."

"I'm doing no such thing." Gigi walked over to the kitchen counter and came back right away with a pitcher of limeade. She filled their glasses as she spoke. "The girl had her reasons for not telling you.

293

I mean, how did you react when you found out what was going on behind the scenes?"

Drew didn't like how convicting his silence was, but he couldn't help it. His response was obviously going to feed right into Gigi's argument.

"Mmm-hmm, I thought so." Gigi set down the pitcher, picked up a chip, and stuck the entire thing in her mouth with no problem. Everything she did seemed like punctuation.

"All right, I got upset with her. But that was only because she… I mean, we've been dating for what, eight months? She's had eight months to tell me. I've never done anything that would signal anger about the house being some big family legacy. I'm a pretty cool customer."

"You said it, bro," Phillip said.

"I always spoke so positively about the house. I put so much love and attention into the remodeling. It was obvious—"

"It was obvious how important the house was *to you*." Gigi used a corn chip to point at Drew with those last two words. "You probably spent the past eight months gushing about how excited you were about *your* house. Am I right? I'm right, aren't I?"

Phillip said, "Now, baby, you can be wrong. Or you can be right. Or you can—"

He abruptly stopped talking when Gigi tilted her head down and gave him a look that said, "Do you really want to go there?" They both laughed for a moment before Drew spoke.

"You're right. I shared every bit of excitement I felt with her. But that's only because I wanted her to feel what I was feeling."

"And you see how she responded?" Gigi set her hand on her hip. "The girl was totally supportive of your buzz on the house. Listen to this, Drew." She leaned forward to deliver her next comment. "The girl helped you decorate the house you had ripped out from under her. Can you imagine how painful that might have been?"

Drew was in the middle of sipping a glass of limeade. He stopped and sat up a little straighter. "So why didn't she just come out and tell me? The whole reason I got upset with her was because I felt like such a jerk for raving about the house she'd set her dreams on. I wouldn't have hurt her for the world."

"Yet that's what you're doing right now, while you stuff corn chips and my amazing salsa guacamole in your face. The poor girl is probably beating herself up even more now than she did the whole time she kept this information from you."

Drew chuckled. "How did Nikki become the poor girl in this and I'm the face-stuffing villain?"

"Classic." Phillip said the word to Drew and then a second of panic crossed his features.

Gigi simply cleared her throat.

Phillip set down his glass and kept his eyes on Drew. "Why did *she* say she didn't tell you?"

"She said she always planned to but just never did. She seemed to be afraid it would cause conflict between us, no matter when she told me." He sighed. "I don't know. Maybe it would have."

Gigi sat across from the men. "So, what now? You don't want to end your relationship over this, do you?"

"No. But sort of, yeah. I've always been a big believer of open communication. This long-running secret bothers me."

Phillip sat back and sighed. "Do you love her, man?"

Drew looked at him and then at Gigi. Their expressions were too knowing. He rested his face in his hands and nearly growled out his next word. "Yes."

"Well, Drew," Gigi said, "if you're not willing to tell her good-bye, you're going to have to use some of that open communication you believe in. And make sure you don't confuse open communication with 'This is how you made me feel.' "

He looked up at her. "What do you mean?"

"Honey, she *knows* she messed up. She knows she hurt you and your view of her. Now she needs to know she doesn't ever have to hold back on you again because you care more about *her* than you do things like some dumb old house."

And it hit him like a slap, what he needed to do. He knew the idea had to have come from the Lord, because not only was it probably the kindest thing he could do, but it was probably the least selfish. That kind of thought didn't often come from his own stubborn heart.

Chapter Twenty-One
....

"I talked with Laura," Drew told Nikki. He stood at Harvey's front door, his kind eyes a little less lively than usual. "I didn't want to stop by while you were making or serving a meal for Harvey. She thought this would be a good time since Harvey had plans away from home."

"Laura encouraged you to come by?" Nikki marveled at the continued positive changes in Laura's personality.

Drew smiled. "She said you definitely needed a picker-upper in your day."

Nikki chuckled. She felt a bit of a pick-me-up just seeing his smile. "Did she now? Well, come on in. I'm actually working in the kitchen, putting together a shopping list. There's a table and chairs where we can sit. I'll make coffee."

He nodded, the small smile still there. He glanced around like a tourist as they walked toward the kitchen. "Gorgeous home."

"Yeah. I'm sure Harvey wouldn't mind if I gave you a little tour. I should have done that a long time ago."

He didn't immediately take her up on the offer. Maybe later.

She noted how polite and friendly they had both become as a result of the silent days that passed since their emotional argument after her parents' dinner. One would never know, to look at them, that there was any conflict at all. Or significant emotional involvement of any kind, even.

But Drew put an end to that shortly after they were shut away in the privacy of the little nook in the kitchen.

Nikki scooped coffee into the coffeemaker, and Drew sat at the table. He looked at his joined hands on the table. "Nikki, I want to sell you the house."

She lost count on the coffee scoops. She studied him to see if he was serious.

He didn't look angry. Or sad. He looked determined.

"But, Drew—" She hardly knew what to say. She shook her head as if she had just come to.

"I'm sorry for the way I reacted the other evening," he said. "I shouldn't have lost my temper, and I apologize for the angry things I said to you."

She started the coffeemaker and sat down across from him at the table. She wanted to place her hand on top of his but thought better of it. "I'm sorry I wasn't up-front with you, Drew. I handled that so poorly."

He put up his hand to stop her. "Let's not dwell on it, okay? Let's forgive each other and let it go. We can talk with financial people and our Realtors and figure out how to best handle the sale. And I'd need you to pay at least what I paid for the place. I mean, I sank a lot of money into the house on top of what I paid by just doing the remodeling, so I can't really afford to cut you a break."

"Drew, no. I absolutely can't do that."

"If you can't afford it just now, we'll wait until you can. I'm sure our financial people can figure out—"

"No, I mean, I can't take your house from you."

He sighed and looked up at her as if he were a father brooking no nonsense from his child. "It will never feel like my house, Nikki."

She could have broken into tears right there. What had she done?

"Of course it will. Look, I meant it when I said I no longer stressed over losing the house. I know you have no reason to believe anything I say ever again, but *please* believe that."

He nodded. "I do. I don't think you're dishonest. I understand now how awkward you felt about the circumstances between us and with the house. But I hope you can understand why I feel really uncomfortable now about living there. I see the place completely differently now. I've prayed about this, Nikki, and I'm 99 percent sure God wants that house to be yours."

She didn't want to speak out of emotion. He had a look about him she'd never seen before. Again, she would characterize him as determined. He seemed unshakable in his decision.

Well, she had prayed too.

"I'm not sure how to put this, Drew, but I'm 99 percent sure God wanted me to get over that house and enjoy your ownership of it quite a while ago. And I've been praying about this a lot longer than you have."

He frowned and studied his hands again. Nikki noticed his hands weren't just joined now. They were clenched.

"I've considered the idea of moving back to San Diego anyway. After my contract here is satisfied."

She couldn't help the tears that sprang to her eyes, and she suddenly had to talk around a swollen feeling in her throat. She got up and took her time in getting cream and sugar, and she took a stealthy swipe at a few tears that escaped. She spoke while looking in the refrigerator.

"Did—did I cause that idea?"

He sighed. "My father's health, well, you know, it hasn't been all that great. It might make sense for me to be closer to my parents right now. Or soon, anyway."

She brought the cream and sugar to the table. "I understand that." She licked her lips and sat back down. "But I'm still not open to taking the house from you. You said it would never feel like it's yours." She looked directly at him. "I feel the same way. I would never feel right about owning it now."

"Why?"

He finally showed a little emotion, but it didn't make Nikki feel any better. If anything, he was getting frustrated. She didn't want this conversation to deteriorate as their last one had.

"Nikki, you can't honestly tell me you weren't duplicating the decor you remembered from when your great-grandparents lived there. I remember how certain you were of what would look good. Now I know why."

She cringed. "Yes, I'll admit I used my old memories for inspiration. But it's *not* the same, Drew. It has your own touches. More modern touches. It looks like it once did but better."

"If it's better, then you should be thrilled about buying the place and bringing it back to the Tronniers. I'm sure your family will appreciate—"

"My family couldn't care less. I'm the only one who ever set her sights on the place. And that was because of the happy memories it held for me. But now my memories would be about taking the house from you. I won't do that. I won't buy the house, Drew."

She got up to pour coffee, but he stood along with her.

He heaved a great sigh. She thought she had finally won their argument.

"If you're really sure."

"I'm totally sure." She nodded.

He walked to the kitchen door. "All right. Then I'm going to put it on the market in a few weeks, once the remodeling work is done."

Nikki gasped. "What? But why?"

"I meant what I said, Nikki." He gave her a resigned smile. "If you change your mind, let me know right away, okay?"

Was this the end, then? Were they over? She wouldn't have the strength to get out any words without a quiver in her voice—she could tell. So she simply nodded and said, "Mmm-hmm."

She saw something shift in his expression in reaction to her wimpy little response. He walked over to her, slowly took hold of her hands, and leaned down to rest his forehead against hers.

He breathed out in some effort, either to keep from getting too emotional himself or to figure out how to let her down easily. She tensed up in dreadful expectation.

"I can't say I know what to expect for us, Nikki. I think we both need to think about how we feel about each other. And pray. I think we could use some guidance right about now. Prayer would probably be a good thing."

Well, that wasn't *necessarily* good-bye. And frankly, he was right. She would have loved it if he had just walked over, taken her hands, and leaned down to kiss away the awkwardness between them. But the fact that she had felt unable to be frank with him these last several months, regardless of her reasoning—that said something. She wasn't sure *what* it said, but she needed to figure that out and make her own decision about her future with Drew. Assuming such a thing existed.

Chapter Twenty-Two

....

Every day of the week after Drew visited her at Harvey's, Nikki found a reason to drive past the Tronnier home. She had started to think of it that way again—the Tronnier home—now that Drew planned to step away from it. But she wasn't driving past to see the house. She was hoping to see him.

Once she had accepted that he honestly planned to put the house back on the market, she actually wondered if she might talk herself back into an interest in it. Yet all she saw now was a lovely building that had caused a wedge between her and a truly beautiful man.

Of course *she* was what had caused the wedge, not the house. She had placed too much value on something she could touch and not enough on someone who had touched her heart in so many ways. Granted, she had never outwardly complained to Drew about her disappointment during the months they dated. Still, had she only known early on how important he would become to her, she might have casually told him about her family history with the house right away and headed off any conflict between them.

She had prayed, as he suggested. She had, at moments, felt a certain peace that everything would work out well. But sometimes she wondered if she was fooling herself about that peace. Maybe she wasn't feeling God's will at all, but simply her own wishful thinking. She trusted God, but she wasn't so sure about herself.

Drew hadn't been there any of the times she drove past. No one had, which made her think the remodeling work was probably done, or pretty close to it. Any day now that FOR SALE sign would go up and they would lose one more connection between them. She could handle the idea of the house falling into someone else's hands. But Drew in someone else's arms? Not so easy to handle.

As she drove by this time, though, the house was full of activity. In fact, two of Drew's workers were actually running out the front door and down the porch steps. They hadn't even put on their jackets.

She turned her BMW around, went back to the house, and parked. As she stepped out of her car and approached, Drew strode quickly out of the house with a shovel in his hand. Draped over the shovel head was one nasty-looking snake.

Nikki had lived in North Carolina all her life. She would recognize those triangular markings and that rusty coloring anywhere. That was a copperhead. Very poisonous.

"Mike!" Drew called to one of the men outside. "Man up and bring one of those lawn and leaf bags over here. The thing's dead now."

Dead *now*? As in, it was in the house *alive*?

"Did you kill it, Drew?" Nikki asked.

He jerked his head toward her. "Oh. Nikki. Hi. Didn't see you there." He looked back at the snake dangling limply across the shovel. "Yeah. It managed to work its way into the basement from somewhere, probably going after mice. I'm going to have to make sure an exterminator gets out here and finds the entryway before I put the house on the market."

Mike approached with a large green bag and held it open for Drew to drop the snake in. "Good old Freddie was the one who found it," Mike said.

As if on cue, Freddie slowly padded out of the house.

"Freddie!" Nikki approached the retriever—she missed him almost as much as she missed Drew. But something was wrong. He didn't try to jump on her or even wag his tail. And when she ruffled the soft fur around his neck, she thought his neck felt swollen.

"Drew?" She turned and saw him tying up the bag and handing it to Mike, who carried it to the Dumpster at the side of the house. Drew looked over at her and finally gave her a smile.

She wasn't in the mood to smile, though. "Did you know Freddie's neck is swollen?"

"Is it?" He frowned and reached down to feel it. "You're right, it's—"

Freddie's legs suddenly gave way, and he plopped onto the porch like a wild animal hit by a tranquilizer dart.

Both Nikki and Drew gasped.

Drew took the dog's head in his hands and looked into his eyes. "He's conscious. But I think the copperhead must have bit him."

Nikki drew her hand to her chest. "Oh, Drew, they're poisonous."

He scooped his arms underneath Freddie and stood; the dog's listless body hung heavily over either side. "I've got to get him to the vet." He glanced toward the garage. "My car doesn't have a backseat."

"We'll take mine." Nikki had her keys in her hand. Her eyes teared up. "You can sit in the back with him."

But when they got to her car, he said, "Let me drive. Is that all right? You sit in the back and let him rest his head in your lap. Do you mind?"

"Of course not." She scooted into the back. Drew leaned in, draped Freddie across the backseat, and gently rested the dog's head in her lap. He glanced into Nikki's eyes before he pulled back out of the car, and for a moment she felt their old connection return, with something more. They shared an unspoken but understood goal.

The combination of fear for Freddie and sadness over whatever she had lost with Drew brought a tightness to her chest that she struggled to breathe away. That little glimmer of hope or love or whatever she had seen in Drew's eyes had vanished as quickly as it had appeared.

She saw him open his phone and place a call before he pulled away from the curb. There wasn't a bit of panic in his voice as he spoke with the vet's receptionist and then the vet himself about the snakebite.

For her part, she kept watch on Freddie. He had closed his eyes, and his breathing was fairly shallow. He was such a sweetheart, and she pictured his making his way to the front door of the house, maybe aware he needed help but not creating a fuss at all. So unlike his usual lively, often intrusive self.

She gently stroked his head and ran her hand across the length of his body, murmuring to him in a soft voice.

"That's a good boy, Freddie. We're going to fix you right up. You hang in there, sweetie."

Until one of her tears dropped onto his coat, she hadn't realized she had started crying again. She swiped at her eyes with the back of her hand. When she glanced up front, Drew had finished his call.

Her eyes went directly to the rearview mirror. He was watching her, his own tears barely glistening enough to see.

* * * * *

By the time they reached the vet's office, Freddie's breathing was labored. Drew quickly reached into the back to retrieve him.

Nikki couldn't help the panic in her voice. "Hurry, Drew. I think his throat's closing up."

She heard a little groan of panic as Drew backed swiftly out of the backseat with Freddie in his arms. He banged his head on the car door jamb before he was able to turn and run to the office door. Nikki slammed the car door shut, ran past Drew, and opened the next door for him.

The staff was ready for them, waiting, when they walked in. They rushed Freddie into one of the small back rooms, and the vet and several assistants went to work.

"You have that antivenin ready, Terri?" The doctor probed Freddie's neck as he spoke.

One of his assistants held up a syringe. "Ready."

The vet shot a look at Drew and Nikki. "I hate to make you leave, folks, but you're in the way. You're going to have to wait out front."

"But…" Drew stood there, his eyes riveted on Freddie. He looked like a ten-year-old kid. Nikki reached up and gently embraced him from behind.

"Come on, babe, we want them to be able to work quickly."

He turned and looked at her with a helpless, sad cast to his eyes and allowed her to pull him out of the room.

They sat together on a love seat in the waiting room, and Drew leaned forward to rest his head in his hands.

Despite his being so much bigger, Nikki reached her arm across his broad back and moved close to him. She closed her eyes and spoke softly.

"Precious Lord, we thank You for being so loving and gracious toward us. We thank You for sweet Freddie. And we ask that You help the doctor to make him well. We trust You to support Freddie's life with the power of Your loving hands."

"Amen," Drew answered. And with a rush of emotion and excitement, Nikki felt his warm, strong hand cover hers and give it a gentle, grateful squeeze.

Chapter Twenty-Three

....

A dusting of snow covered the yard in front of the Tronnier home on Christmas morning. Nikki took a moment, once she got out of her car, to appreciate the house in its renewed glory. Drew had mounted a beautiful wreath on the front door. Prospective buyers would like that touch.

Her plans for the day included a cozy family brunch and the opening of gifts at her parents' home in a few hours. Hannah would bring her latest boyfriend, Ronaldo, who was unable to take time to travel to his hometown in Sintra, Portugal, to be with his own family.

Drew would come too. His parents' plans had worked out nicely for Nikki.

"This last heart attack really woke Dad up about his priorities," Drew told her this past week. "They want to get in some of the travel they've always *talked* about doing, and they're starting with a winter cruise in the Caribbean."

So Drew didn't have to leave to spend Christmas in San Diego. And he hadn't said anything else about moving out there to live closer to them. After what happened at the vet's, Nikki and Drew had naturally been drawn back into their mutual trust and need for each other's company.

Drew's parents scheduled a stop in Cary and asked that he and Nikki come have Christmas dinner with them at their hotel.

As she studied the front porch of the Tronnier home, Nikki felt a little sad about the idea of having Christmas dinner at a hotel. This would be Drew's only Christmas as owner of Grampa William and

Granny Lillian's beautiful home, and Nikki knew how memorable the holiday could be when celebrated there with family.

And this time she had talked with him about it, regardless of any annoyance she might cause. She had learned her lesson about holding back information, her thoughts, or her feelings.

"A hotel is so...cold," she had said about the evening's plans. "Don't you want to get at least a *little* bit of enjoyment out of your house before it sells?"

He chuckled. "Nikki, it might be beautiful and new inside, but it's also empty. I'm not about to move furniture in just for a few days' use. I love your idea, but I want us to be comfortable. So Christmas evening at the hotel it is."

She had given in. Nothing was going to spoil her mood, regardless of the hotel idea. Just the fact that Drew wanted to meet her here at the house to exchange their gifts in private was a thrill for her. It would be somewhat bittersweet, saying hello and good-bye to Christmas at the Tronnier home at the same time.

But the romance in Drew's gesture was unmistakable. And that was all she cared about now: Drew. And the fact that he seemed to want to repair and rebuild their relationship. In that they were agreed. They shared a common goal, as they had when Freddie needed rescue. As they had in bringing the Tronnier home back to life—without realizing it at first.

The front door opened, and he stood there with a smile on his face. "You going to stand out there all morning?"

She tucked his gift under her arm—just a sweater, a book, and a couple of CDs he wanted—and sauntered up the walk toward him. She sighed at the sight of him, tall and handsome, dressed in his jeans and a rich burgundy V-neck. The winter sun highlighted the sheen in his dark hair and the color of his forest-green eyes.

"The wreath looks beautiful, Drew. Merry Christmas."

Freddie suddenly appeared at Drew's side, looking more energetic than she had seen him since their close call at the vet's.

In her dogs-and-small-children voice, Nikki said, "Freddie! Merry Christmas, Freddie!"

But before she could get close enough to touch the dog, Drew pulled her into his arms. They hadn't even stepped inside, but he wrapped his arms around her and leaned in to give her the one thing she'd hoped for this Christmas. A long, warm, totally-committed-to-her kind of kiss. All question of whether he had forgiven her was fully answered by the time he released her and said, "Okay. *Now* you can hug the dog."

She played up the sweet dopiness in her expression. "What dog?"

Freddie's impatient whine made her laugh. She pulled away from Drew, handed his present to him, and rubbed her hands through Freddie's lush golden fur. "Merry Christmas, Freddie boy!"

Drew pulled her inside, shut the front door, and took a few steps back.

When Nikki looked up, she gasped. The house was still empty, save the living room. There, a fire crackled in the fireplace, an old-fashioned couch and two chairs sat atop a beautiful, ornate Persian rug, and a small, fat Christmas tree sparkled with a sparse handful of ornaments hanging from its boughs.

Nikki looked from the room to Drew, whose eager expression broke into a satisfied grin at her obvious pleasure and surprise.

"What did you do?" she said. "I thought you didn't want to bother bringing furniture in here for the short-term."

He shrugged. "I thought this little bit was the least I could do for our Christmas morning. It's not much, but—"

"No." She put up her hand and looked at the room again. "It *is* much." She couldn't help but feel a connection to her childhood Christmases now, and her eyes stung with tears.

She gestured at her gift to him. "*That* isn't much. But this—" She pointed to the living room. "This is the nicest Christmas present you could have given me, Drew." She gave him another hug and buried her face into his warm, spicy-smelling neck.

He pulled back and chuckled. "Oh, that's not my gift to you." He walked away from her, entered the living room, and stood in front of the Christmas tree. He spread out his arms as if he were king of the living room, presenting his domain. "This is the *setting* for my gift to you."

She grinned. She loved his playful side. She loved all of his sides.

Mischief suddenly brightened his eyes, and he crooked his finger to beckon her toward him. Looking the way he did, he was definitely her pied piper. No question—she'd follow him anywhere.

But his expression changed, as if he suddenly remembered something, and he put up his hand to stop her.

"Oh, you need to bring the dog with you."

She frowned. "Freddie?"

Freddie, who had already settled into a comfy heap in front of the fire, lifted his head at the sound of his name. But he didn't get up.

Drew nodded. "It's best that you take hold of his collar and tug him over here. He's not going to want to leave that fire."

Nikki gave Drew a suspicious side glance and smiled. She walked over to Freddie, slipped her fingers under his collar, and said, "Come on, Freddie. Let's go sit with your crazy master over there."

Freddie didn't put up any of the fight Drew predicted, but once Nikki had her fingers under the collar, she noticed a ribbon tied to the buckle. And tied to the ribbon—

She gasped and straightened, her hands quickly covering her mouth.

Freddie trotted in Drew's direction, so she turned to stop him. "No, wait, Freddie—"

And there was Drew, right behind her, down on one knee, with his trusty best friend trying to jump all over him.

"Stop!" Drew said to Freddie, in mock crazed frustration. He had to put his other knee to the floor to avoid getting knocked over. "Crazy mutt!"

Nikki laughed and cried at the same time.

Once Drew managed to free the ring from Freddie's collar, he got back into the traditional position. "I kind of pictured this working out a little differently."

They simply laughed together, a moment's embarrassment lingering between them before Drew spoke again.

"Nikki, I've been thinking along these lines for quite some time now. I just hadn't been aware of it. And I let our conflict about this house sidetrack me...but only for a little while. There was something about that day—the way we were when Freddie was sick—that reminded me of why I love you. I love the things you care about, Nikki. And in a weird way, I know that whole thing with the house happened because you cared about the house but also because you cared about me. And how I'd feel. And what I'd think."

She couldn't speak. She simply nodded. He was absolutely right.

"And what I think," he said, "is that I want to be with you forever, no matter *where* we live."

She wiped the tears from her cheeks.

"So I'm asking you, right here in your great-grandparents' living room: Nikki Tronnier, will you marry me?"

She practically knocked him down when she fell to her knees and wrapped her arms around him. "Yes!" She laughed and pulled back, and she repeated herself before kissing him. "Definitely, yes!"

He returned her kiss, and she decided she never wanted to get up from where they were. This was heaven on earth, right here, kneeling on the floor with him.

When they drew back from each other, he slid the ring onto her finger. "We'll get it sized tomorrow." He smiled at her. "I love you, Nikki."

"I love you, Drew."

"Oh, there's one more thing," he said. He reached into his back pocket. "We can get married whenever you want, however you want, *wherever* you want. You just let me know. But after we do, you're going to need this."

He took her hand, turned it palm-up, and placed a shiny brass house key there.

"That goes with the rest of the house." He leaned forward and kissed her right below her ear. "Welcome home."

About the Author

....

Award-winning novelist Trish Perry has published eight inspirational romances as well as two devotionals. Before writing novels, she published numerous short stories, essays, devotions, and poetry in Christian and general market media. Over the years she has served as a columnist, a newsletter editor, and a stockbroker. She currently serves on the board of directors of Capital Christian Writers in Washington, D.C., and she is a member of both the American Christian Fiction Writers and the Romance Writers of America organizations. She holds a degree in psychology.

Trish's nostalgic romance novel, *Unforgettable*, released in March 2011. She and Debby Mayne were both contributing authors of the devotional *Delight Yourself in the Lord...Even on Bad Hair Days*.

Trish invites you to visit her at www.TrishPerry.com.

Want a peek into local American life—past and present?
The *Love Finds You*™ series published by Summerside Press
features real towns and combines travel, romance,
and faith in one irresistible package!

The novels in the series—uniquely titled after American towns with romantic
or intriguing names—inspire romance and fun. Each fictional story draws on
the compelling history or the unique character of a real place. Stories center on
romances kindled in small towns, lost and found again on the high plains, or newly
discovered at exciting vacation getaways. Summerside Press plans to publish at
least one novel set in each of the fifty states. Be sure to catch them all!

NOW AVAILABLE

Love Finds You in Miracle, Kentucky
by Andrea Boeshaar
ISBN: 978-1-934770-37-5

*Love Finds You in
Snowball, Arkansas*
by Sandra D. Bricker
ISBN: 978-1-934770-45-0

Love Finds You in Romeo, Colorado
by Gwen Ford Faulkenberry
ISBN: 978-1-934770-46-7

*Love Finds You in
Valentine, Nebraska*
by Irene Brand
ISBN: 978-1-934770-38-2

Love Finds You in Humble, Texas
by Anita Higman
ISBN: 978-1-934770-61-0

*Love Finds You in
Last Chance, California*
by Miralee Ferrell
ISBN: 978-1-934770-39-9

*Love Finds You in
Maiden, North Carolina*
by Tamela Hancock Murray
ISBN: 978-1-934770-65-8

*Love Finds You in
Paradise, Pennsylvania*
by Loree Lough
ISBN: 978-1-934770-66-5

*Love Finds You in
Treasure Island, Florida*
by Debby Mayne
ISBN: 978-1-934770-80-1

Love Finds You in Liberty, Indiana
by Melanie Dobson
ISBN: 978-1-934770-74-0

Love Finds You in Revenge, Ohio
by Lisa Harris
ISBN: 978-1-934770-81-8

Love Finds You in Poetry, Texas
by Janice Hanna
ISBN: 978-1-935416-16-6

Love Finds You in
Tombstone, Arizona
by Miralee Ferrell
ISBN: 978-1-60936-104-4

Love Finds You in Martha's
Vineyard, Massachusetts
by Melody Carlson
ISBN: 978-1-60936-110-5

Love Finds You in
Prince Edward Island, Canada
by Susan Page Davis
ISBN: 978-1-60936-109-9

Love Finds You in Groom, Texas
by Janice Hanna
ISBN: 978-1-60936-006-1

Love Finds You in Amana, Iowa
by Melanie Dobson
ISBN: 978-1-60936-135-8

Love Finds You in Lancaster
County, Pennsylvania
by Annalisa Daughety
ISBN: 97-8-160936-212-6

Love Finds You in Branson, Missouri
by Gwen Ford Faulkenberry
ISBN: 978-1-60936-191-4

Love Finds You
in Sundance, Wyoming
by Miralee, Ferrell
ISBN: 978-1-60936-277-5

COMING SOON

Love Finds You in
Nazareth, Pennsylvania
by Melanie Dobson
ISBN: 978-1-60936-194-5

Love Finds You in
Sunset Beach, Hawaii
by Robin Jones Gunn
ISBN: 978-1-60936-028-3

Love Finds You in
Annapolis, Maryland
by Roseanna M. White
ISBN: 978-1-60936-313-0

Love Finds You in
Folly Beach, South Carolina
by Loree Lough
ISBN: 97-8-160936-214-0